# STILL A Mistress

## The Saga Continues

By Tiphani

A Life Changing Book in conjunction with Power Play Media
**Published by Life Changing Books**
P.O. Box 423 Brandywine, MD 20613

Library of Congress Cataloging-in-Publication Data:  2007939105

www.lifechangingbooks.net

ISBN - (10) 1-934230-89-8 (13) 978-1-934230-89-3
Copyright ® 2007

# _Dedication_

TO GOD,

YOUR LOVE HUMBLES ME.

# Acknowledgements

It's 2:03 a.m. and the world around me is finally quiet. I'm down to the last minute of having to send off my acknowledgements, which is ironically, the only time I feel like doing them. There are so many to thank, and yet so many I'm intentionally trying not to remember. Not for any specific reasons, just that the season of my life has changed. So, I'll start off by saying…PLEASE FORGIVE ME if your name isn't mentioned. It's late and I'm tired and wide-awake at the same time.

Almost delusional, but still sane.

What a combination.

People often wonder why certain people thank God when they write the kind of books I write. Well, the reality is that none of this would be possible without Him. He breathes life into me, wakes me up every morning, allows me the strength to take care of my daughter, provides us shelter and blesses me with wisdom (that I still only sometimes use). Without Him, I am nothing. And, so God, I thank You for your unconditional grace, mercy, and your promise of Psalm 91, that keeps us protected. Because you're You, I'm me…and that Rocks!

Brenda "Mom" Ellison, I swear this laptop was the best gift yet! I appreciate your unselfishness and your dedication to make me greater. And I also want to thank you for your brutal honesty about the book at its beginning stages. Whoever said that moms sugar coat has never met mine-LOL. I love you. Larry Ellison, thanks for all your support also! It meant a lot.

To my lovely sister, Carrie "Yah Yah" Montgomery, you've grown up so much! I love you and wish you the best in life.

Jaedah Kiss, my first born, you're the reason I wake up everyday and hustle so hard. Thank you for all your promotional work! At only seven years old, you're the greatest!

To my darling brothers, T-Tom Evans, Cyrus "Spunge" Procter, my other mother, Pam Evans Montgomery, Gail Evans and Pam Johnson, I love you all very much! My brother and sister, Tex and Chey, thanks for cheering me on when my ADD kicks in-LOL. It really takes someone special to know when it's creeping up on me, and you catch it every time. I love y'all unconditionally.

To Azarel, we did it again! God seems to always put me in the presence of excellent people, and you're a great example of what that person is. Leslie Allen, a presence like yours is rare. You're incredibly enjoyable, and yet so serious, all at the same time. If they had a Best Editor of the Year Award, I'd be the first to vote for you. Thanks for everything!

Tonya Ridley, you're so funny. Thanks for believing in me. I love you. Davida Baldwin, my sister in another life, you're one of the hottest graphic designers out there! I really appreciate all your hard work. To my publicist, Nakea Murray, thanks for your dedication to my project. To my other editor, Kathleen Jackson, I know you had to pull this off at the last minute, so I thank you for your hard work as well.

Keisha George (Poole Rd) thanks for your tips. You have the eye of a tiger, (I'm assuming they see very well), and honesty like yours is rare. Thanks for being by my side!

To my Power Play/Life Changing Book Family-Tonya Ridley (Talk of the Town, The Takeover), Danette Majette (Deep, I Shoulda Seen It Comin'), Darren Coleman (Taste of Honey), J. Tremble (Secrets of a Housewife, More Secrets More Lies), Tyrone Wallace (Nothin' Personal, Double Life), Mike G. (Young Assassins), Mike Warren (A Private Affair), Ericka Williams (All That Glitters), and Azarel (Bruised, Bruised 2, and Daddy's House); just wanted to say that we make a great team! Kim Pae (www.kimpae.com) you did another amazing job on the cover!! I wish you the best in everything you do.

To my cousins, Shameika "Goldie" Moore, Bridget Johnson, Shawn, Gayla and Juan Yarborough, Wally and Brandon Evans,

Sherri, Stan Evans, Destiny and Alphonso Daniels, Baby Sammy, Stacey Mathis, Kimiko, Teddy and Teresa Kenney, Junebug, V-Jay, Butch, Marcat, and all the other eighty cousins I have, I love y'all!!

Uncle E, you are a hot damn mess, but I love ya! Samzelle, I look forward to seeing some movies from you in 2008!! Mo Vega, Sunrise, Kim and El, thanks for all the love and support.

To my friend since the fourth grade, Christie Monique Linton, boy look at how time flies. I love you very much, and I wish you and your growing family all the favor in the world.

To my BFFs, Marla Dinkle, Khara "Sweet Muffins" Grant, Yolanda "Pooh" Richardson, Shaunita "Skinny" Randolph, Karza "Friend" Walton, and Jacque Harris, I love all of you!!

To my other literary friends, Shannon Holmes (B-More Careful, Dirty Games), you are a wealth of information…thank you for taking the time to share it with me. KiKi Swinson (Wifey, Still Wifey, and Life After Wifey), you are so sweet. Thanks for all your words of encouragement! Nicolette (Paper Dolls), JM Benjamin, Kurin, SC Dikens, and Freeze, I wish you all nothing but prosperity.

Rochester, New York…my first love! The love y'all showed me was unbelievable. I want to give a shout out to the person that started it all, Flo Anthony. Thanks for picking up my book in the first place and reading it. To 104 WDKX (103.9 fm), you all are incredible!! I thank everyone at the station for the outburst of support I got. Words can't explain how much it all meant! I'll be at the #1 morning show, The Water Cooler, soon without totaling the car this time-LOL! Tavirus (Mad Flavors) you were my first stop in the ROC with my book! Thanks for welcoming me with open arms.☺

The illest bookstore in the city of Rochester... It's Official, located on 197 Genesee St., held me down BIG TIME!! JaGood and Jerome, thanks for keeping my book in the streets! I want everyone in Rochester to call them for a copy of the book (585) 529-9829.

Big thanks to Venu Lounge and Nightclub, for a banging

book release party. Sossity, I appreciate your help! Shout out to Will Mongeon and The Prepstar Movement...love ya!

To Nicole Dixon, Yoshida Baldwin, Nkosana Turner, and Tia Linton, thanks for everything!

A special thanks to the members of the Rochester City School District, especially the Young Mother's Program, for the tremendous support you all showed me for my first novel! To Minnie Lee and Jackie Williams, you guys are unbelievable! Thank you so much for your help.

Raleigh, North Carolina...my new love! Your southern hospitality has been beyond words. Thanks to K97.5's Shena J for the radio love!! Can't wait to read your book soon.☺

To Oakwood Mini Mart King and Queen, Tisha and Eron, thanks for opening up your hearts to let me hustle my book in front of the store and even pushing them for me when I wasn't around. Your generosity will never be forgotten. And E, thanks for the good look on the hood DVD! Hustle hard! Hey Tawanna!

To all my friends that are locked up, LaKeya Williams, Latoya Lee, and Country, I can't wait to ya'll get out!! You deserve another chance.

A big thanks to my neighbors from Brooklyn, Gloria and Kia, for proofreading my book and coming up with some great ideas.

To all the Karibu Bookstores, you really made me feel like I was family, so thank you. DC Bookman, you are the bomb...can't wait to come back and get it in at Foggy Bottom. Dynasty Books(Charlotte, NC), African American Bookstore (Greensboro, NC), Black and Nobel, Horizon, As The Page Turns Book Club (Philadelphia, PA), Waldenbooks, Borders, and Barnes and Nobles, thanks for pushing my book. A special thanks to Xanielle (PA), Tiffany (PA), Tasha (Military Circle Mall, VA). To all the other independent black bookstores that showed me love, please forgive me for not naming you...I really appreciate your help too.

To Essence Magazine, thank you for having an outlet for African-American authors to be recognized. It was an honor. Thanks to blackpressradio.com, artistfirst.com, Venom (South Carolina's first lady) for the love.

Wendy Williams and Charlamagne the God...I love you guys! Dad, I love you too. And to Quency Hawkins and Antonio, thank you both for your financial savvy. I've come a long way-LOL. Kory Hill...there.

Torrez and Chuck with A-List (www.alistnc.com), Shawn with the City Commentary, and J Flexx with 7-NC Ent. (www.7-nc.com), thanks for the love!

Boy, was the world upset with me when they got to the end of The Millionaire Mistress. I really had all intentions on doing a sequel...guess I just forgot to tell everyone about it-LOL. Thanks for being so patient!
Hope you enjoy...

Please feel free to write me and send your comments to PO BOX 40133, Raleigh, NC 27629. Also visit me at www.myspace.com/tiphanitheauthor and www.lifechanging-books.net. I would love to hear your thoughts.

Three very long excruciating hours later,
*Tiphani Montgomery*
'ROC' Star forever!!

# 1 CHLOE

"I want that bitch dead!" was the first thing he said about his mistress, after cumming on top of my stomach. The murder that rested in his eyes revealed how serious he actually was as he collapsed on the bed. His sour, stale breath seemed to have climbed on my face, as his breathing got heavier. He continued to lie next to me, while I looked over his shoulders and saw the culprit, a large bottle of expensive whiskey. Macallan Seventeen to be exact.

The bottle, that was only sips away from being empty, sat on the table with less than half left. It told me that he was pissy drunk, but he held his liquor well. Most crooked politicians did.

Asheville, North Carolina's most hated Mayor had made a request of me that wasn't in my job description. But as he kept talking, I found myself up for the task, and besides, the longer he talked, the more expensive the perks got. I'd been offered any luxury vehicle of my choice, a house that was big enough for a small army, and an all day shopping spree at Bergdorf

Goodman.

My nipples became even stiffer every time he mentioned an elaborate perk. I was that much closer to closing the deal, and the thought of murderess for hire was intriguing to me. I figured that it wouldn't hurt to add another skill to my resume, other than fucking everybody. Besides, I could use the practice. This contract was definitely what I needed to prepare me for my next big plan.

"Chloe," he said, looking at me with glassy eyes. "I really like you, and once she's out of the way, I want you to step up."

I let out a slight laugh. "Step up? Who the fuck do you think you're talking to?" I asked. "I don't step up, I move bitches aside!"

"No, baby, I didn't mean it like that," he blurted out, in an attempt not to piss me off. "It's just that you do things for me that nobody has ever done, and I want to make sure that you stay by my side."

Bullshit.

Everything that he'd just said was one hundred percent bullshit. I wanted to ask him what made tonight different. What sparked the sudden change of heart that wanted him to finally make me his main bitch? We'd been fucking for a little over six months now, and he'd never said this to me before, even though I knew he was pussy whipped.

My shit was powerful.

I was sure it was the liquor talking, and I wasn't upset at his suggestion for my new role, because the only position I'd ever played was the one of a mistress. Hell, I enjoyed being a mistress. It was the only thing I knew how to do. The thought of fucking men who belonged to other women was the ultimate turn on. Especially since there were no strings attached, and I always got the same benefits or even more. I wouldn't even know how to be a housewife.

It was just the fact that he thought he was doing me some

type of fucking favor that made me mad. Maybe he felt that pacifying me would make murdering his former mistress easier. Little did he know that he could've saved his breath. His weak promises of love didn't matter, because money was my motivator.

"By your side, huh?" I looked at him, and rolled my eyes at the thought of what his plan was once he was through with me. His sorry ass would probably do me the same way. "Baby, I would never leave you," I mustered up, giving him a brief kiss on his cheek. If this was the game he wanted to play, I was down.

"That's what I want to hear," he responded.

"What about your wife? Where does she stand?" I asked, even though I didn't give a fuck.

"My wife stays for now," he said, with remorse in his tone. I poked out my lower lip, pretending to be upset with his decision. "Don't worry though, I'll never treat you like my mistress. I'll always treat you like number one."

That was all I needed to hear. "So, why do you want this woman out of your life?"

I tried my best not to get personal, but my nosiness took over, and I had questions that needed to be answered. The Mayor's breath was on fire, and the scent almost melted my nose off as he continued.

"This bitch has been trying to ruin my life from the beginning, and now with her getting pregnant on purpose, I know things are about to get ugly. I want her ass dead before my wife and the public finds out. She's already promised to blackmail me, and I need her stopped before it's too late!"

I inserted my index finger into my wet pussy, pulled it out, and rubbed it against his full lips. "How do you know that I won't ruin your life?"

His smile could be seen a mile away. "Because I trust you, baby. Besides, there simply isn't enough room for the both of you, and she's the one I want out of the picture. I couldn't imagine you gone."

*There you go again with more bullshit*, I thought. *This dude must think I'm some type of rooky.* Game recognizes game, and I was a professional when it came down to this shit. I knew in the end, he wouldn't give a fuck about me. It would always be about his wife.

"I'm glad you chose me, daddy," I replied, in an assuring tone.

We snuggled on his beautiful white Goose Down duvet, at his cottage on The Biltmore Estate. This was a piece of luxury that not even his rich ass socialite wife knew about. The only part of the house that I despised was the two story library that held thousands of books. It was an instant memory of my bitch ass sister, Oshyn. Ever since we were little, books had always been her first love. Long ago I waged a war against anything she loved, and literature of any kind had now become my enemy.

I'd made myself at home in Asheville a year ago, right after I left Raleigh. I needed to get out of town after all the chaos, but I also wanted to stay as close as I could to Oshyn. My plan was to get her back for everything she'd done to me. I'd never been to Asheville before, and the mountains seemed to clear my head. Shit, even the Uni Bomber, Timothy McVay, came here to hide, so I knew it had to be something special about the place. There wasn't any drama here, any worries, and any problems...or so I thought.

I was renting a cabin, and down to my last two hundred dollars when I met the Mayor at a restaurant downtown. I knew it was only a matter of time before he would be taking care of me, but I had no idea he would be the one to bring back my killer instincts.

"You're so much prettier than that other bitch I deal with," he said, stroking my hair. "And your body is to die for!"

I looked at his small grey afro and smiled. I knew he was

referring to my perky 36 C cups and big round ass. "Is she white?" I asked.

He seemed surprised by my question. "Why would you ask me that? Besides, what difference does it make?"

"Actually I could care less, but I'm just curious. For some reason, you look like the type of black man who would have a white girl on the side. Shit, I'm probably the closest thing to black pussy you've ever had. You're probably tired of being with a woman with an ironing board for an ass."

"Well, if you must know, yes she's white."

I wasn't surprised by his comment, but I hated that I had to kill someone who sounded like a woman after my own heart. I started feeling kind of bad that I had to betray one of my fellow blackmailers. Women in this business had to stick together, but I was sure she would do the same thing if she were in my shoes. It was always business before pleasure.

My thoughts were distracted by what looked like a large deforming burn that was shaped like the boot of Italy, sitting on the right side of his face. The miniature country, which had melted away on his brown skin, was too gross to ignore. I tried my best to avoid that side of his face when we got together, but it was hard not to look at. Something about its monstrous feature scared me.

Reminded me of the boogey man.

Reminded me of my past.

My childhood always had a way of doing that. I tried not to let it bother me too much, because he was filthy...filthy rich!

I'd done my research, so I knew Mayors normally didn't make tons of money, but this one did. His sleazy political deals netted him millions in various crooked investment deals, and his ties to the mob didn't hurt his rapidly growing pockets either.

"How much?" I whispered, while rubbing his huge potbelly. After recalling all of the wealth I was surrounded by, I was ready to seal this deal, but I needed him to be as comfortable as possible with his decision.

He sat up, took another swig of his whiskey and said, "A hundred thousand."

I paused and thought about accepting the offer, but my mind quickly wondered away again and got the best of me. I couldn't believe a hundred grand was all his mistress was worth. She also carried his unborn child, and he wanted them both to disappear. I immediately saw myself in her.

It was only a year ago that Oshyn had stolen my baby's life, and now I had agreed to do it to someone else. A little bit of emotion started to rise in my chest, but I quickly suppressed it. Emotion wasn't part of my resume. If this was what he wanted, the bitch would simply have to go.

Not only did I need the money, but this would also make what I planned on doing to Oshyn, a total walk in the park. I was sure that no one knew whether I was dead or alive, even after everyone died at Oshyn's house, except me and her. I left out of her home that night bullet ridden and broke. All the money I'd stacked up went right down the drain, and Brooklyn was the reason for most of it. I'd given Brooklyn the million dollars I'd blackmailed from Mr. Bourdeaux, and he took it all, leaving me with nothing.

Since then, my more generous clients had offered me permanent housing in their mansions and penthouses, but I reluctantly declined their offers. From the bullet hole Oshyn had put in my stomach, to the one Brooklyn put in my shoulder, along with the broken nose I sported, all those things were just too much to explain. With all these gunshot wounds, I was starting to feel like a female version of Fifty Cent. As it turned out, I definitely had more than nine lives, minus the budding music career.

"Is a hundred thousand enough?" the Mayor asked, probably uncomfortable with my long pause.

"Nah, you're gonna have to come larger than that. I'll do

the bitch for a hundred, but the baby is gonna cost you another two, making it three hundred even."

"Two hundred thousand for a fucking kid that's not even born? You're out of your damn mind, Chloe. Abortions don't even cost a tenth of that!" He became enraged, and the alcohol didn't help.

"Three hundred. Take it or leave it, but it's my final offer." Even though I could've really used the hundred grand, my offer was set in stone, and I wouldn't take anything less. I just couldn't bring myself to kill the baby, born or not. Maybe with me being twenty-six now, I was beginning to gain a conscious, but this was something that truly bothered me. "Take it or leave it," I said again.

"Alright. Three hundred, but not a dime more than that. After everything is done, I need you to skip town for a few weeks. You know, just until everything cools down. I've already arranged for your trip to Jamaica."

"Jamaica? That wasn't in my plans. I have things to do," I whined.

"Baby, just trust me," he begged, with a sinister smile that screamed just the opposite.

That was the problem...I didn't trust anybody.

# 2 CHLOE

It was ten thirty at night when I arrived in a development called Crest Mountain. As soon as I entered the neighborhood of brand new homes, I could tell you had to have money to live in this area.

"I guess the mountains are where he keeps all his whores," I said, as I admired the beautiful waterfall entrance.

Feeling more at ease in the midst of darkness, I was glad that I'd waited until the sun went down before I decided to go ahead with my assignment. I figured there was nothing worse than murdering someone in broad daylight, which was an idea that the dumb ass Mayor first suggested.

I cruised fast enough through the neighborhood not to raise suspicion, but slow enough so I wouldn't miss her house. Surprisingly, I drove past the expensive homes in a 2007 Sapphire Blue Lexus ES 350, that the Mayor purchased just for this occasion. I suggested driving a hooptie, but after checking out the area, I was glad I didn't. Any vehicle other than a luxury one would've stuck out like a sore thumb, and I didn't need that kind of attention. I thought it was too bad that he had ordered for the car to be torched after the murder, but I guess it was necessary. A senseless and brutal demise for a car of this caliber hurt like hell. My pussy got wet just thinking about me cruising around town in this beauty.

When I finally pulled up in front of her house, I was quite impressed. The Mayor's directions were on point as I reviewed the house that was in a picture he'd given me, and compared it to the one I sat in front of. I was relieved that I didn't have to rely on looking for the address, because the numbers were barely visible from all the huge manicured trees.

"Wow, it looks like she makes a good living from being a sideline hoe," I said, as I continued to look at the brick million-dollar estate.

Call it jealously, but I began to wonder what she had that I didn't for the Mayor to put her up for so long.

*Now I'm beginning to think she should've been out the fucking picture a long time ago.* Her living conditions spoke volumes of her pussy game. Most bitches were lucky if they got their rent paid, and this one had managed to get herself a kingdom. *I knew I should've demanded more money,* I thought, as I realized how little three hundred thousand dollars was to him. *By the looks of this house, his ass could afford it.* I decided not to dwell on the numbers too much, and stick to what I was here for. I was content with the deal we'd worked out, which was eighty thousand in cash before I left him this morning, and the rest when the deal was closed.

I turned off my car and sat in the dark, trying to peep the scenery. The Mayor tried to assure me that no one was ever at her house, but I was still cautious. I knew that women in our profession always kept our options open. In the midst of my thoughts, I noticed her silhouette in the second story window. *Damn! White people never have blinds for some damn reason,* I thought, after realizing that most of the houses in the neighborhood had windows that weren't covered either.

I looked as discreetly as I could in my rearview mirror, and readjusted the long burgundy wig that covered my jet black hair. I also wore a pair of Gucci shades so it wouldn't show any parts of my Asian decent. I patted my hip to make sure that my weapon was still in place, and grabbed the spare key to her crib; compliments of the Mayor. I slid out of the car, barely closing the door, when my phone rang.

"Damn it," I whispered softly, wondering why I'd been so careless as to leave the phone at the highest ring volume. "Hello?"

"Are you there yet?" the Mayor asked, slurring his words. "Did you kill her?"

"Are you fucking serious? Did you really just say that to me over the damn phone?" I was pissed. I treated every call like it was being tapped, and this asshole mentions some stupid shit like that over the phone. He was definitely out of it. "Stop calling me. You asked me to do something for you, and it's getting done. Don't fucking call this phone again!" I warned, before hanging up.

Too much time had been wasted already from that meaningless phone call. I just hoped I hadn't brought any unwanted attention to myself. I turned my phone off and ran to the front of her house.

I hesitated for a second, wondering if it was a good idea to enter through the front door. However, those thoughts quickly went away when I remembered that it had to appear as though she knew her killer. It would be a lot cleaner than a break in. The Mayor had informed me that her alarm was always disarmed, and only turned on when she went to sleep, so I hoped her ass hadn't called it a night since I saw her in the window. I thought that to be pretty backwards, wondering why she just didn't set it as soon as she walked in. But he said she was a creature of habit, and that was something she'd done for years.

I hope he was right.

Seconds later, I quietly let myself into her house, and braced myself for the piercing sound of the alarm, but surprisingly everything was silent.

*This broad is crazy, doesn't she watch scary movies*, I thought, as I entered the huge foyer. I slowly tiptoed across the cream colored marble floor, toward the spiral staircase that sat in the middle of the room, and looked up to make sure no one was there. With my Pumas on, I was quiet as a mouse as I crept up the staircase until I reached the top.

Once I planted my feet quietly on the plush carpet, I immediately came to an obstacle, trying to figure out what room she was actually in. There had to be at least ten closed doors and not a sound came from either of them.

*Damn, why do all the doors have to be closed? She could be in any of these rooms.*

I instinctively started checking my surroundings, afraid that she may have found out that someone was in her home, and was now hiding. From the silhouette I saw, I thought she might've been in the room I stood directly in front of, but wasn't positive. It seemed as though I'd lost all sense of direction, and now couldn't figure out anything.

I quickly whipped my head to the right after hearing what sounded like water trickling down a drain. I pulled away a few strands of the wig that got stuck on my lip-gloss, and went to investigate where the noise was coming from. I crept up to a room that was enhanced with French double doors, protecting the room from my view. It didn't take a genius to know that it was the master bedroom.

I waited with my ear to the door until I heard the sounds of water coming from the shower. That gave me the go ahead to enter the room. I was sure, at that point, she was actually in the shower, or at least in the bathroom, and I wouldn't have any surprises. I crept in her room, and followed the sweet aroma of the vanilla scented candles, but couldn't help noticing a few pictures of her and the Mayor that sat on the night-stand as I passed by.

She was a beautiful woman who looked to be in her early twenties, with long blonde hair and an infectious smile, which made her look like she belonged in Paris Hilton's clique.

Who knows, maybe she did.

Too bad the smile she held in the photos would be her last moment of happiness.

Suddenly, her soft humming that echoed throughout the room broke me out of my daze, and I quickly made my way over to the bathroom. My adrenaline began pumping and sweat began pouring down my face. I knew that I had to get this over with and get out as fast as I could.

"Ahh," I gasped, as my right pocket began to vibrate. I took out the phone that I thought was completely off, and saw the Mayor's number lit up in the caller ID window. *This fucking guy*, I thought, as I hesitated whether or not to answer it.

"What!" I said, in a tone that was barely a whisper. I was taking a big risk of being heard right now, so whatever he wanted, it needed to be good.

"Are you finished yet?" he asked, sounding even more intoxicated than before.

"Why are you still calling me?" I was so irritated at this point and was beginning to think this was all a set up. "Are you trying to get me caught or some shit?"

"No. I...love you...Chloe. I can't wait to see you again," he answered.

"If you call me one more fucking time, the whole thing is off," I warned, meaning every word I said. I figured eighty thousand dollars would suffice for a deed that wasn't finished, and it was a headache I wouldn't have to worry about.

"Okay, okay, I won't call you again...I promise!"

I hung up the phone before he had a chance to say anything else, and made sure to turn off the power this time. I couldn't afford to get locked up because of his dumb ass.

Her shower glass door was covered with fog, and I didn't want to risk her screaming when I opened it, so I waited until she was finished. After several more minutes of her off tune melody, she stepped out onto her bathroom floor, dripping wet. As she took a few steps forward to reach for her towel, I took a quick second to admire her small protruding stomach before grabbing the twenty-five caliber Berretta off my side, and put one bullet in her forehead. The state of shock that was left on her face made for a quiet ending, and the silencer that was attached to the gun luckily hadn't let me down.

My job was done, and I felt no remorse...none!

Before I left out of the house, I dug through the antique jewelry box that sat on her vanity, and took one of the biggest diamonds I'd ever seen in my life. Since I didn't feel like I was paid what this job was worth, I considered it my incentive.

"She won't be needing this anymore," I said, placing the huge emerald cut diamond ring in my pocket. "Damn, that beauty has to be at least five carats."

Within seconds, I was out of the house as fast as I came in, and made my way back to the getaway car.

As planned, I dumped the car at an abandoned factory, setting it, along with the weapon on fire, and hopped into the silver 1998 Honda that had been left for me. The plan had turned out to be easier than I thought, and I drove back to my cabin with a huge smile on my face. I hadn't been this happy in months. I was back to the old me, and loving every minute of it.

# 3 CHLOE

The next morning, I went to the dealership to purchase myself a crispy new luxury SUV, and I knew no other company could do it better than Mercedes. When I made my way into the dealership, I immediately walked up to a Platinum 2008 GL450 truck, and it was love at first sight. The shiny metallic exterior seemed to illuminate the whole showroom floor, and the smoky colored buttery interior topped it off.

"I can definitely see myself in this," I said, as I ran my hand across the familiar silver emblem on the grill.

After looking at the cheap $57,000 price tag, I knew I had more than enough to pay for the car in cash, and pay the salesmen off too. Finally, I was back at the level where I belonged…the top.

Not wanting to appear unaccustomed to such elegance, I resisted the urge to test drive my new love. I lifted my head and stared in the direction of one particular salesperson. I'd become quite skilled at reading people, so I knew he wouldn't give me any problems. Not to my surprise, he hurried over in my direction.

"How fast can the paperwork be drawn up on her?" I asked, gliding my fingers along the truck I was standing beside.

The older black man wasn't discreet, as he scanned me with his eyes to see how serious I was about making the purchase. Little did he know, I was fully prepared to buy what I wanted. I arrived at the dealership decked out in an all white St. John sundress that I'd bought earlier that morning, along with my studded Bvlgari shades, and Jude Frances diamond and cross bracelet that ran me thirty-three hundred bucks. With all the money that the Mayor gave me for his dirty work, I was back to my old ways, spending money like it was water, and it felt good.

"I see you have great taste, but you seem like a lady who likes top of the line things. Are you sure you're not interested in the G500?" he asked, pointing to another truck. "That one retails for $87,000."

My face began to frown as I turned my head. Even though it cost more, the ugly metal vehicle reminded me of a mail truck. "No, that's okay. I don't work for the post office." Besides, I couldn't buy that one until I met up with the Mayor to get the rest of my money.

He let out a huge smile. "Okay then, right this way, ma'am," the salesman instructed, after giving me an interrogation with his eyes. He led me into a rather large cubicle and took a seat in a hard looking leather chair.

"How are you prepared to finance this vehicle, Mrs…"

"Jones. My name is Mrs. Jones, and I'm not financing it. I would like to pay for it in cash. However, I'm fully aware that any purchase over ten thousand, you have to report to the IRS," I said, as I uncrossed and crossed my legs, trying to find a more suitable position for seduction.

"Yes I do, but…"

"That's why I'm prepared to pay you fifteen thousand in

cash, to overlook it," I added, cutting him off.

He rubbed his chin in deep thought for a few seconds, before looking down at the briefcase that he was sure carried the money. The offer I laid out on the table was too good to be true, and I knew he couldn't turn it down.

"And I get the money now?" he asked, looking around trying to make sure that he wasn't being overheard by an unsuspecting bystander.

"Yep!"

He drafted up the paperwork within a matter of minutes, and proceeded to have me fill out the necessary forms. I signed the borrowed name, Oshyn Jones, on all the documents, and opened up the briefcase to reveal my gratitude for a job well done. As I placed my hand on the money, he stood up and made his way over to a small coffee machine. He looked around and over his shoulder, as the thought of being caught obviously consumed him. Though fear resided in his eyes, I was sure that his greed would conquer his other feelings, and I was right.

I watched as his shaky hands managed to pour the steaming hot coffee into the cup without spilling it. I could tell he was trying to maintain control.

"Would you like some?" he asked, forgetting that he never offered.

"No thank you. I just want to get on with the process."

I was supposed to be in Jamaica by now, but I'd overslept and missed my plane. The Mayor would've been pissed had he known, but I still had all intentions on going. It would just have to be after I tied up some loose ends.

"Here you go," I said, extending my hand toward him with the fifteen grand. He snatched it up quickly, still looking around nervously.

After putting the money in his desk, he said, "Follow me."

I gave him a slight frown. "Where are we going?"

"To the finance department."

"Why?" I asked, confused. "I thought you were going to handle everything right here? I just told you I didn't want to finance!"

"Well, unfortunately, the rest of the paperwork has to get taken care of in the finance department. I can't complete the transaction here. But don't worry, I have a connect that will finalize the sale without any hassles."

"I'm not paying any more money," I warned.

"No, ma'am, it's okay," he assured me. "I'm gonna give him a portion of my money."

I finally agreed to his terms, seeing as though I had no choice, and followed him down the hall.

"Wait right here," he instructed, as he walked out of the office. It was only seconds before he came back, accompanied with another guy, who appeared to be around the same age as my salesman. By the wrinkles that formed on their faces like vines, I'd give them both late forties.

"Lovely meeting you, Mrs. Jones. My name is Terry Boon, and I'll be helping you from this point." He reached out and gave me a soft feminine handshake. At that point, I knew he was a bitch.

"Well, it was nice meeting you, and congratulations on your new purchase," my salesman said, right before walking away. He seemed to be a little too eager to get away from me.

"Now, Mrs. Jones, back to you," Boon said, redirecting my attention to him. "The total purchase price for this vehicle comes out to sixty-two thousand one hundred and eighteen dollars. I understand that you'll be making the total payment today with cash?" He never looked me in the eyes, as he waited for my answer. Just fumbled through papers, pretending to be overly occupied.

"Yes, that's correct." I pulled out my briefcase again, placing it on his table, and opened it. I counted out the money he asked for and handed it to him, nicely stacked. He didn't seem fazed by the large amount of money that was in front of him. It was like he'd done this several times before.

He excused himself and walked out of his office, taking the stacks of money with him. I'd now been in the dealership for more than forty minutes, and I needed the process to hurry up so that I could catch my plane. Ten minutes turned into thirty before I got any sign of life again.

"What's taking so long? Is this how you treat all your customers?" I asked, standing up as Mr. Boon returned to his office.

The finance guy cleared his throat before looking at me with a concerned look. "Mrs. Jones, I'm afraid some of this money is counterfeit," he said, in a whisper-like tone. It was like he thought he was being set up. He pushed the money back toward me, as beads of sweat began forming on his slim face.

"Counterfeit, what the hell are you talking about? This money isn't fake!" I replied, while inspecting every last detail of the bills. It smelled real and the texture was consistent, which made me even more confused.

"The money marker indicates that these bills aren't real," he informed, while pointing to the pile on the right. "However, the bills on the left are fine." He wiped his face off with a handkerchief.

The proof was right in front of my face and he was right. The Mayor had obviously played me like a fool, and I fell for it. It was all starting to make sense to me. I was supposed to be in Jamaica by now, which probably would've been a death sentence. I was positive at that point the Mayor would send someone else to kill me in order to cover his tracks. This was all a set up, that he was hoping wouldn't be figured out until it was too late.

I quickly stuffed all the money back in the briefcase, and stomped out of the dealership on a war path. My anger increased as I drove off in the cheap ass silver Honda that the Mayor gave me the night before. I sped furiously to his favorite hang out, the restaurant where we'd met.

When I arrived twenty minutes later, I wasn't surprised to see his driver's car sitting outside. You would think that after fucking me over, he would be long gone by now, but he had bigger balls than I thought.

Too bad they were about to be cut off.

The high end Italian restaurant was closed to the public, but I knew the front door would still be open. I walked in the dimly lit building and startled the maitre'd when I walked up on him.

"SShhhh," I said, putting my finger over my lips. "Who's in the restaurant?" I asked him, waving a stack of money in his face.

He hesitated a moment before answering. "Only the Mayor and his wife," he answered, hypnotized by the smell of currency. "It's their anniversary, so he had the restaurant closed."

*Oh really*, I thought, before handing over a stack of counterfeit money. "Here's twenty grand. I want you to leave, and don't tell anyone that you were ever here today. Do you understand?"

The middle aged white man nodded his head up and down. "Mums the word," he said, as he grabbed the money and smiled all the way out the door. I knew that he would spill the beans once he found out the cash was fake, but his silence would give me enough time to at least get out of town.

Once inside the dining area, I made my way to the Mayor's private room where I heard laughter. "Oh, you won't be laughing for long," I said quietly, as I walked up to the door to peek inside. They were alone. As I watched the two of them making a toast, I thought that was the best time to make my presence known.

"Steak, my favorite!" I said, rubbing my stomach as I pulled up a chair and sat between the two lovebirds. From the look on the Mayor's face, you would've thought he'd seen a ghost. Perhaps he had.

"Hi honey," I said to the woman, who joined him in such an intimate setting. She was a little older, yet gorgeous like all the others, and was dripping in diamonds. Diamonds really were every girl's best friend. I turned my attention back toward the Mayor, who seemed more jittery than a child who needed Ritalin.

"I knew you loved yourself some white women," I joked.

"What are you doing here?" he asked, in an attempt to take control of the situation.

"Well, I *would* be long gone by now, but there seems to have been a mix up," I replied, opening up the briefcase. "You see, all the money you gave me isn't real."

"What?" he asked, pretending to be confused. "I don't know what you're talking about? I didn't give you any money!"

"What's going on here, sweetheart?" his wife interjected. "Who is this woman?" Those were words from a woman who held a position, a woman who got what she wanted.

"She's nobody, and I'm getting ready to call the police," he threatened, with his phone in hand.

"Nobody? Oh, since your wife is here, now I'm nobody?" I asked. I directed my attention toward her. "I've been fucking your husband for almost a year now, and I just killed his other mistress, who by the way, was pregnant with his child."

She stared at me, telling me through her eyes that she didn't believe a word I'd said. I guess there had been so many mistresses in the past who'd tried to break up their happy home, that she wasn't taking it anymore.

"Honey, she's lying. I don't know who this psychotic woman is!" He looked in my direction. "Are you on drugs, young lady?"

I was speechless. I knew he would lie about the money and

our affair, but he should've known not to disrespect me like that.

He grabbed his wife's hand and said, "Come on, sweetie, let's get out of here."

Before he stood up completely, I swooped the oversized steak knife off the table and stabbed him in the chest over and over again, until I was sure he wouldn't make it. In horror, his wife began screaming, but quickly stopped when I placed the same blood drenched knife under her neck.

"Is everything okay?" the teenage waitress asked, in regards to all the noise. Once she realized what she'd walked in on, she too began to scream in horror. The beautifully designed desserts that she carried in her hand, now decorated the floor. She backed herself up, trying to get away from the mayhem, until she hit the wall.

"Scream one more time and you'll both die," I warned the women, while the Mayor gasped for air on the floor. I moved the knife from his wife's neck, making sure to graze her skin with its blade and sat down. I took a sip of the Mayor's wine, while he fought for his life, then looked up at both women, who were obviously afraid to fight back. Back in the day, I probably would've let him go with a warning, but now I refused to play any more games. Anyone who crossed me from this day on would die. The Mayor could thank Oshyn for his pain and suffering.

"Wait, please don't kill us!" the Mayor's wife begged. She reminded me of Oshyn the night she begged for mercy once everything came tumbling down. I saw my sister's fear in this woman's tears. All I wanted was revenge for what Oshyn had done to me. I hated her. With every bone that I had in me, I hated her existence, and I wanted her dead. She stole my past from me, and killed my future. The Mayor's wife reminded me of my enemy, and unfortunately, she would have to pay the cost.

I snatched the same knife I used to stab the Mayor, and

without hesitation, ended the frail woman's life with one swing. I turned and looked at my only witness, and decided to kill her too. There was no need for anyone to be able to pick me out in a line up.

"Where's the cook?" I asked her, expecting him to pop out at any moment.

"He…he's out back taking out the trash," the teenage waitress stammered.

For some reason, she didn't seem as afraid of my presence anymore. I sensed that she hoped the cook would sneak in from the back and save her from death. I was pissed that she'd tested my strength.

"Hold out your hands," I instructed her. She obliged. I took the knife that was now responsible for two deaths, and made a clean cut through the main arteries in her arms. It was only a matter of minutes before she would lose consciousness and die. However, once she dropped to her knees, I realized that she wasn't dying fast enough. I was afraid that she'd be able to get help once I left.

While she cried for mercy on the floor, I stabbed her in the throat, ending her life instantaneously. I took the knife and ran out the restaurant before someone else showed up. Killing the Mayor was almost as satisfying as making money, and it was something I was starting to feign. I didn't know what the feeling was, but every time I took someone's life, I got a high that was unexplainable. It was exciting in a fulfilling sort of way. It was sort of like an out of body experience, and I was beginning to crave it.

With the Mayor being killed, I knew that it wouldn't be long before there was a nationwide manhunt put in place to find the killer. Even though he was a politician that everyone seemed to hate, the authorities would still do everything within their power to bring me down.

As I jumped in the car and sped off, all I could think about was how Oshyn was the reason I was in this mess in the first place.

"If that bitch hadn't ruined my life, I wouldn't be going through this shit," I said, as I made my way to the highway. It was finally time for Oshyn to pay for what she'd done. It was time to put my family back together again.

# 4 CHLOE

Two hours later, I arrived in Charlotte as the gas light in the car began to come on. I would've driven the full four hours straight to Raleigh, but I had to make a pit stop, because there was some pertinent information that I needed from this city. While on the road, I called in a favor from an old client of mine, and he put a meeting together with someone named Mr. Tate, who agreed to help me.

After stopping at a gas station to fill up and grab a donut, I decided to change my clothes. I'd been in the same blood splattered sundress for hours, so a new set of clothing was well overdue. I walked into the filthy bathroom and placed my duffel bag on the sink. I decided to put on my short black Stella McCartney dress, which had a plunging neckline. If I wanted heads to turn when I walked in the room, this was the dress. I proceeded to take off my clothes, and could've cared less if someone walked into the bathroom at that moment. I was on a mission, and wasn't about to go into one of those small ass stalls. Once I sprayed a few squirts of my favorite Vera Wang perfume, and played with my hair, I was back in business and ready to take on whatever Charlotte had to offer.

Minutes later, I pulled up in front of the strip club, *Swallow*, and decided to go in, even though I had at least thirty minutes before my meeting. Little did Mr. Tate know, he couldn't have picked a better place to talk business. Strip clubs were next to heaven in my opinion. As I walked in, several eyes were on me as I made my way to the stage and took a seat in the front.

The best seat in the house.

At three o'clock in the afternoon, the high end titty bar was jammed packed, and the dancers were nasty, just the way I liked them. They even danced fully nude. *Someone pinch me, because now I really am in heaven.*

I immediately noticed a gorgeous dancer, as she climbed up the famous silver pole like a cheetah, and worked her way down, while her pussy seemed to talk to the audience. Her gigantic round ass clapped with every move she made, almost sending me into cardiac arrest. I could tell she'd been doing this for a while. Though her face said, early twenties, I knew she was a pro. She moved the black wig that came down to her waist, over her shoulder, and crawled her way over to me. Her skin was the color of a cardboard box, and the barb wire tattoo that lined her lower back was sexy as hell.

When she stopped and showed me what she was working with, I licked my lips at the thought of the goddess that was before me. I hadn't been this close to pussy since my last girlfriend, Joy. While all the men howled for more, she took her smooth hand and rubbed her kitty in a circular motion. My clit began to throb as I admired her perfectly toned body.

"Come and rub your pussy against my tongue," I insisted, as I held it out. "I promise I won't bite!"

She pretended to be getting fucked as she humped the air and moaned in ecstasy. I took some of the fake money that I couldn't seem to get rid of, and placed it in the crack of her ass. I craved to feel the warmth and dampness of her shaved goodies. As the crowd cheered, she looked me in my eyes and dared me to fondle her. I instantly became mesmerized by her beautiful body.

Her kitty looked divine as she bent over and grabbed her ankles. At that moment, I was so turned on, I began to make circular motions in the chair while my clit begged to be licked. I wanted to cum immediately.

"Let me touch it," I mouthed to her.

As she did her final seductive moves, she rolled her eyes, and said, "I'm strictly dickly!"

"Next on stage is La La," the DJ said, interrupting whatever was about to go down. Little did he know he'd just saved her ass from a butt naked beat down. The bitch that played me was now on her six-inch heels and strutting off the stage. *I hope that dumb bitch has a great time spending that fake money.* I was furious. I wanted her to come back out, so she could put out the fire she'd started. With nothing left but time on my hands, and a soaking wet pussy, I went to the bar.

"What you drinking, beautiful?" a man asked, who was surrounded by hoes.

"Ace of Spades."

"What the hell is Ace of Spades?" he asked, as all the girls chuckled.

"What's your name, playa?"

"Boo...Boo Brown."

If the girls wanted to laugh, now was the time because his name was hilarious. "Well...Boo Brown, here is a little lesson since it seems like you're here to be a baller. Ace of Spades is a champagne, that could be seen in Jay-Z's new video, and that's what I like to drink. So, if you can't afford it...I understand!"

"Can't afford it? Are you serious? These bitches aren't around me for nothing, sweetheart," he said, getting obscenely loud. "I'm buying out the whole bar right now!" he screamed, slamming a few stacks on the bar. The bartender ran and grabbed the money, and moved as fast as he could to take everybody's order.

I walked away, not really wanting to entertain him. I knew that if I got hyped enough, things would get ugly. I was more concerned with finding my new friend. I looked down at my watch and saw that it was almost time for him to arrive. I went and sat back down in front of the stage. I was hornier than ever, so I was expecting the next dancer to put me in the same zone as the previous girl did. *Maybe this time, I can have an orgasm.*

"Chloe?" someone said to me, over the loud rap music. When I turned around, a humongous bouncer stood in my view. *I could sure use him on my team,* I thought, wondering how many heads he'd smashed over the years. "Mr. Tate is ready to see you now."

*Damn, this dude must be pretty important, anytime he sends someone to come get me.* I got up and followed the massive man to the VIP section of the club. When I arrived, I noticed an attractive guy in a buttoned up polo shirt, a pair of glasses, and some Dockers. He looked way out of place, and more importantly, I was expecting some thug type dude. Everybody knows you can't be a gangsta with four eyes.

"Thanks, Pete," he said, as the bouncer announced my presence before turning around to leave. "So, how can I help you today, Ms. Chloe?" he asked, keeping his focus directed toward the stage.

"I need a little help finding someone, and I know that you have the resources I need." I wanted to destroy Oshyn's whole life, and he was the only man who could do it.

"Don't you have enough trouble on your hands after what you did in Asheville?" he asked, never looking my way.

I could've shitted on myself. I'd just killed the Mayor earlier today, so there was no way anyone could've known about it.

"How…how did you know?"

He finally looked at me. "I check out everyone before I fuck with them. But trust me, I'm the only one who knows."

*Nigga, are you crazy? I don't trust anybody.* "Well, since you know so much about me, I hope you can help with my situation."

"I'll be more than happy to help, but for a small fee of course."

I sighed, because I didn't have a lot of money since the Mayor had played me for a fool. "How much do you want? I don't have a lot of money."

He stood up and walked over to me. "I don't need your money. However, you can pay me in other ways," he said, stroking my arm.

At that point, I knew exactly what he was talking about, and that was my type of payment. *Thank goodness I decided to put on this short ass dress.* "So, what would your wife say if she found out," I replied, tapping his wedding band.

He pushed the glasses up on his nose and smiled. "Stop acting like you give a fuck about her because I don't."

I returned the smile. "You've got a point."

*     *     *

It was the very next day, and fifteen hundred dollars an hour is what he agreed to pay for my services. Besides, he didn't complain once when I mentioned my three-hour minimum. The plan wasn't to fuck Mr. Tate at first, but I needed to get this monkey off my back. Even though I tried to maintain a low profile, the money sounded too good to pass up. This man not only had a lot of money, but he was also a huge asset to me. Little did he know that he was going to help me kill two birds with one stone.

I peeked out the window of my lavish hotel suite in the Hilton, and admired Charlotte's downtown area. *This shit looks just like a little Atlanta,* I thought, still surprised that I'd ended up here from Asheville. I was supposed to be somewhere in Jamaica lying in the sun, three hundred thousand dollars richer. But now, because of his mistake, the Mayor was somewhere laid down, six feet under.

My new client, Stanford Tate, had me stay in a hotel, which was several minutes away from his Corporate Headquarters. I guess he didn't want to risk running into any of his co-workers. After applying some makeup, and adding my favorite lip gloss, I checked the camera I'd hidden inside a stuffed animal which sat on the desk one more time, to make sure that everything was in place.

Earlier that morning, I'd gone down to the gift shop, to purchase something to hide the high-tech camera in, and the stuffed bear with a *I Love Charlotte* t-shirt on, was the only thing I could find. Since he knew about the Mayor, I needed something on him. I just hoped like hell he didn't catch on.

I went to my duffel bag that was underneath the bed, and pulled out a slightly tattered birth certificate that read:

OFFICE OF VITAL STATISTICS
Certificate of Birth
Name: Oshyn Mone Rodriguez
Date of Birth: 7/4/81      Sex: Female
Place of Birth: Monroe County, New York
Certificate Number: 123-00-022400
Date Filed: 7/8/81
Mother s Maiden Name: Mahogany Rodriguez
Father s Name: Unknown

I laid the worthless piece of paper that I couldn't seem to throw away, on the bed next to an old yellowish newspaper article that was dated back to October 10, 1981, that read: SERIAL RAPIST CAPTURED!

I looked over the two documents, as I'd done several times

since my grandmother's death, and wondered for the millionth time how Oshyn and I shared the same womb. I also couldn't understand how, even after the loss of one mother, she still seemed to have another one. Now I understood why my grandmother had been hiding the important documents in her closet all these years. If I hadn't been searching for money the day of her funeral, I would've never run across it. I guess she knew we were never meant to be sisters.

After I found out that my mother gave birth to Oshyn, I was so angry. That little bitch got everything, including the only one who ever loved me...my mom. My main purpose for living now had become to get revenge for all the things that Oshyn had stolen from me. She would pay, and that's something that I would bet my life on.

*KNOCK!*

His timing couldn't have been better. I remembered him requesting that the door not be opened, unless there was only a single knock. Before I made my way to the door, I pulled up my black bustier that looked radiant against my golden brown skin, and made sure that my matching thong and garter belt were in place. The sexy lingerie had been delivered to my room that morning, with a note for me to have it on once he got there. This type of shit obviously turned him on, and if he wanted freaky, then I was the right one to give it to him. I admired myself in the mirror one more time. "I should teach a class," I said, shaking my head at the thought of what some of these dumb ass wives thought they were too good to do. I'm sure his wife was the stuck up type.

"Who is it?" I asked, as seductively as possible.

"Superman," he answered, giving me the password that we agreed upon.

I opened the door slowly, making sure he caught a good view of my sexy attire, and smiled. Even though he didn't look like Clark Kent, he still looked good, as his goatee and smooth bald head turned me on.

I grabbed him by the hand and led him to the bed, where the camera would have the best view. I couldn't afford to miss any part of the action, and had to make sure that I got it right the first time. I decided to start a brief conversation to make him feel comfortable.

"How's your day been so far?" I asked, while slithering behind him. I massaged his shoulders, which were a little tense, and waited for an answer. I knew in his line of work, that he was stressed big time.

"Long and hard!" he answered, looking down at his dick. "Long and hard!"

*Damn, that shit is huge!* I thought, as I did a double take over his shoulder. His dick literally looked like it touched his knee even through his pants. *No wonder his wife won't fuck him!* I thought to myself, after concluding how much damage his dick was going to do. By the size, I estimated that I would suffer from a swollen pussy for weeks.

"How do you want it?" I whispered seductively in his ear, never showing how unenthused I was about fucking him. I'd made up my mind, and was going to take it like a champ.

He smiled, showing off a set of nice teeth. "Long and hard!" he repeated for the second time. Since he didn't seem like much of a talker, I decided to go on with the show. I slid off his shirt and began nibbling on his neck. Without warning, I grabbed his shoulders, causing him to fall back on the bed.

"Wow, I see you like it a little rough," he said, allowing me to take charge.

"You haven't seen anything yet." I got up and stood in front of him, so I could take off his pants. I couldn't wait to see the monster that was hidden under his clothes. After unbuckling his belt, I slid his pants down to his ankles, and surprisingly, he wasn't wearing any underwear. *He really is a freak*, I thought, as I watched his huge dick stand at attention. I guess he could tell I was excited, because he immediately began pulling on my bustier.

"Slow down, Papi. I promise, we'll get to that in a second," I assured, while I started dancing for him to a tune that only I could hear. As he smiled and ran his masculine, hard working hands over his face, the phone on the side of his pants began to vibrate.

He snatched the phone off of his pants, as I continued to do sexy moves with my hips.

"Hello?" he said, with urgency in his voice.

*Oh hell no! I need your full attention*, I thought, as I immediately dropped down to my knees, and managed to stick what felt like twelve inches down my throat. I could tell he was trying to concentrate on the caller, but it was hard. Long and hard, as he would say.

"Umm…the…body was where? Okay, I'm on…my… way!"

"What's wrong?" I asked, in between gulps of air. I didn't care what anyone else said, I was the real super head.

"I have to go back to work," he replied, paralyzed by the champion brain I was giving him. "Umm…it's an emergency."

I stopped right in the middle of what I was doing, and insisted that he go on about his business. Besides, I'd already been paid my three-hour minimum, and I was sure the camera had captured him in a compromised position, so whatever he decided to do was fine with me. As he stood up to get dressed, I noticed his rock hard dick standing firm like a missile. It resembled a ten-ounce water bottle.

"It's not going to go down," he said hopelessly.

"Well, put it in here and I'll see what I can do," I teased, while I lay back on the bed, pulling my thong to the side.

My pussy had been recently waxed, and looked so pretty with the new tattoo of my name written in cursive. I could've sworn I almost saw drool come out of his mouth as he forgot what he had to do, and jumped on top of me. His facial hairs pricked me, while his mouth ravished my kitty with strokes from his tongue.

He didn't even bother to take my thongs off, as he licked every inch of me, and sucked on my clit for at least ten minutes. He couldn't eat pussy as good as Joy, but he was a very close candidate. After having my second orgasm, he quickly inserted his massive dick inside of me before I even had a chance to lube up. I just knew I was gonna need some KY in order for his humongous dick to glide in as effortlessly as possible, and I was right.

I winced in pain, while he pounded my pussy with long deep strokes and grunted spontaneously. However, after a few more minutes, he finally slowed down. I was surprised at his sudden attempt to be gentle, as he placed my fingers in his mouth and played with each one of them with his tongue. I found it easier to manage his dick at this speed, so I slowly moved my hips to catch his rhythm, enjoying this a little more than before. For a moment, I closed my eyes and went somewhere else.

I took myself to all the nights my baby, Brooklyn, made love to me. I fell in love with each of Brooklyn's strokes, as I imagined him in my arms again. Brooklyn was the only man who never fucked me, we always made love. He took care of my pussy like a delicate flower, so I made sure my pussy took care of him. I knew that meant he loved me, and we would've been together if it wasn't for Oshyn's ass.

Superman's dick began to throb, bringing me back to reality. I knew he was getting ready to erupt. Within a matter of minutes, he pulled out and busted a nut all over my chest. I could care less where any of my clients put their baby makers, as long as it wasn't inside of me. He was up in no time, putting on his clothes as fast as he could. After putting on his shirt, he reached in his pocket and handed me a stack of hundred dollar bills.

"Damn, is this my tip?" I asked, counting the money. There

were fifteen bills in all.

"Yeah, you deserve that and even more. I can't tell you the last time my wife was able to take my dick like that."

I smiled. Little did he know I almost failed at the challenge myself.

On his way out the door he said, "The first part of your request has been done. I'll need a little more time to get that other information to you. Keep in touch."

As he closed the door, I counted my extra money for the second time, and then blew kisses at the camera. *Federal Agent Tate, you're going to pay me much more then you think!*

# 5 OSHYN

We sat in silence for what seemed like an eternity, while eight dark suited pallbearers placed the two coffins, one platinum and one baby blue, on the gurney. I couldn't believe this was happening. I shook my head back and forth, as I watched the rain beat down on a pair of coffins that shouldn't even exist. The water that fell out of the sky, replaced the tears that once fell from my eyes. The weather was fitting for this type of event. The clouds were grey, the birds weren't singing, and the ground had turned to mush, just like my life.

The coffin my son laid in was so small. The thought of him being six feet under by himself was enough to send me to the crazy house, that's why I made the decision to bury Apples at the same time. It brought me, and hopefully Bella, what little comfort the world had left, to know they weren't alone. Although I selfishly wished at least one of them had been left behind.

I thought my mind was playing tricks on me, as I noticed an image that once resembled happiness. I closed my eyes, shook my head again and looked a little closer. There was no mistaking his frame even from miles away. The man I once called my husband, the only one that had ever truly won my heart, was standing a far distance at his car to pay his respect.

Suddenly, a sharp pain cut through my forehead where Chloe had hit me with the butt of her gun. It was a wound I'd received the day everyone died. Without realizing it, I pressed my hands roughly against the gauge, loosening a couple of stitches, and causing it to bleed profusely.

As the nurse cleaned the blood that ran down my face, which had turned a hint of purple due to all the bruising, the minister laid a comforting hand on my shoulder, as he concluded his prayer. He placed a long stem red rose in my grieving hands, to toss on my baby's coffin that rested above his freshly dug home.

The rose.

A flower I once loved.

It now created a sense of uneasiness for me. Just the smell of them almost made me a bit nauseous and dizzy. I had a feeling that I would eventually grow to hate them.

I stood up the best I could, elbowing all those that came to lend an unwanted hand. This, I was determined to do on my own. Using my crutch as a balance, I got ready to place the flower on the hard metal coffin, when something came over me. I looked over to where Brooklyn once was, and noticed that he was gone.

I hated myself for yearning for his hug.

His kiss.

His smell.

That's all I wanted...love. It was the one thing that would convince me that this was just a cruel joke.

I missed them all so much that I could literally feel my heart breaking into pieces. Micah, Apples and Brooklyn were all gone forever. I felt the rough touches of Brian, and a few others, cupping my elbow to keep me from fainting. I was so frail, and in so much anguish, that I started seeing double.

Angry at life, and determined to stand on my own, I took what little strength I had left, and yanked myself out of their grasp, losing my balance and falling on top of the casket…

*BEEP! BEEP! BEEP! BEEP!*

I woke up for the third night in a row drenched in my own sweat. The dream with me almost falling into the ditch just wouldn't leave my mind. The bright red numbers that read seven a.m., looked me dead in my eyes, as I stared at the custom made alarm clock that carried the photos of a family that no longer existed.

Everyday I woke up to the pictures that seemed to drown me deeper into depression, but I just couldn't put them away. I'd made a promise to remember them forever. Even after a year, I still couldn't seem to let go. I forced a smile on my face as I watched Bella stroll into my room.

"Hey auntie," Bella said, kissing me on the cheek.

I motioned for her to hop in the bed with me, and when she did, I gave her the biggest hug I could. I couldn't imagine anyone, especially a girl her age, going through anything like this.

"You…are…hurting me!" she managed to get out, while I crushed her with all one hundred and thirty pounds of me.

"Sorry, baby, that's just how much I love you!"

"I know, auntie…I know," she replied, rolling her eyes. I'd started noticing a little attitude from her lately, but really hadn't paid too much attention to it. I figured she was just going through an emotional roller coaster and assumed it would soon pass. My roller coaster ride hadn't managed to stop yet, but I was sure that God wouldn't let her go through this for long. "I miss my mom," she confessed, shocking me half to death.

After my best friend, Apples passed away, Bella rarely showed any emotions or even spoke of what happened. The psychiatrist told me that it was normal for a child her age to withdraw after going through so many traumas. I guess with her turning seven years old, she'd finally decided to grieve in her own way.

"I miss Micah too. Auntie, do you think they can still see me?"

"Oh baby, of course they can see you. Your mom is looking down on you all the time, making sure that you're okay. So is Micah! They're your angels."

I wanted her to believe me.

I wanted me to believe myself.

Her light skin made her nose light up like Rudolph, as small tears ran down her slightly freckled face. I wasn't sure if it was because I missed Apples so much, but Bella was beginning to look more like her mother everyday. Her eyes had even started to change to a hint of green. Talk about spooky!

The baby monitor startled us both, as cries from Mye's screaming whaled through the speakers.

"Pumpkin, go brush your teeth and get dressed before you're late for school," I instructed, slightly pushing her aside as I ran to console my son. "And hurry up!"

My baby, now three months old, looked up at me and smiled as soon as I stood over his crib. My grandmother probably would've said that it was gas, but I knew he was smiling at me. He inherited his deep dimples from me, and his grey eyes were a constant reminder of the love that I once knew. I still thought about Brooklyn from time to time, but I never let myself get too far.

After I told him that Chloe was really my sister, I never heard from him again. The last sign that told me he even existed was when I received the million dollars he'd put into a bank account for Mye. I didn't even know that he was holding that kind of money, but after everything happened, nothing surprised me anymore.

I prepared myself to get me and my son ready for the day in a house that I still hadn't gotten use to. The first house I bought when I moved to Raleigh was perfect, but after it turned into a morgue, I had to move. The new three thousand square foot pad that I'd purchased for my new family, wasn't much of a home, but it would have to do for now. After taking a shower, I finished preparing Bella's lunch, Mye's diaper bag, and stuffed an egg sandwich down my throat, before quickly putting the finishing touches on myself.

I stood in front of the bathroom mirror and took off my black Chanel headscarf, combing down my wrap. My black hair fell down my back, as I brushed it away from my face. After putting my trademark part in the center of my head, I looked at my forehead and ran my fingers across a scar that I had for life. *Memories*, I thought to myself, wondering why everywhere I looked reminded me of that night.

At twenty-five, I still looked the same, despite the twenty pounds I'd put on from being pregnant with Mye. I was now a hundred and thirty pounds, and loving every minute of it. I grabbed my bottle of Aveeno lotion and squeezed a generous amount in my palm. I started on my chest area, and began to admire what the years had done to me. Although my stomach showed no signs of my childbearing years, my once perky breasts now had visible sags, accompanied with stretch marks.

"Who knew thirty-two B's could hang so low?" I said, as I continued to inspect my pitiful looking breast. I was tempted to get plastic surgery, but what would be the use if I didn't have a man.

I turned around and glanced in the mirror, focusing in on my butt, which had grown considerably. I finally had the ass that I'd always wanted, and I was going to eat everything I could to keep it there. After I finished moisturizing my butt, I turned back around and looked at my vagina, which had been completely neglected over the past few months. It was a hairy mess, and I refused to shave.

There was no point.

She was now vacant.

When I was finished greasing down my body, I opened the

jar of Vaseline and rubbed a thin dab of it on my face. It was something that I'd done since I was a child. I smoothed out my perfect eyebrows that had never been arched, and slapped some on my lips. There it was again, another memory. It was a scar that sat on the left side of my upper lip. I was beginning to feel less like a lady, and more like a war veteran.

I threw on a grey Yum Couture velour sweatsuit to work in today. Instead of business meetings, my top agent Brian and I had a few renovations to do for a couple of properties, and to cut cost, we decided to do the work ourselves.

"I've got to get a bigger car," I said, as I struggled to stuff everyone into my black CL600 Coupe.

The overpriced, under sized Mercedes was really starting to be a pain in my ass but at the time, it seemed like a perfect trade-in for the Aston Martin Brooklyn gave me as a wedding gift. I was trying to relieve myself of any memories from him. Besides, the one I already had for life.

After sitting in a little bit of morning traffic, we finally pulled up in front of Turner Christian Academy, a private school that I'd enrolled Bella into, and I smothered her with kisses, fighting with her long, curly blondish brown locks that covered her face. Forgetting to do her hair, I quickly tied her thick hair in a ponytail before she got out of the car.

"I love you, Bella."

"I love you too, auntie," she replied, as she hurried to catch up with her friends.

*Second grade. Micah would've been in the second grade too.* I glanced in my rearview mirror at Mye Storie trying to find reasons other than Bella to live.

Fifteen minutes later, I dropped Mye off at Brian's mother's house, which was a blessing, because she was the only person left in this world I trusted. Most people thought I'd lost my mind to go back to work so soon, but I had to. It was the only thing that kept my mind occupied on something other than what happened. It was a decision that I knew no one else would understand, and I didn't expect them to.

Ms. Sara offered her services to me, and it seemed like a perfect match. Brian and his new wife were living the high life, and still hadn't given her any grandchildren, so Mye and Bella was the closest thing she had. The money I offered was another great incentive, and seeing what a great person Brian turned out to be, I knew that Mye was in great hands.

*When it hurt so bad...when it hurt so bad why it feels so good...when it hurts so bad...when it hurts...*

"Hello?" I answered, wondering for the millionth time why I hadn't changed Lauryn Hill's depressing song off my ring tone. I actually hated the song now.

"Hey Oshyn, mom told me that you just left her house, and I need you to stop by Home Depot and price some granite countertops for the kitchen. I already bought some, but they were a bit expensive, so if you can find a better deal then I can take these back and..."

"Okay, okay!" I said, rushing Brian off the phone, "Anything else?"

"Nope, that's it. See you when you get here." Brian had a habit of talking longer than he actually had to, so when I cut him off, he knew why.

I pulled up to Home Depot that was located two traffic lights from Ms. Sara's house, and walked inside, hoping that this venture wasn't going to take long. I took a deep breath as soon as I entered the building that looked like an organized construction sight. I didn't know what it was, but the spicy smell of sawdust mixed with wood was so inviting. I had a thing for woody scents. Call it weird, but it was what it was.

The renovations needed to cost about thirty percent or less of the home's market value, and Brian wasn't too great at staying under budget. I thought about asking one of the workers, dressed in bright orange aprons for help, but instead I picked up my phone and dialed Brian's number.

"Hey Brian," I said, hating that I had to call him back for more information.

"Uh huh, guess I wasn't talking too much after all," he boasted in between his 'I know it all' laughs.

"Oh shut up. I forgot to ask you what color the countertop needs to be, and what kind of edge were we looking to put on it?" I asked, looking at a beautiful ceiling fan, as I continued to walk.

"The material is Golden Valley with a water fall edge. You got that, or do you need me to stay on the phone and hold your hand while you find it?" He had a little too much sarcasm in his voice.

"You win, now shut up and leave me...*OUCH!*" I yelled as I bumped into a complete stranger. My phone immediately fell to the ground from the collision.

"Are you okay?" a man asked, as he picked my overpriced I-Phone off the dusty floor. I was one of the idiots that had bought the high tech phone as soon as it was released. A few of the rhinestones I'd glued on the back were lying on the floor.

"Yeah, I'm fine, thanks. Guess I should've been watching where I was going. I'm sorry."

"Oh, don't worry about it, I'll live."

I quickly started throwing miscellaneous things in my basket to appear lost in my shopping, and like I planned, it caused him to turn in the other direction. The white man was drop dead gorgeous. Had to be in his late twenties, maybe early thirties, and had the prettiest ice blue eyes, I'd ever seen. His hair was jet black and cut short on the sides, which made his small and fashionable mohawk very stylish.

Before I knew it, I ran back into him as soon as I entered the appliance section. Smoothly, he said, "I've got to ask, what's a beautiful woman like yourself doing with plywood, grout, and a tile cutting saw in your basket?"

I was kind of insulted. "I'm working, or did you forget that women work these days!" I proceeded to walk away, when he put his hand on my arm to stop me. I looked at him, then at his hand and he quickly got the hint.

"I didn't mean it like that at all, it's just that…never mind," he said, probably thinking that whatever he wanted to know was best left unsaid. "So, if you don't mind me asking, what do you do?"

"I own a real estate company, so one of my agents and I are doing some renovations on one of our properties," I answered, in a softer tone this time. I made a decision to give being nice a chance, since I was the reason that we'd bumped into each other in the first place.

"Ah, that's awesome! Maybe we can get together sometime and…"

"I'm straight, white boy! Look, I'm not interested at all in your advances, so I suggest that you keep it moving! I'm not looking for a man, nor if one came around, would I even want one! I already said sorry for bumping into you, so please, leave me alone!" I knew that I was being a bitch, but for some reason, didn't care.

"Please excuse me if I insulted you in any way, but I was never intending on asking you out," he snapped back, with a straight face. At this point, I wanted to crawl under a rock. "I am however, new to the area and was looking for some properties to invest in. If my research is correct, the market in North Carolina, Raleigh to be specific, is booming and I want in. Do you mind if I take your business card, and use it when I'm in need of your services?"

I looked at him for a few seconds without saying a word. I tried my best to figure him out, but nothing came to me. *I guess I didn't inherit my grandmother's intuitive genes.* I reached in my Chanel purse and handed him my business card.

"And by the way, my name is Cody," he said, extending his hand forward.

"Oshyn," I replied, ignoring his welcoming hand as my phone rang. "Hey Brian, sorry I…"

"Oh my God, Oshyn, you have to get here now! The FEDS are here!"

"Wait….slow down…FEDS? What are you talking about?" I asked, feeling out of control.

"Oshyn, they're seizing everything! You have to come now!"

I dropped everything I was doing, never saying goodbye to Cody, and ran out of the store as fast as I could, imitating a scene straight from the Cinderella movie. I guess now I didn't need my intuition to tell me that this situation wasn't good.

# 6 OSHYN

I couldn't believe what my eyes were witnessing when I pulled up to my office. There were at least fifteen unmarked police cars in the parking lot of my business. Oshyn Realty had built a great name for itself, and with the reputable clients my firm brought in, we couldn't afford for our reputation to be tarnished.

I walked around in a fury, trying to figure out what was going on. I was sure that if you looked close enough, you could see the steam that rose from my head. I was beyond mad, and determined to get to the bottom of this. I noticed that Brian was nowhere in sight, as I watched a pudgy agent walk toward me. She, unlike everyone else, was a black woman in a suit, and looked to be in charge of the whole operation. I was a bit relieved to see her face, reassuring myself that she would understand the 'black woman's struggle', and clue me in as to what was going on.

"Are you Oshyn Rodriguez-Jones?" she asked, as she peeked over at my hundred thousand dollar car.

"Yes I am. What in the world is going on here?" I stopped

and helplessly watched, as countless officers removed papers and files out of my building.

"I'm Federal Agent Tompkins of the FBI, and we have a court ordered warrant issued to seize all records and properties to investigate allegations of tax evasion and money laundering."

"Tax evasion? Money laundering? What are you talking about?" I asked, as I pretended to read over the warrant she handed me. There was so much legal jargon in it, I felt like I was reading a document written in Chinese. "All of my transactions are legit!" There was too much on the warrant to read, and I was so mad that I couldn't concentrate on what it said anyway.

"Well, apparently not Mrs. Rodriguez-Jones, because we have proof that your *husband,* Mr. Brooklyn Jones, used his drug money to expand your business. Not only that, he introduced you to a few of his big time partners, who also benefited from your services, so that they could clean up their money, as well using you as a scapegoat."

"That's not true, everything I did was with my money. It was all legal, I swear!"

"Admit it, you knew what was going on from the start, and it's going to be my pleasure to take you down!" The hairs on my neck rose as she came a little closer. "Guess it really didn't pay to be a hustler's wife, did it?" she whispered in my ear.

"Bitch, fuck you!" I yelled, as Brian came out of nowhere. His six foot three shadow towered over me as he pulled me away from her.

I could tell that she had no intention on arresting me, or it would've been done as soon as I stepped out of my car. The agent, that turned out to be the devil in disguise, just stood there and smiled. I returned her stare, and we instantly became like two pit bulls ready to engage in a fight...to kill.

Brian tried his best to get my attention, but all of his attempts failed, because I refused to lose whatever battle we were fighting. Finally, one of her agents tapped her on the shoulder, distracting her from our eye-engaging brawl, making me an instant winner.

"Oshyn!" I finally heard Brian say. This was the first time I looked at his pale face, which was red as an apple. "What in the hell is going on? They're freezing up everything!"

"I don't know. It feels like I'm being set up but…they said something about tax evasion. Not only do I pay my taxes on time, I have two accountants going over everything to make sure the numbers are accurate." I thought for a second about the seventy thousand dollars I forked over to Uncle Sam last year. "That bitch also said something about Brooklyn laundering some money, but I just don't believe it. He would never do something like that to…" I paused, not being able to bring myself to finish the sentence. There were a lot of things that I thought Brooklyn wouldn't do. "Oh my God, I don't know what's going on! I feel like I'm being raped," I added, as I buried my head on his chest.

I shivered as the sharp wind blew on my neck. It was unseasonably cold in May, making me grateful that I decided to wear my velour sweatsuit. Brian held me as we stood in silence, watching everything we worked so hard for being stripped away. We also watched as two different news stations parked their vehicles, and headed in whatever direction they could to be the first in capturing a headlining story. They were the same reporters that set up at Micah and Apple's funeral, trying to bring 'breaking news' on the conclusion of a triple homicide that took the city of Raleigh by storm.

"Brian, I just can't do this," I gasped, immediately cupping my hand over my mouth. "I'm not strong enough yet," I whispered, as I watched the FEDS take another baby from me.

"Go Oshyn, leave. I'll handle everything," he promised, giving me a nudge. I put my shades on and ran to my car, comfortable with Brian handling the press. He was truly a friend.

As I sped off, I watched the press through the rearview mirror bombard Brian with questions. I was sure that his handsome Calvin Klein image would soften the story a little. Our society was so vain, I was hoping that the world would focus more on his top model dark features, as opposed to these lies. I was pissed about the whole situation, but what infuriated me the most was Agent Tompkin's accusatory tone. I got none of the 'sister girl' love I expected, which made me believe that in the midst of all those white men, she forgot that she was the minority.

I forced myself to clear my mind and to think of my next move. *Money!* I didn't quite know what to do next, but I was fully aware that it was going to take some money to get it done. I made a sharp u-turn on Capital Boulevard and pulled into Bank of America's parking lot like a bat out of hell. I had three banks that I kept my money in, but I chose this one because it was the closest. I walked straight up to my banker, bypassing all the customers that had been waiting patiently in line, and firmly suggested that we speak in private.

"Mrs. Rodriguez-Jones," he said, sensing my urgency. "Is everything okay?" He closed the door to his office and took a seat behind his desk.

"Um, yeah," I muttered, wiping the sweat off my upper lip. I hated that I still carried Brooklyn's last name. I forced myself to believe that I'd been too busy to file for a divorce, so I could be one step closer to using my maiden name again. Deep down, I guess I still wanted to be Mrs. Jones. "I need to withdraw forty thousand dollars out of my savings account."

I knew the money was there, because I kept at least a hundred thousand dollars in each bank account. This was my emergency cash.

"Are you sure?" he asked suspiciously, while typing a few things on his computer. I'd been dealing exclusively with Tommy since my business began, and we'd developed a great business relationship. Now definitely wasn't the time to get personal.

"I'm sure, Tom. I just need my money," I snapped. He looked at me and then at his computer. I watched his eyes as they went back and forth, reading something on the screen intensely. He bit his lower lip nervously, and then again. He looked at me and then back to his computer.

"Mrs. Rodriguez-Jones…"

"Mrs. Rodriguez! Just call me Ms. Rodriguez!" I hated that I was so short with him, but I refused to be called Jones one more time.

"Okay, well Ms. *Rodriguez*," he replied, finally ending whatever ritual he conducted. He looked me dead in my eyes as he continued. "The FBI has seized your bank account, so we're unable to conduct any activity on it at this time. I'm sorry," he added, letting me know there was nothing else that he could do.

"No! Look again. There has to be something that you can do. I have *over* a hundred thousand dollars in here." My tone had softened. If there was anyone who could help me right now, he was the one.

"I'm sorry, but once the FEDS seize your accounts, there's nothing we can do. As a matter of fact, they've probably seized all of your bank accounts."

*All my bank accounts,* was all that ran through my mind as I imagined every last dime that I'd worked so hard for being gone. It was only then did I wish I'd taken my grandmother's advice about the bank. This was the reason that none of her money touched the financial institutions. It felt like my heart had completely stopped. I stood up, stumbling back a bit. Tommy jumped up from behind his desk to help me gain my balance.

With all that was happening, I'd become nauseous and lightheaded. Thieves with badges were stealing my livelihood from me, and I didn't know why. With no warning at all, I suddenly threw up everywhere.

"Oh my!" Tommy said, as he jumped out of the way. A little bit of vomit splattered on his black Gucci loafers. "Mrs. Rodriguez, are you okay?"

"No, I'm not." I answered, what I thought was the obvious. I took the back of my hand and wiped the residue of my egg sandwich from my mouth. Everything I had for breakfast had come up. "What's happening to me?" I asked, with tears everywhere. I got up, still a little dizzy from confusion, and headed toward the door.

"Mrs. Rodriguez, do you need me to call the paramedics?"

Tommy's question was sincere and I could tell. I stared at him with a look that screamed *HELPLESS,* but I never said a word.

I wiped the juices off my mouth one more time, before putting my Gucci shades back on, and headed to my car.

*When it hurt so bad...when it hurt so bad why it feels so good...when it hurts so bad...* The played out song seemed louder than ever as it continued. I'd just noticed that I forgot my phone while I was in the bank and had seventeen missed calls. *Damn news,* I thought, as I was sure it had hit all the stations by now. Out of all the missed calls, Brian seemed to have been the most, topping everyone else off with eleven calls. I decided to hit him back because right now, he was the most important.

"Oshyn, I've called you a million times! Are you okay?" he asked, seemingly out of breath. I struggled to keep the phone up to my ear while my hand trembled out of control.

"Brian, what's happening? Everything is gone!" I sat in the bank's parking lot with snot pouring out of my nose, crying my eyes out.

"I don't know what's going on, but they've frozen all my accounts too! Listen, come straight to my mom's house. Don't go anywhere else!"

"The kids, are they okay?" I asked, wanting to know why he was being so stern.

"They're fine. Just come now, and don't go anywhere else!"

*      *      *

It took me nearly twenty minutes in traffic to get to Ms. Sara's house, but I finally made it. I spotted Brian leaning up against his mom's brand new white Range Rover that he'd gotten her as a birthday gift. He was smoking a cigarette, and I could tell he was stressed from the twenty cigarette butts that decorated his shoes. As soon as he saw me, he ran up to my car.

"They took it all; computers, documents, the properties, everything. Is there something that you're not telling me?" Brian asked, very upset. But who could blame him. He had every right to ask me that question, but this time something wasn't right. He spoke to me like someone who'd been deceived. He spoke to me like I was his enemy. I sensed that he'd already blamed me for what happened. But again, I couldn't blame him.

"Brian, you have to believe me. Everything that I ever did with this business was legit. I followed every single code in the book!"

"Yeah, well, what about Brooklyn? The FEDS said…"

"Fuck the FEDS!" I screamed, forcing a couple of birds to fly away. "Brooklyn got my whole family killed! My son, my best friend, and my grandma are all dead, and you want to ask me about him?"

Brian slammed his face in his hands and made a muffled sound as he screamed in them. "I'm so sorry, Oshyn. That was totally uncalled for. I just…"

"It's alright. We're both stressed out," I replied, in a calmer tone.

"Look, I went by your house looking for you when you wouldn't answer your phone, and the FEDS have seized that too."

Tears welled up in my eyes. "My house?" I asked, not believing what he'd just said.

"Yeah, I'm sorry," he answered, as he looked at the ground. He then came over and held me as my body went limp in his arms.

"How am I going to take care of Bella and the baby?" I said, as I tried to figure out how I was going to get use to the world of homelessness.

Brian let go and walked a few feet away from me. "I'm so sorry, Oshyn. I told you from the beginning that I had your back, and I'm a man of my word, but they took everything I have too."

"No, this isn't your responsibility. I'll find a way." It was a lie that even I didn't believe.

"Because of the wedding, I'm a little broke, but I have five hundred dollars inside my mother's house. I want you to have it."

"No," I replied, shaking my head. "You have a wife to take care of, you keep…"

"Don't worry about that, my mother will take care of us. You have to take care of those children. It's not about your pride anymore, Oshyn. You have mouths to feed."

I followed him in the house, and assisted Ms. Sara in getting the kids ready to go. She was a beautiful woman inside and out, and looked like Brian's sister instead of his mom. She aged like a black woman, and didn't look a minute over thirty-five. Brian had told her what happened as soon as everything went down, so she took it upon herself to pick Bella up from school. I was so glad I'd decided to put her on Bella's 'pickup list', because with all the ruckus that was going on, I simply forgot.

"Oshyn, you're a strong woman. You've been through things I'm not sure I would've been able to tackle. You're a survivor! Don't let this beat you." I took heed to her advice, but my worried expression told her otherwise. "These children need you. Remember, they are all you have left!"

"What about me?" I screamed, throwing a childlike temper tantrum.

"You?" she asked, without remorse. "*You* no longer exist when *you* have children to look after! *You* will get over it! *You* will find a way to make it work, and in the midst of all of that, *you* will survive! *You* have no other option!"

I felt so stupid. She was absolutely right. I was responsible for other lives, and this was no time to consider myself.

"Oshyn, you and the kids are more than welcome to stay here until you can get on your feet. There's more than enough room, and I could use the company."

"Thank you, Ms. Sara, for all you've done, really. I just need a little bit of space. You know, just a little time to think things through. But I thank you so much for even offering."

Brian returned to the room, interrupting our moment, and headed in my direction. He handed me a folded up wad of money and winked at me. Minutes later, I said my goodbyes as I headed to my car with my children, and promised both of them that I would be strong. However, I faked it pretty well, because I still had no idea what was happening or what I was going to do next.

# 7 CHLOE

"Several agents from the Federal Bureau of Investigation seized hundreds of records yesterday from the office of one of Raleigh's largest real estate companies, Oshyn Realty, for allegations of tax evasion and money laundering. The FBI currently have control of over fourteen properties in the Raleigh and Knightdale areas, seven acres of land in Wake Forest, and an undisclosed amount of money.

"Just last year, the twenty-five year old owner, Oshyn Rodriguez-Jones, lost her son in a horrific homicide that left three dead and a six-year-old girl critically injured. An alleged suspect involved in that crime was found missing at the scene. With one suspect dead, investigators still haven't found a motive or the victim's cousin, Chloe Rodriguez, who was said to be involved in the murders. Stay tuned as we keep you updated on the latest information involving this case."

A devilish smile appeared on my face while watching the results of what a simple blow job could do. "The FEDS are just as corrupt as hood niggas in the street!" I said, still smiling. I knew crooked ass Agent Tate would jump on the idea of setting Oshyn up, if he and other dirty agents could make some money. All it took was a little pussy, mixed with a dose of blackmail, and things were already working in my favor.

I grabbed the remote and flipped through a few channels, trying to see what other information I could find. Just my luck, on one of the stations, I caught a reporter trying to catch up to Oshyn as she ran to her car. I bit my bottom lip several times, as I watched her open the door to her expensive luxury vehicle. *That bitch still doesn't look broke. Why didn't they take the fucking car too?* I stood up and paced the hotel room floor back and forth.

"How is it that every time I try to destroy that bitch, she always manages to bounce back?" I wanted her left with nothing, just like she'd left me.

I knew other families had sibling rivalries, but I was positive that none could compare to my fucked up family. This was definitely some Jerry Springer type shit. We were already at war as cousins, but now since I'd found out that we were really sisters, the game had changed drastically. As a matter of fact, finding out that piece of information made me hate her even more. Whatever Cain and Abel had going on, would be considered minor after I was done with her ass. I guaranteed it.

Along with ruining Oshyn's life, which was just the beginning, this deal was also going to make me a lot of money. Agent Tate had informed me that by law, his agency was allowed to take a cut, and therefore profit from whatever assets they seized before Oshyn even went to court, which was mind blowing. However, in the deal I made with Tate, I was in line to get some of the proceeds he'd managed to keep from turning in. So I could care less what they did to her.

But I'm no fool.

The FEDS are just like the mob, if not worse, so I knew it was only a matter of time before they killed me. I'd be stupid if I walked around thinking they were going to let me get away with knowing some of their crooked tactics. There wasn't one person who knew where I was, so if I happened to disappear, I couldn't expect a missing person's report, especially since everybody thought I was dead anyway. I probably would end up like Joy, my former lover, decomposed and alone.

It was quite a shame that even a year later, no one had yet to find her body, much less file a police report. Joy didn't talk to her family, and since I was the only person in North Carolina that knew her, no suspicion of her disappearance was aroused. It was fucked up what Bella's father, Quon, did to her, but hey, business was business. However, that still wasn't the ending I wanted for her.

My thoughts were interrupted when I heard my phone vibrating on the table beside me. "May I help you?" I asked, knowing exactly who it was.

"I'll be at the meeting place we talked about in five hours. Don't keep me waiting!" He was testing me, but that wasn't how I played my games. I had to put his ass in check.

"Well, since you like to throw out demands, I'll be there in six hours, and it'll probably be in *your* best interest if *you* wait!" *CLICK*!

I could tell that he was more than upset about the videotape I'd sent to his office with us fucking from every angle, but what did he expect. He had to know that I wasn't the one to be fucked with. *Did he actually think that I was gonna go through this whole thing without any insurance?* With this six hour wait, he had plenty of time to figure out how everything went wrong.

I immediately went to the closet, pulled out my bags and started packing. I wasn't sure when I was gonna have to pick up and leave, but I knew that it would be soon. While stuffing whatever would fit inside my small luggage, a picture of Oshyn's son, Micah, fell out. I picked up the picture that captured a smile that unfortunately, no one would ever see again.

I remembered standing behind my digital camera like it was yesterday. Micah had just lost his two front teeth, and he was so excited to show the world his toothless smile, along with the five bucks the tooth fairy gave him. If it was one person in this world I truly loved, it was Micah. My heart sank like a weight at the memories I'd created. I shoved the picture back in my bag before my misty eyes got any worse.

After putting my bags by the door, I hopped in the shower, and proceeded to get dressed. I had a stop to make before meeting up with Tate.

"Fuck!" I said, as I struggled to pull up my Rock and Republic Jeans minutes later. "I really need to do some shopping." After losing almost fifteen pounds during the time I got shot, I'd gradually started putting my weight back on. I was now thicker and juicier than ever. My hair had also been deprived, since it hadn't been professionally done in over a year, so now it was damaged beyond repair. I didn't just need clothes, I needed an extreme makeover.

I took a seat on the bed, grabbed a pair of scissors off of the nightstand that I'd bought earlier, and before I talked myself out of it, made the first cut. I watched as my precious locks fell lifelessly to the ground. I got up and went to the bathroom to see how much damage I'd actually done. My silky tresses that once fell to the middle of my back, now barely touched my ears.

I was a bit surprised, because it was much more flattering than I thought it would be, considering I'd hacked it off myself. After I polished it up a bit, I was satisfied with my new choppy style. *I look just like Nas's wife, Kelis,* I thought, while I ran my fingers through my hair. My trademark Asian eyes stood out more than ever, and my cheekbones, which I must've inherited from whoever my father was, were now very distinct. Not the best idea that I'd had all day, but it was going to have to do for now.

*       *       *

Six hours passed, and I was more anxious than I wanted to admit as I drove to our meeting spot. I knew I could never trust crooked ass Tate, so I really didn't know what to expect once I got there. After pulling into the diner parking lot, I watched Tate as he sipped a cup of coffee. Looking around, I knew there was a reason why he'd chosen a window seat, because we were already taking a risk being seen in public. However, this was the only way I knew I would walk out alive, so if Tate wanted to play games then I was the right candidate. I reached in the back seat and pulled out the fake navy blue jacket that read FBI in bright gold letters on the back, and quickly put it on. The guy at the costume shop had informed me that it was really close to an authentic FBI jacket, so I was sure I'd fool at least one idiot.

I walked in and sat down at the table. He hesitated for a second, and stared at me like he wasn't sure who I was. I guess the haircut had turned out to be pretty good after all.

"Why in the hell do you have that jacket on?" he asked, still looking at me like I was a stranger.

"Well, it's a little nippy out today, so I decided to put it on. Isn't it cute?" I asked, with a huge smile, "Besides, I wanted to feel like a dirty ass FED today, which I'm sure you can relate to." I knew that comment would push a few of his buttons.

He looked around the diner and tapped the coffee cup with his fingers, but didn't say anything.

"Where's my money?" I asked, breaking the silence.

"You're a slimy bitch!"

"I'm no slimier than you. Now, where's my money?" I asked again. Bitch or no bitch, I wasn't here for small talk. He looked at me, rubbed his goatee, and then looked around again. I did the same. "What the fuck do you keep looking around for, and why are we sitting by this window?" Before he could respond, I continued. "I had an idea that you'd try something funny, so it's been arranged that if I don't meet with two specific people after this meeting, the videotape will be broadcasted on every station over the country."

"You're a dirty bitch!" he replied, clenching his jaw. "Trust me, you're gonna pay for this shit!"

"Not before you do!" I answered back confidently. This whole blackmailing thing had turned out to be quite a lucrative business. "Besides, there are tons of people who hate me and want to get me back for something, so get in line."

"I mean, I thought we had a pretty good thing going on. Why would you do some shit like that?"

"Come on, Tate. I mean why blame me for looking out for myself. I needed insurance since you knew about my problems in Asheville. How did I know that you wouldn't set me up?"

He took another sip of his coffee. "I asked you to trust me, and look what you did."

"Well, like the old saying goes, it's just business, nothing personal."

I was still shocked at the fact that Tate was as careless as he was. Since he studied criminals for a living, I was sure that he would've covered all all tracks, to make sure this wouldn't happen to him. I guess he was so overwhelmed with the whiff of new pussy that he'd become lazy. Too bad, but his mistake was going to cost him…big time!

He reluctantly slid me a metallic briefcase and said, "There's a hundred thousand in there. That's some of the money we got from her bank accounts. Everything else, the properties and the land, haven't been appraised yet. When they do, I'll make sure you get your cut."

I was pissed that I couldn't get all the money at once, but I couldn't complain. A hundred grand wasn't bad for a few minutes of fucking the right person. Little did Tate know, this was his last time seeing me. I knew that it was only because he didn't know who else had the videotapes that I was still alive, and that the next time I went to pick up money, I wouldn't be so lucky.

"And where's Oshyn's information?" I asked sarcastically, looking around as if it fell on the floor.

"What information?" he asked.

*Oh, now he wants to play games.* "You know what the fuck I'm talking about. And why didn't you all take everything from her? I see she's still driving around in her fancy car."

Tate shook his head. "We have to take this slow, Chloe. Did you forget that it's just a few agents involved in this thing, and not the entire bureau? We don't want them catching on, so we had to use our discretion about a few things," he responded. "Besides, she has kids. She needs a car to get around."

"I don't give a fuck about her or those snotty nose kids!"

Tate shook his head again. "Do you have to be so fucking cold?"

"Where's her information?" I asked for the second time. I'd lost all my patience at this point.

"Right now she's staying in a motel. That's all we got so far," he said, gritting through his teeth. He was mad as hell and I knew it. "I'll get you the rest of that information, along with the remainder of your money. Just let me know where you'll be."

"What do you mean that's all you got so far? I need that information!"

I hated the fact that I needed him, but the truth was I did. That was the whole reason for our initial contact. The money was great, but Oshyn's information was all that really mattered. I was willing to take a chance on my life, by getting that information, so I guess I would be seeing him again after all.

"Well, it looks like you're just going to have to wait!" He seemed satisfied that I didn't get what I wanted. "I hope you don't think that you're gonna get away with this," he warned, barely able to contain himself.

"*You* better hope I get away with this!" I answered back, as I stood up and headed out of the door. Information or not, I was on my way to Raleigh.

# 8 OSHYN

"I want to go home!" Bella whined for the hundredth time since waking up. "It stinks in here!"

Call it spoiled, but we'd become so accustomed to living in a nice and comfortable home, that this small, cramped and cheap motel room felt like we were living in a matchbox. The walls were closing in on us, and the damp musky scent of old cigarettes, had started to suffocate us. Like the saying goes, you never realize what you have until it's gone.

With only five hundred bucks to live off of, I didn't have any other choice but to stay here. The motel offered their rooms at fifty dollars a night, and at this point, that was all I could afford. With groceries and other essentials to buy, I had less than ten days to make more money, or we'd be in a home-less shelter. However, that was a fate I just couldn't let happen.

I chose not to let Bella go to school today, because I knew that she'd be bombarded with questions from her friends, and I wouldn't doubt, a couple of nosey ass teachers. I didn't have many possessions anymore, but no one would ever steal the right to protect my children.

"Sweets, we all want to go home, but we just can't right now," I said, while trying to do the best I could to keep the tears in. "But don't worry," I continued, "I'm going to figure this all out, and we'll all be home and in our own beds in no time."

She rolled her eyes and flung her little body on the bed in a fit of rage.

I wanted to fuck her up.

Thoughts raced through my mind to do something bad, but I calmed myself down before I acted on them. I backed away from her, almost in a trance, wondering where my sanity was going. I'd never hit her before. I always threatened her, but there was never the urge to physically hurt her.

With all the commotion that Bella and I made, even Mye woke up crying. He too had become a little fussier than usual, and it had started to weigh me down. There was nothing worse than a colicky baby, and with all this pressure I was under, he was definitely working my nerves. We were all stressed and on the edge. Age didn't matter.

I would've given everything I had for my grandmother to be here right now. I was sure that she would have all the answers to the mess I seemed to have made of my life. I still didn't have any answers as to why the FEDS had stolen a part of my life, and I couldn't figure out what my next move would be. All I needed was time to think. With no additional income coming in, I was on an extremely tight budget, and had no choice but to use the money that Brian had given me wisely.

Bella grabbed the remote to turn on the TV, but I quickly removed it from her hands. "Hey, why did you do that?" she whined. I could hear the resentment in her voice. I just didn't want all of that bad news invading our space.

"No television!" I yelled.

As far as I knew, she didn't know what was going on, and I wanted to keep it that way. I powered up my phone, which had been turned off all night, and saw that I had twenty-seven voicemails. *What a way to start my day*, I thought, while instantly feeling a headache coming on.

Mye's constant screaming only increased my tension, as I tried whatever remedy I could think of to shut him up. I gently picked him up and began rocking him in my arms, noticing that his diaper was wet.

"I'm sorry stank," I said to him, wondering why I didn't notice his dirty diaper the first time I picked him up. My mind was, without a doubt, somewhere else. "Bella, go and get me a diaper," I instructed, while undressing him.

I watched her as she moved as slow as humanly possible, dragging her sixty pound body to his diaper bag. "Bella, I need you to move a little faster than that," I replied, trying to be as patient as possible. Her freckled face looked me dead in the eyes, and sucked her teeth so hard, I could've sworn I heard an echo.

I jumped up, leaving Mye on the bed butt naked, and before I knew it, I had slapped Bella so hard that she landed a few feet away from where she once stood. She looked up at me with blood in her mouth, as tears immediately began to fall. I panicked. All that ran through my mind was Apple's reaction the day I punched her in the face for the lies that Chloe had told me about her and Brooklyn. I'd never hit Bella before, and to say I felt bad is an understatement. Her frightened body trembled and she began to cry uncontrollably.

As I went to help her up off of the filthy dingy carpet, she flinched. I backed away slowly, uttering the words, "I'm sorry," over and over again. She'd been incredibly rebellious lately, but that didn't warrant me hitting her as hard as I did. The more I thought about it, that hit wasn't really intended for her, it was intended for the world.

I went to go look for the diaper that had started this mess, and realized that there were no more. Feeling guilty as ever, I walked back over to Mye, who'd finally calmed down, and picked him up. For the first time all morning, he was at peace, and for a moment, I got lost in his grey eyes, wishing that everything were back to normal. After everything Brooklyn did to me, I still hated to admit to myself that I still loved him, and I wanted things back to the way they were. *I wish he was here right now to see how handsome his son is.*

My daydream was interrupted by the warm liquid I felt running down my arms. I lifted Mye off of my chest to find that he had peed on me, and remembered that he didn't have on a diaper. I wanted to kick myself for not having an extra supply on hand, because the last thing I wanted to do right now was to go out in public.

"Bella, come in here," I told her, hoping that she'd follow me into the bathroom, without me having to say it again. She scooped herself off the floor, and was quick on my trail. Since the faucets weren't working on the rusted old sink, I turned on the water in the bathtub that was corroded with mildew and fungus.

I grabbed a worn washcloth that the motel supplied, and held it under the water. When it was thoroughly wet, I took it and lightly pressed it on her mouth. She didn't fight back like I expected her to. Instead, she just sat there, whimpering like a wounded animal.

"Please forgive me," I begged, forcing her to look into my eyes. "It'll never happen again," I promised.

"Who killed my mother?" Bella asked. It was as if the last ten minutes of our lives never happened. This question came from out of the blue, and I wasn't sure if I could answer it or not. "Who killed my mother?" she asked again. The whimpering had gone away, and she'd gained her strength back from somewhere.

"Baby, maybe we'll talk about it another time," I suggested, trying to brush her off. I held the cloth under the water again, and then placed it back on her mouth.

"I want to know now!" she demanded, turning her head

away from the blood stained cloth. "Who killed my mother?"

"It doesn't matter anymore, Bella. Nothing matters any-more."

"It *does* matter. Just tell me…who killed her!" she yelled, becoming very furious. This was a conversation I didn't want to have. Not here…not now. She'd never asked me this before, and I guess up until now, I thought she never would. I felt obligated to protect her from the truth, but today I knew the time had come.

"Chloe. Chloe was the one who killed your mother."

"My dad didn't do it?" she asked surprised.

"Um…I don't know…maybe it was him. Everything hap-pened so fast that night…I wasn't there…maybe it was him…" Now I found myself in a ball of confusion. I didn't want to relive that night, and Bella was forcing me to go there. She never talked about it and I wanted to know why.

"What's going on, babe? What are all these questions about?"

She crossed her arms and tuned me out. "I want to go home," she repeated, never answering my question.

"We can't," I confessed. "We have no home."

That was the first time I'd admitted that to myself since all of this happened. I stood up from the bathtub, so I could get Mye together, when an unexpected crunch made way under my foot. Bella turned her head to see what happened, and I closed my eyes in disgust at what I assumed it was.

I lifted my foot up slowly, and watched as the antenna on a half dead cockroach quivered. Bits of its two inch body was still stuck to my heel from the slime that now oozed out of its body.

"Oh my God!" I shouted, as I allowed my panic attack to get the best of me. I was deathly afraid of bugs, and to have one dead on my foot was just too much to handle. I ran to the motel phone and called the front desk for help.

"Front desk, what do you need?" the uneducated employee asked.

"I need someone up here quickly!" I screamed.

"Oh my goodness. Is y'all straight?"

"Roaches, there are roaches…big ones all over the place and…we just need some help!"

"Oh," she said laughing. "Them ain't nothing but some water bugs. Y'all be okay. Just step on them bastards!"

"I can't stay in here like this! Is there another room available?"

She let out another piercing laugh. "Where do you think you staying at, The Hyatt? You in a working girl area," she informed me.

Her sarcasm pissed me off.

"Well, what about a discount?" I asked, trying to get some comfort from this awful ordeal.

"We don't give them out neither. You can leave if you want."

*What happened to customer service?* I wondered, while brushing the bottom of my foot on the thin comforter. I had to get the roach off my foot one way or another. I instantly hung up the phone, figuring I wasn't going to get any help and decided to head to the store.

Using a shirt as a diaper for Mye, I got everyone dressed and headed out the door. After making it to the store, and picking up a few necessities, we headed back to the motel, parking my car in the same secluded location that it was in before.

While walking to the only ice machine in the motel lobby, I noticed a man at the check out counter who looked oddly familiar. He was an older white man with short salt and pepper hair. I don't know why, but for some reason, he reminded me of George Clooney. I couldn't figure it out, but his presence was out of place. I wasn't in the best of motels, and from the way he looked, he wouldn't be caught dead in a one star such as this. *Maybe he's here for one of those working girls,* I figured, while I continued to walk by.

"Oshyn?" he called out, scaring me almost half to death. I stared him down like a hawk, trying to ignite those intuitive genes that my grandmother was blessed with. All I came up with was his high fashion sense, as I priced his charcoal cashmere Brioni suit at being around six thousand dollars.

Still not sure about who he was, I chose to ignore him, but he insisted on getting my attention. I yanked Bella behind me for protection, as a lion would her cubs, as he got closer.

"Oshyn," he said again, this time not in a question format. I could tell that he was trying to get me to confirm my identity, but I remained silent until he revealed who he was. "I know that you may not remember me, but I'm Shannon Bourdeux. I met you last year at your grandmother's funeral."

*That's where I knew him from,* I thought, instantly remembering the exact day I met him. He was at my grandma's funeral, and had purchased the majority of her floral arrangements. That was a generous act coming from a man I didn't know. But I still kept my guards up until I could figure out what his motives were. I was convinced that everybody had one.

The scent of Brooklyn's favorite cologne, Clive Christian, danced around in my nose as I inhaled the subtle smell of lime, mandarin and sandalwood. Whoever this Mr. Bourdeaux was, he had money, and lots of it. There weren't too many people that would pay twenty-four hundred dollars for one ounce of fragrance.

"What do you want from me?" I asked, cutting to the chase.

"I came here to find out how I could help you," he replied. Even with the patches of grey and white hair that covered his head, he was extremely handsome. His face still carried its youth gracefully, and I could tell that he kept his body in great shape.

"How did you know that I was here?" I asked defensively. I just knew my cover was blown. If this complete stranger could find me, anyone could.

"Don't worry, nobody else knows where you are," he guaranteed, as if he was reading my mind. I could tell he was trying his best to assure me that he was trustworthy. However, that's what made me watch him more. "Is there somewhere we can talk in private? I think that I can be of some assistance to the situation you're in."

"How do you know?"

"Who doesn't?" We both just stood there until he broke the silence again. "Chloe. Does that name ring a bell?" he asked arrogantly. Bella instantly become alert, and the hairs on the back of my neck rose. "She's responsible for all of this, and I can explain everything to you, but not right here," he insisted, as he looked around to the girl at the first desk, who was breaking her neck to eavesdrop.

*Wow, I guess she's not dead after all.* Thoughts of all the drama I'd gone through with her filled my mind, as I agreed to meet him back at the motel in an hour. I didn't want Bella to witness our conversation either, so after watching Mr. Bourdeux leave, I called Ms. Sara to see if she could watch the kids. Once she agreed, I quickly put the kids back in the car, and headed toward North Raleigh.

Of course Bella whined all the way there, saying over and over that she wanted to know about Chloe. But I made sure to shut her down, by saying the conversation was between adults. After arriving at Ms. Sara's house, and thanking her for watching them on such short notice, she handed me a bundle of mail. Seems that Brian had taken on the duty of driving by my old house to get the mail out of the box for me.

*What would I do without him?* "Thank you," I said, heading back to the car in a rush.

"Oshyn, wait!" Ms. Sara yelled.

When I turned around to see what she wanted, I noticed an

envelope in her hand that she'd obviously separated from everything else. As I walked back toward her, she placed the envelope in my hand and smiled.

"This one is probably unexpected, so it deserves to be read first," she said.

*Albion Correctional Facility* is what the envelope read, and an unexpected letter to say the least. I knew it was from my mother, and although I didn't have anything against her, I hadn't spoken to her in awhile. Not since I found out that she was really my aunt. However, I was still anxious to see what the letter said, so I ripped it open right in front of Ms. Sara.

*Hi my baby,*
*So much has happened since we've last spoken, where do I begin? I can only imagine how upset you were when I decided not to come to my mother's funeral. As you've probably heard, the prison lets you out to a funeral for immediate family, but I chose not to come. Not because I didn't want to see you, but because I didn't want to see her in that coffin. I hadn't seen your grandmother in so long, that I didn't want that to be my last memory of her. I hope you understand.*

I put the letter down for a second and thought about her apology. I didn't realize it until now, but my grudge was deeper than I thought. I *was* aware that she was able to come to the funeral, and had always wondered why she didn't show up. After hearing her reasoning, I guess I understood. The letter continued:

*Although I've wanted to get that off of my chest for some time now, that is not my reason for writing you today. I wanted you to know that my lawyer's found a technicality in my case, and by the grace of God, after almost nineteen years, your mother is coming home! Did you hear that? I'm coming home! I chose*

to write you before I called, because I wanted to give you a chance to take this all in. I'll be in Raleigh in two weeks. The Greyhound that I'll be taking will arrive at ten o'clock in the morning. I don't have a number for you, or else I would've called, so hopefully this will get to you in time. I have no where else to go, but anywhere is better than this place. If you're not there to pick me up, I will understand.
I love you,
Your mother...Roslyn R.

Here I go again. My life was about to take on yet another twist. My mother was coming home, and I wondered if I was even ready. Or more importantly, if I was even happy.

"Thanks again, Ms. Sara," I said quietly, before turning around to leave. "I'll be back for the kids, shortly."

"I know you'll never forget, Oshyn," she responded. "But learn how to forgive."

I turned around and looked at Ms. Sara, who at that moment, instantly reminded me of my grandmother. Although we both didn't say anything, I knew she was right. I couldn't continue to carry around those feelings. I managed to give her a smile before walking back to my car to meet a man, who could possibly help me get my life back on track.

I got back to the motel a little later than expected, and immediately noticed a black 2008 Koenigsegg sitting out front. I knew that six hundred and fifty thousand dollar Swedish car didn't belong to anyone else other than the stranger with great taste. I walked into the building, and like clockwork, he was right where I left him.

"First rule of thumb when having important meetings is to be on time, young lady," Mr. Bourdeux said.

"Yeah, girl, you can't keep this fine man waiting," the nosey desk clerk added.

Mr. Bourdeux turned around and laughed. "This place has

character."

"So, would you like to come to my room?" I asked, rolling my eyes at the desk clerk. I knew it was crazy to invite a strange man to my room, but maybe the nosey ass desk clerk would call the police if she heard me scream or something.

"Sure, that's probably the best place."

As we turned to leave, I shook my head as the desk clerk said, "Y'all have fun, now."

I wanted to tell her to shut up and to mind her business, but I didn't want to scare Mr. Bourdeux away at the first meeting. He'd offered to help me, and I could use his services. Besides, there was no time for having pride now. I had two children to look after. After walking into the room, I turned on the TV, just in case the person in the next room was nosey too.

"So, you mentioned something about Chloe being responsible for all of this?" I asked, jumping right into the conversation.

"Yes. She's the reason you're living in this shit hole!" He scanned the dirty room, and turned his nose up at my filthy living quarters. "Oshyn, I'm a very busy man, so let's get straight to the point."

"Who are you, seriously? Is your name really Shannon Bourdeux?" I was starting to feel uncomfortable with his presence. The hairs on my neck that rose earlier never went down, and my goose bumps were evident, even in the humid room.

"Don't worry about all of that. Let's just say, I'm your new best friend."

It was at that moment, I regretted not having a weapon on me. One would think that my past would've taught me something, but it didn't.

"When I saw you on the news, I took it upon myself to pull a couple of strings to get some information about your case. You see, I have friends in the Bureau as well." I sat up on the sagging bed, anxious to hear the details. "It seems there was an anonymous call put in a couple of days ago from a young man claiming illegal activity going on at your business. Now whether it's true or not doesn't even matter, because unfortunately with our laws, the FEDS can take anything from you on probable cause, and your word has no relevance. I tried having the agent I work with trace the number, but it had been erased. He said that it must've been a glitch in the system, but I knew better. They're the FEDS, there's never a glitch in the system. That comment let me know that this was an inside job. It appears that a crooked agent set you up."

"So let's say I do believe you, how did you find me?" I asked, still skeptical.

"I'm a resourceful man," he replied, with a smile. He had some of the prettiest set of teeth I had ever seen in my life. "I kept tabs on both you and Chloe."

"Why, what do you want from us?"

"Well, let's just say…Chloe owes me big time! There was a one million dollar misunderstanding, and I want it back!"

"So, go and get it! I don't have time for this. I'm trying to get my life back together and…"

"And what a fine job of that you're doing so far Mrs. *Jones*!" He applauded me in sarcasm, while looking around. "You *will* help me find that bitch!" he said, getting volatile.

Now I was scared.

It seemed like I'd let a violent stranger in my room, in a part of town where the police didn't visit often. His whole demeanor had changed, which instantly made me fearful. I'd done my best to erase Chloe out of my mind, and here this man was, bringing her back to life. *I should've killed that bitch when I had the chance.* His sudden anger kept me drawn, so to appease him, I continued to listen to what he had to say.

"I'm offering you a deal, and there are no options!"

"You have a lot of fucking nerve coming in here and…*OUCH*!" I yelled, as he cupped my chin with his hand.

"Again, there are no options!" He flung my face out of his grasp, and walked over to the window as I rubbed my face. My heart began to pound, and my instincts told me that something wasn't right. "I'll put you and your family into one of my homes, so you can get out of this dump."

"What do you want from me?" I asked, as my voice cracked.

"I want Chloe and…" he paused, as his eyes scanned my entire body.

"No," I said, backing up from him. "I want you to leave now!"

"I don't think so. I told you there were no options."

"Please, don't do this."

"Listen, I'm getting ready to spend a lot of money on you, so you have to repay me with something until you find Chloe. So, your pussy will have to do for now."

"Get the fuck out of my room!" I screamed, hoping someone would hear me. *Where was that nosey ass desk clerk when I needed her?*

I'd been threatened.

In my own territory, I had been preyed upon.

"You're gonna give me what I want," he insisted, coming a little closer. He grabbed the front of my pants with his hands. "You have kids to feed remember…you don't have any other choice!" I fought back, trying to break free of his grasp, and he seemed to be enjoying every minute. "If you don't give me what I want, let's see how safe the kids are at Ms. Sara's house!"

I stopped struggling with him and froze.

"How did you know?" I asked, wondering how he knew the name of Brian's mom.

He held a huge smile. "I know everything."

Suicide didn't seem like such a bad thing after all that I'd been through, but I quickly erased the thoughts out of my head.

I had to make it.

Not for myself, but for my children. They needed me.

I bent down, with my hands wrapped around my stomach and just rocked myself for comfort. Five hundred dollars wasn't going to last me longer than a couple more days. With everything that he'd just mentioned, I began to feel overwhelmed all over again. The sadness that I carried started to feel like a weight in the pit of my stomach. He placed his hand on my back and moved it around in a circular motion. The goose bumps that I should've listened to when we were in the lobby wouldn't go away.

I watched as he moved a little closer and placed his thin dry lips on top of mine. I quickly snatched my face away, and I could immediately tell that he was pissed. My heartbeat began to beat at a rapid pace, and at that point, I wasn't sure what he planned to do. Before I could get my mind together, he took the bottom of my lip and sucked on it, before forcing his tongue into my mouth. He was fast, hard and rough.

When he realized that I wasn't going to submit to his advances, he ripped my shirt open and forcefully took off my bra, exposing my small sagging breasts. I sat in front of him like I was a virgin being sold to a sex slave. When I looked back up, Mr. Bourdeaux had taken off all of his clothes, and stood before me with a fit body to be his age. His erect penis was an average size, but at this point, it didn't even matter. He laid down on me and continued to kiss my body.

"Get off me!" I cried, as I struggled to get free.

He grabbed me by the neck, and for a slight second, cut off my air passage. "Don't try me, bitch...I'll kill your fucking kids! You're gonna give me what I want! Chloe and everything else!"

I stopped struggling as his body applied more pressure. I wasn't sure whether or not to continue to fight back or to let him have his way.

I was losing; vulnerable and unsure what to do.

He unbuttoned my pants and forced them down my legs, along with the sheer underwear I wore. I could tell he liked what he saw, by the smile he displayed once he saw my goodies.

"Aren't you at least going to wear a condom?" I asked.

"I don't do condoms, sweetheart," he replied, spreading my legs apart. "Besides, it'll feel much better without it," he whispered, as he forced himself into me. My dry pussy didn't make way for easy entrance, as he rocked roughly back and forth on top of me, trying to get it in further. His raw dick felt so nasty against my skin. I stared at the ceiling as a tear dropped down the side of my face. This is what my life had amounted to.

Me, on my back, at a motel where whores frequented...

I was a working girl now.

I was Chloe.

# 9CHLOE

I sat on a hard metal bench in front of the courthouse in downtown Raleigh, waiting for Agent Tate to bring me the rest of my money, which had come quicker than I originally expected. I knew I was risking my freedom by being around the many police in this area, but I figured it was better than risking my life with the FBI in a secluded part of town.

It was eighty degrees, and my skin tight business suit was beginning to be a little uncomfortable. I could've kicked myself for not wearing a pair of booty shorts, but I had to look the part of a businesswoman instead of a hooker. My Louis Vuitton briefcase rested against my leg, as I looked around my shoulder one more time for Tate. However, all I saw were couples holding hands, out of touch with the rest of society, and in love.

It had been a week since I'd moved back to Raleigh, and already I was sick of it. The air I inhaled always reminded me of Oshyn, and any man I came close to carried the scent of Brooklyn. Their legacy lingered on in the city's air, and it was making me sick to my stomach. I couldn't wait to get this over with, so I could leave this place forever, and never come back.

One of the love struck couples stopped in front of me to order a hotdog from the stand, and as they stood there, they kissed the entire time. As sick as all of that was, it was what I wanted.

I blamed Oshyn for taking that love away from me, because I know Brooklyn truly loved me. I looked at my phone, wishing I still had his number. I wanted to call and shout in the phone how much I loved him. How much I missed him. He was the only one that I didn't want to be a mistress to. I wanted to be his wife, and I knew that he wanted the same.

"Pssst!" I turned around to see who that was, and noticed Agent Tate standing behind me looking nerdy as ever. After looking around a few times, he handed me a large manila envelope and said, "That's the last of it, the information and the rest of the money. Now, where's the tape?" He held his hand out, expecting a fair exchange.

"Tape?" I asked confused.

"Don't fucking play with me, you little cunt! I just drove two hours out of my way to meet your ass here, now give me the damn tape!"

"That wasn't a nice word, Agent," I said, while watching the pedestrians walking up and down the street. "I have the tape in a very safe place. Trust me, no one will get to it…unless of course, I'm harmed in any way."

I was bluffing big time, but that wasn't something that he needed to know. I decided to peek in the folder to make sure everything I requested was there. Before I got a good look at what was inside, I felt someone staring at me. When I found the culprit, who stood a few feet away, I batted my lashes and waved.

"If you don't give me the fucking tape, I'm gonna cut your head off, bitch!" Tate moved closer, allowing me to get a whiff of the musk that followed him. It smelled like he hadn't showered in weeks.

"Hey, is everything okay here?" My admirer asked, making himself known. I guess with all that eavesdropping he was doing, he couldn't contain himself any longer. In his eyes, he probably saw a scary villain and a damsel in distress. Little did he know that the tables were turned, and I wasn't the damsel.

I frowned my face up in fear and pretended to be helpless. I looked up at the stranger with my puppy dog eyes and then at Agent Tate, but said nothing, hoping that his intervention would calm the agent down. I didn't need any more attention.

"I said, is everything okay?" the older man asked again. He was a bit more aggressive the second time. He turned his body toward the agent, and waited for an answer. The black man with a crown of white hair on his head was not letting up so easy.

"This is not the end," Tate said, as he walked away. I was just glad that he decided not to cause a scene.

"Thank you so much," I managed to let out in a childish tone.

"I heard him talking to you roughly, and that's no way to speak to a woman." His voice was deep and he spoke eloquently, being very respectful of my space. "Now that I'm sure you're safe, I must be on my way."

I put my hand on his arm, noticing his gold crocodile cuff-links, pricing his Jan Leslie's at twenty-five hundred dollars. I got the sense that he wasn't from here, and while I was just here on business, I didn't want to let him get away. I could smell the money coming off of his breath.

"Please, let me thank you appropriately. I promise you won't be disappointed."

"No, I was just doing my duty," he laughed nervously. "I really must be going." He moved his arm away from my grasp and began walking away.

He didn't know who he was fucking with. Here I was practically throwing the pussy at him, and he walked away. I picked up my package and empty briefcase, and followed the stranger to his car.

"Excuse me, sir," I said, trying to flag him down. He turned around reluctantly. "I never got your name."

"My name is Mason...Mason Grey."

"And I'm Chloe. Chloe Jones." I was getting used to using my alias instead of my real last name. I no longer felt like a Rodriguez, and I wanted to start practicing using Brooklyn's last name. I extended my hand out for a friendly shake, and he finally bit the bait. "I really want to thank you again for saving the day. Please, I insist."

"Okay. I was just on my way to run a few errands. You're more than welcome to join me."

I agreed and walked by his side until we reached a black stretched limo with a driver by the door. "Good afternoon, Mr. Grey," the driver said, as he opened the door to let us inside.

"Good afternoon, Thomas," Mr. Grey replied, as he extended his hand for me to go first before he got in.

As the car pulled off, and we settled onto the plush leather seats, I instantly became even more curious about this man. "Is there a reason you don't drive yourself around?" I asked, trying to get more information about what he did for a living.

"I get more work done this way. People spend too much time behind the wheel and not enough time making deals."

I watched as the driver put up the divider, giving us our privacy. Mason had a pleasing countenance about him, and I could tell that he had to at least be in his sixties. There was something mysterious about him, but it seemed to turn me on. I rested my hand on his knee and began stroking it softly.

"How can I ever repay you for saving my life?" I moaned, in a Marilyn Monroe sort of way. I moved my hand up a little, brushing my fingertips across his penis.

He jumped as if I'd startled him, moving his leg away from my touch and loosened his tie for more air. I began unbuttoning my shirt, exposing my Dolce and Gabbana leopard print bra. I was hoping the 'DG' hardware would tell him that I had great taste as well. I hiked up my skirt, and lifted myself off of the leather chair to straddle him.

He just sat there motionless, as if I were bothering him. I sucked on his neck and grinded my pussy against him, expecting him to get hard any minute, but nothing happened.

"Please, Ms. Jones!" He took his hands and lifted me off of him in one swoop, then brushed off his pants, attempting to get the wrinkles out. "I'm sorry, but you just don't have to do that. Why would such a beautiful woman such as yourself lower your standards for sex?"

*Damn that was a low blow.* I bent over, putting my head in my lap, and pretended to cry uncontrollably. I'd even managed to muster up a couple of tears for my show. "I'm sorry, sir! That was so unlike me," I lied. "I'm just under so much stress. The man you saw me with was my fiancé, and I just found out that he was cheating. He moved me here from California, but he kicked me out of the house just before you walked up." I took my shirt that once covered my breast and used it as a handkerchief. "I have no where to go."

"Please, put your shirt back on," he insisted, before saying what I wanted to hear. "I tell you what, you're more than welcome to stay with me. I have a pretty big house, and I could use the company. What do you say? You can stay as long as you want and leave when you're ready."

Out of all the years of me fucking men for perks, getting into a house had never been so easy. "What about your wife?" I asked, pointing to the diamond wedding band that hugged his finger. He rotated the ring around with his other hand. Seemed like I'd asked him a tough question, but I needed to know where the bitch was at.

"My wife of over twenty years was in a horrible car accident, leaving her paralyzed and brain damaged. She's been in that condition for the last five years."

"Is she still at the hospital?" I questioned.

"No, she lives in the other wing of the house with her full-time nurses."

*Wing*, I thought, as I fastened up the last button on my shirt and thought about his proposal for a second. He had great taste, and from the sounds of it, I was sure that he lived just as well. He didn't want to fuck now, but I was sure that would change over time. This sounded like the perfect living conditions. Better than wasting my money at some hotel. I would be his mistress in no time.

"Are you sure?" I asked, pretending to be nervous. "I don't have any money."

"Money? Don't be ridiculous, I would never take money from you. It would be my pleasure to have you stay."

I deserved better than an Oscar for that performance. *I wondered if they would give a bitch like me a Nobel Peace Prize or some shit.* We made plans to meet up later that night, so that he could direct me to my new living quarters. I went back to my room, packed the little bit of stuff I brought with me, and headed to Mason's house.

*        *        *

After driving twenty minutes and taking Exit-75 to Dunn, North Carolina, my eyes almost popped out of my head when I witnessed one of the biggest houses I'd ever seen in my life. It looked to be the size of a shopping center, and sat on the street by itself. I'd never been to a house that didn't have neighbors. Once I arrived and got out of the car, I was met by Mason at the door, who seemed happy to see me.

"I'm so glad you're here," he said, taking my bags. "Let me show you where you'll be staying."

As he led me through the house, I felt like I was at a museum from all the expensive rare paintings that lined the walls and bizarre statues. Not to mention that everything was extremely clean.

"This is your room," he said, finally leading me inside a room that was almost the size of an apartment.

Everything in the room was lavishly custom designed. From the polished stone floors, to the gold threaded curtains from Morocco, I knew that his pockets ran deep. My money senses told me that the whole room was furnished by Versace, and not too far away was the bathroom, which was graced with Chinese onyx, that covered the heated floors. I fell in love instantly.

"If you don't mind me asking, what is it that you do for a living?"

He smiled bashfully and humbly told me, "I started a dot com company a few years back, that seems to be working out quite well for me."

"Are you sure there's nothing I can do to repay you for everything you've done?" I began undoing my shirt, hoping to seduce him this time, but it wasn't working.

"Just have a good night, and I'll see you in the morning," he said, right before walking out.

In a way I was sort of offended, because I'd never had a man turn me down before. But then I thought back to Brooklyn, who definitely played hard to get when we first met. I knew at that moment, it was only a matter of time before Mason would be eating out the palm of my hands, or should I say my pussy.

# 10OSHYN

"Bella, hurry up and let's go! You're going to be late for school!"

It had been two weeks since I allowed Shannon Bourdeaux to fuck me. Two weeks since my self respect had vanished. Two weeks since I was willingly raped. I'd been very uneasy about everything. I never exchanged pussy for money. It was out of character for me, and though I was weak with no other options, I still blamed myself for giving in.

In all actuality, I still had no idea where he lived, or even what kind of occupation he was involved in that allowed him to be so violent toward me. I wanted to call the police, but at this point, they weren't my friends either. With no place to go and two mouths to feed, there was nothing else I felt that I could do. To ease all these questions that I didn't have an answer to, I forced myself to make it okay, as long as the children and I were safe, and prayed that I'd find another way in due time.

Me, Bella and Mye had settled into our lavish, fully furnished house in Wake Forest. His harsh character was totally different from the beautiful view of the top rated golf course that covered over a thousand acres in land. Even though I had no clue how to play, I figured I had a lot of unwanted free time on my hands to learn.

We also had access to a bank account where he put in a thousand dollars a week. I was used to much more, but it's all I had for now. I also hated to admit it, but for first time since all this crap started, I felt safe...sort of. I mean, since the government had raped me of something that was rightfully mine, I wasn't sure if my sense of security would ever come back.

"Bella, let's go, it's time for school!" I yelled again, wanting to know why I had to repeat myself. Lately, Bella's behavior had become strange, and I just didn't get it. I walked up the stairs to her room, only to be greeted by a closed door.

I burst into her new pink princess room and asked, "Bella, what in the hell are you doing? In my house you don't close doors," I reminded her.

"This ain't your house!" she said defiantly, while laying in her bed, still in her pajamas.

"What the fuck did you just say to me?" I demanded, forgetting that I was talking to a seven year old.

She wouldn't answer me.

Even refused to acknowledge my presence.

"Don't you hear me talking to you?" I asked, with my hand on my hips. I was failing miserably at my attempt in gaining her attention, or respect for that matter.

I stood in front of her, while her green eyes stared right through me as if I was glass. Still, she never said a word. Her rebellion toward me was starting to get out of control, and my patience was diminishing with each second. I grabbed a belt that sat on the floor, and tried incorporating a little fear and respect to get her to talk. Again, I got nothing. Before I knew it, the anger of her defiance erupted in me like a volcano, and I hit her as hard as I could over and over with a belt that I'd now made into a weapon. With all the welts that almost immediately appeared on her legs, not once did she shed a tear or show any sign of weakness. I was losing her fast, and I didn't know what else to do.

I kind of felt bad for her, because she probably felt like I was trying to take her mother's place. She missed her dearly, and I understood. My mother was ripped from my arms when I was around her age, so I felt her pain.

"You have ten minutes to wash up and get dressed, or you'll be going to school looking like that," I told her as I walked out her room, panting from exhaustion and feeling defeated. I went to check on Mye, who was still in his car seat sound asleep. *I'm so glad I don't smoke weed, cause I'd be high as a bitch right now!* It was days like this that I was truly glad that I didn't have an addiction like Micah's dad did.

Bella forced herself out of her room before her deadline, fully dressed and prepared to go to school. We rode in the car in silence. Even though we weren't blood, she seemed to be inheriting my stubbornness, which was not a good trait.

"Bella…please. You have to work with me on this," I begged. "I'm sorry for hitting you." I continued driving, occasionally looking in the rearview mirror for some sign of life. I hated to hear myself apologizing to her for the same thing. I was beginning to feel like an abusive spouse. "Bella, say something…anything!"

I was pleading with her.

I silently hoped that she would talk to me before we pulled up at her school, but so far there was no luck. Her school was about ten miles from the house, and before I knew it, we were pulling up in the circular driveway. As I turned around to say goodbye, she was already out the car and on her way to the front door. I didn't have the energy to chase after her for being disrespectful, so I decided to let it go.

On the way back to the house, I stopped by the grocery store to stock up on some food and a few other things. I'd been craving some Beef Jerky badly, so to suppress my desires, I thought it was best to buy a bag. It had been a long time since I overindulged on the dry, hard beef, so I was going to enjoy treating myself. I put Mye's car seat in my shopping cart and proceeded to walk down the aisles, one by one, until I had everything that I wanted.

Just as I went for the checkout line, something caught my attention. I reached for the pink box of satin glide tampons and attempted to fling them into my cart, but my fingers hung onto them as if they were super glue. They just wouldn't let go. My heart chose to ignore the fact that my period, which was quite regular, hadn't been seen in three days. It had been two weeks since I had sex with Shannon, and I was fighting hard to stay positive.

My heart put a band-aid over the problem, telling me not to worry, that I was just stressed out, and that it would come in no time.

My mind told me that my heart was in denial.

I put the tampons in the cart just in case my heart was right, and against my wishes, dropped a pregnancy test in along side it just to be sure. My heart seemed to have forgotten that, in the heat of the moment, I let a man that I didn't know stick his dick in me without protection. I suddenly got a sinking feeling at the bottom of my stomach that something wasn't right.

"Oshyn?"

I flung my body around, trying to see who it was calling my name. I wasn't in a familiar location, but I did know quite a few people, so it could've been anyone. That was what I was afraid of. I gasped at the face I saw, almost losing control of all my bowels.

"Brooklyn?"

"Oshyn," he repeated.

Life treated him well, as I looked and witnessed how well a year had treated him. He smiled, showing me his precious gap that I once loved so much and asked, "How have you been?"

I took my hand and brushed it through my hair. I didn't know why, but I had the sudden urge to look presentable. The urge to feel like the woman I once was, had resurfaced. I hadn't spoken to him since that dreadful night, and I didn't expect to ever see him again. This meeting came as a total surprise. I secretly wondered if he had another identity, a new life.

"Is everything okay with you?" he asked in a whisper. His concern was prevalent in the way he frowned his eyebrows.

He knew.

Everyone did.

"I'm straight," I snapped, not really knowing what else to do. I tried to deny it, but I knew that running into him only confirmed that I was still deeply in love. I immediately crossed my arms, and looked away, feeling uncomfortable about our conversation.

He betrayed me.

The whole world had betrayed me, and he was trying to get too close. He had been too close before. Fucking my own sister.

I drug my eyes from the dirty grocery store tile and forced myself to look at him. I wanted to force myself to be strong. He wore a black New York fitted cap that covered his wavy hair. It sat low on his face, leaving the new mustache he'd grown to be seen clearly. Even his slightly ashy lips were a turn on.

His short sleeve Crooks and Castle t-shirt barely stayed together with all his muscles that were bulging out. I looked at his arms that displayed his new tattoo and smiled. 'Brooklyn's Oshyn' and 'RIP Micah' had been indented into his skin forever.

He noticed that I was noticing.

He took his left hand, the hand that once wore our symbol

of forever, and rubbed his tattoos that were a tribute to my life. "Oshyn, please just listen," he begged. "I love you. I always have, and I always will. Please…believe me!"

"Believe you? Are you serious? You fucked Chloe remember? Stay the fuck away from me! You were never honest with me. You were never honest with yourself. Fuck you!" I screamed at the top of my lungs.

I wanted to run away from him, but my feet wouldn't carry me. I wanted him to say something magical like he always did to make me smile, to make me forgive him. He lifted the hat off his head and wiped the beads of sweat that suddenly appeared. I stared into those big grey eyes that once hypnotized me, and fell into his trance. He was more handsome than ever. He'd put on a couple of pounds since I last saw him at the funeral, but his six four height carried it well.

"Oshyn, I'm sorry," he whispered, while he looked away. I noticed a tear roll down his face, as he tried his best to conceal his emotions. "I'm sorry."

We both stood in an awkward silence, as customers walked by to see who was causing such a big scene. In a quick attempt to appear normal, Brooklyn wiped his eyes and focused his attention into the cart.

"Oh, that's for a friend," I blurted out in a panic, referring to the pregnancy test.

"Um, I was just smiling at our son in the car seat. I can't believe how big he's getting."

"Yeah, he looks a lot like you."

He glanced at me as though he wished we were together. Everything that was going on was beginning to make me really paranoid. "Can I hold him?"

"I have to go," I lied.

"Well, if you ever need anything, just…"

"I don't need your fucking charity! Just leave me alone!"

Right on cue, as if he knew that I needed a little more aggravation, Mye started screaming. I ran away from

Brooklyn as quick as I could, purchased the items and listened to my son cry all the way home. Once there, I changed his pamper and fed him until he dozed off again. He was simple to please. I began to wonder why all men couldn't be.

I paced back and forth with the EPT test in my hand, trying to figure out if I was going to use it or not. I wasn't sure what I was so anxious about, but deep down inside, I knew. After ten minutes of over evaluating the situation, I finally took the test that revealed what I was afraid of all along. My heart was wrong. I was pregnant.

# 11OSHYN

All kinds of thoughts ran through my head. If I was pregnant, there was a chance that I could've contracted AIDS or anything else from this man. I couldn't believe I was so stupid and weak to allow something like this to happen. *I could've fought back,* was all I kept thinking about, as I stared at the positive symbol on the narrow stick. But then my thoughts went to survival, and the fact that my kids and I would be out the street if I had.

I'd turned into the person I hated the most…Chloe.

This was her character, something that she would do.

I picked up the yellow pages and found the number to the nearest clinic. I dialed the number on my cell phone without hesitation, and waited for what seemed like an eternity, for someone to answer. There was no question about it, I just couldn't give birth to another child, especially by a man I didn't know.

"Hello… Hello?" the underpaid receptionist said repeatedly, on the other end of the phone.

It was at that exact moment when I remembered my grandmother making me promise that I wouldn't abort Mye. It was also in that same breath that she revealed to me that I myself had been seconds away from being aborted, until she and my 'mom' intervened. In the back of my mind, I could hear my grandmother saying how precious life was under any circumstance, so before I made a decision that I wouldn't be able to live with, and in honor of my grandma, I hung up the phone.

*God must really have something against me,* I figured while, I cried in hopelessness. I was facing the burden of having a child that I didn't want, by a man I didn't know. I desperately needed someone to talk to, and when reality hit that I'd be doing this all alone, it hit harder than ever.

My grandmother always knew all the answers, Apples always found the good in every situation, and Micah just simply made me laugh. I put Mye back in his car seat and headed to the one place I knew would bring me comfort, the graveyard. To most, this was a place opposite to what comfort was. This was a place that resembled loss, loneliness, death, and even though it was in fact all three of those things, I still saw the light. My family was here, so in it I found what love was left.

I pulled into the cemetery, which seemed sunnier than normal, and drove up to where all three of them rested. It was about seventy degrees, which made this visit a little more pleasant than it was. I made my way out of the car, taking Mye with me, and took a few steps in the dusty gravel to their well-manicured granite plots.

I gazed at Micah's custom baby blue marbled tombstone that had the last picture he'd taken engraved in it. I forced myself to smile.

"Hey, little man. Mommy misses you so much."

I found myself not being able to finish my sentences. *Maybe this was a mistake after all*, I thought, after realizing how weak I was. I allowed myself to wallow in my pity party only for a few seconds, until I forced myself to chalk it up. "I wish you were here to straighten out your home girl, Bella! She's trippin," I added, trying to lighten up the mood. I let out a tender laugh and wiped a few tears from my eyes. "Baby, I know that you're watching over me, and I love you very much!"

I stood there quietly, waiting for some dialogue I knew would never come. My six-year old son was dead, and I had to come to grips with that.

I took a few steps away from Micah and ran my hand on the stone that towered over Apples. I also had her picture engraved inside the tombstone, and it did the best it could to reflect her beauty. Her trademark freckles and green eyes that now lived on through her daughter, made the picture so real.

"What's up, chicka? Your little girl is bad as hell. I had to beat her ass this morning," I said laughing. "But I got it all under control. You made me her godmother, and I told you that I'd hold it down, so don't worry, I got it all under control."

It was all lies.

I really didn't have it all under control, but she didn't have to know, unless she already did.

"I love you, Apples, and I wish you were here."

I walked away before I started crying again, and took a few more steps over to my beloved grandmother. Not that I wasn't here to see anyone else, it was just that this visit was especially for her. I needed her guidance so bad that I could taste it. All the days of her life I overlooked her advice, and even though she proved herself to be right ninety-nine percent of the time, I still didn't appreciate her gifts.

I needed her now though. I was pregnant again by a man I didn't know, and had a thriving business that the government now owned.

I needed answers…her answers.

"Hola, Mama," I whispered, knowing that she'd be happy

to hear me speak in her native tongue. "I'm not doing too good right now," I continued, still maintaining a low tone. I didn't want to start feeling like I was going crazy, but I didn't want Micah and Apples to know that I was losing this battle called life. They were counting on me to win, and I refused to let them hear me lose.

"I know it's been a while since I've come to see you, but a lot is going on right now. I know that's no excuse, but coming here is just too hard and I…I needed a break." I paused and shook my head after realizing how selfish I sounded. "Look, I just really need you right now. My whole life is shattering before my eyes, and I'm losing all the pieces. Mama, I'm pregnant," I said, waiting for her inaudible English accent to comment. I grabbed my stomach for the first time since I found out and rubbed it.

"Mama, did you hear me? I said I'm pregnant, and I don't know what to do next. I want to get an abortion, but I know that you wouldn't approve, so I need to know what my next move is."

I thought about telling her who the father was, but I was sure that she already knew. I stood in the graveyard in silence and waited for a sign, anything to let me know that she was here.

I got nothing.

She wasn't here.

I spoke to her in the same way she'd taught me to seek God. If I knew her as well as I thought I did, I knew she probably wouldn't answer my questions just on principle. She would instruct me to seek God's face and wait for an answer. While that may have worked in her day, I needed answers now. I hated to say it, but God wasn't moving fast enough for me. I quietly waited a little longer for one of her solutions, but all I heard was Mye's piercing cries from my arms.

"Please, answer me!" I cried, feeling suffocated. It felt like I was running out of time, and in a sense I was.

I said my goodbyes to each of them, and I walked back to my car feeling defeated for the third time today, coming to the conclusion that maybe I really was on my own. I looked back at my family as I drove away. I would come back to see them another day, under better circumstances.

*       *       *

I ran into the mailman as I pulled into my borrowed driveway. I recently had all of my mail transferred here from my house. I figured there was no reason in running from my bills anymore, when I had someone to take care of them for me. I thanked the old man as he handed the bundle of mail to me, and made my way inside the house.

I played with Mye for a while until he dozed back off. *This looks good,* I thought, as I looked at a book that read *The Success Principles* by Jack Canfield. I could have definitely used some words of encouragement, but it had been a while since I'd picked up a book. I remembered the feelings I got when I went into a bookstore. It was unexplainable how excited I got just to be surrounded by all that literature, but Brooklyn had tainted my views on books. Ever since he sent me that gift of almost three hundred of my favorite books, I couldn't bear to read one. It was like when I saw a book, I physically saw him, and just like today, it made me sick to my stomach.

I put the book off to the side, making a mental note to skim through it later, and continued scrimmaging through the rest of the mail. I heard my phone vibrating in my purse, so I stopped what I was doing to retrieve it.

"Hello?"

My tone was harsh.

I was frustrated.

All I needed was at least a couple of minutes to think over

my day, and I couldn't even get that. Not only had the government taken everything that I owned, but time seemed to have slipped out of my grasp as well.

"Hello, this is Mrs. Sanderson from Turner Christian Academy. Am I speaking with Mrs. Jones?" she asked, in a stern voice.

"It's *Ms. Rodriguez,* and how can I help you?" I answered back, challenging her.

"This call is in regards to your daughter, Bella. We need for you come down to the school as soon as possible."

"Why, is everything okay?" I asked, due to the lack of information she was giving over the phone.

She repeated herself by saying, "We need for you to come as soon as you can, Mrs. Rodriguez." I got the hint that she was avoiding my question.

"I'm on the way," I replied, right before hanging up on her.

# 12CHLOE

Separated from the long hair that once rested on my back, I ran my fingers through what was left, trying to shove it in place, and readjusted the brown wig that sat right below my earlobes. My red lipstick was dark as blood, and I added a Cindy Crawford mole to my face just for humor. I also sported a pair of Louis Vuitton shades, hoping it would conceal me from the bright sun that beamed through the windshield of the car. With all the effort I went through to look different, I was sure Oshyn wouldn't recognize me.

It was early in the afternoon, and I was parked a couple of houses down from her house. As I slid the sunglasses down the bridge of my nose to get a better view of her new home, my blood began to boil. I looked down at the paper Agent Tate had given me with her address on it several times, before confirming that I was in the right place. I was furious at how well she was doing, despite my attempts of fucking up her life. *This bitch must have nine lives or some shit.* I hated the fact that Tate and I were no longer on good terms, because I desperately needed to know how she'd managed to pull this off without any money. *Maybe she pulled one of my moves, and fucked her way into the house*, I thought for a few minutes, then quickly changed my mind. *No, she couldn't pull that off in two weeks. I doubt if her pussy is that good.*

As I continued to rule out different reasons, my heart stopped for a second, as I watched the person I hated so much running out of the house. The car seat she carried slowed her down a bit, but she still moved pretty fast, considering the load she had. After putting the baby in the car, she jumped into her Mercedes CL and my blood began to boil even more. Here I was, stalking her in an old ass Honda.

"I wish I knew someone that would blow up that bitch's car," I said to myself. I wanted it to explode, like a classic episode of an old Italian movie.

Despite the fact that she lost her business, her home, and all of her family, Oshyn still looked good. She always had a natural beauty that allowed her the option to never wear make-up and she still had it. She'd maintained a nice shape too, and even looked like she'd put on a few much needed pounds since the last time I saw her. *We'll fix that*! I immediately began imagining her eating through a tube for the rest of her life.

As hard as I tried, I still couldn't figure out how she managed to live in a nice house, and seemed to have money. I couldn't figure out what she had that I didn't. *That shit will all change soon.*

When she finally hopped in her car and pulled out of the driveway, I made sure to stay a few feet away, as I followed Oshyn to her next destination. It was obvious she was in a rush, the way she zoomed in and out of traffic, and barely paid attention to any traffic signs. It took a while before we got there, but I was right on her tracks when she parked in front of a school. *Must be where Bella goes*, I thought, making sure to take a mental note.

As Oshyn parked her car, grabbed her baby and ran inside,

I knew that was my cue to quickly put my plan in motion. Just before I parked, I made sure the gun I carried was still in place under the passenger's seat.

My gun was the only thing that protected me.

When I thought the coast was clear, I jumped out of my car with the gun by my side, and ran up to her passenger door, hoping that through all of her excitement she'd forgotten to lock the doors. The adrenaline rushed through my body as I placed my hand on the door handle and pulled.

Bingo.

Unfortunately for Oshyn, she had no idea how much she'd helped me out by forgetting to lock her car. I quickly opened up her glove compartment, and placed a black 9mm inside. With that in place, I closed the passenger door and kneeled down on the pavement.

With the tiny transmitter in hand, I carefully placed the tracking device under her car, near one of the front tires. Now I could pin point where she was at all times. At that moment, I felt like some sort of spy out of a James Bond movie, and I loved it.

It was amazing what you could get off Ebay.

I walked back to my car and sat there for a few more minutes, waiting to see what was next. In the meantime, I had a phone call to make.

"911, what's your emergency?"

"Oh my goodness," I cried hysterically. "I would like to report a hit and run. This woman just hit me and almost pushed me off a bridge. She just drove off and..."

"Ma'am, just try and stay calm. Is everything okay?" the operator asked, cutting me off.

"Yeah, I have a huge cut on my head, but I'm fine."

"Do you need the paramedics?"

"No, I'll be fine...just please find her. She shouldn't be on the road...I think she's drunk! She was swerving all over the road when she drove off. She's gonna kill somebody!" I acted out a phenomenal scene, and she seemed to believe everything I said.

"Did you get her license plate number, ma'am?"

"Yes, I wrote it down. It's NCX5478."

"Let me repeat that, it's NCX5478?" the operator confirmed.

"Correct, please do something." I hung up the phone, as if my cell phone battery had died, and with me blocking my number, hopefully the call couldn't be traced. I got off the phone feeling completely satisfied, and even though I wish I could've pushed Oshyn's ass off a bridge, this would have to do for now.

# 13 OSHYN

Mye and I waited patiently in the office of Bella's school, as Mrs. Sanderson took her time to come and greet me. From the strange way everybody looked at me, and refused to give me direct eye contact, I could tell that something was wrong. I could feel it in my bones.

"Mrs. Jones?" Mrs. Sanderson asked, not sure if I was the right parent. There were two other adults in the office that I assumed were waiting for the same thing I was…reports about their bad ass kids.

"I've told everyone in this office repeatedly that my name is *Ms. Rodriguez*. Is everyone going to blatantly disregard my request for the use of my proper name? I'm beginning to feel disrespected that you all refuse to acknowledge me by my right name. Who do I need to speak with to correct this right now?"

"Ms. Rodriguez, I do apologize for the misunderstanding. I'll be sure to correct the problem as soon as we speak, but until then, please follow me."

She turned her back to me, and started walking in the

direction she wanted me to follow. For some reason, I felt brushed off and disregarded.

"I'm sorry, maybe you didn't hear me," I added, when I realized she wasn't going to stop. "I said that I wasn't going anywhere until this was resolved *right now*." I was tired of playing the Ms. Nice Guy role. My days of compromising with the world were over. It was my way or no way.

Realizing how serious this issue was to me, she walked over to the secretary, and asked her to replace the old information in the computer, with the updated version. It was a shame how much fuss I made over Brooklyn's last name, when I was the one who wouldn't even go file for the divorce. I knew that I was only fooling myself, but the world didn't have to know.

After I made a scene in the school's office, we walked into a rather large room that had two additional people at the table. Both women extended their hands to greet me, and I grabbed them with the hardest grip I could display. I knew my arrogant handshake was unnecessary in an elementary school, but I gave it to them so they would know I meant business. After I bruised their ego, I took a seat at the boardroom table, and placed Mye's car seat next to my feet.

"What's going on?" I demanded to know. I had enough of the run around, and I wanted to know exactly why I was here.

"Ms. Rodriguez, this is the school Principal, Mrs. Johnson, and this is Ms. Starks, a caseworker from Child Protective Services. Today Bella came into school and told me that you beat her."

*That little bitch,* I thought. Back in the day, calling the police was unheard of. As a matter of fact, the police normally sided with the parents, and told the children to behave themselves.

"She pulled up her shirt, which revealed some rather large bruises on her body. We're very concerned about her well being, and we need to know what's going on in your house?"

"In my house?" I questioned them, offended by whichever

way they were coming at me. "In *my* house, I beat her little ass with a belt when she got out of line!"

"Well, Ms. Rodriguez," Miss Starks replied, taking over. "We're all aware of your present situation, and can imagine the stress this can put on a person. Sometimes even the best parents can take their stress out on their children without even realizing it," she said, in a soft childlike tone.

"Don't patronize me!" I lashed out, feeling insulted. "You all are aware of my present situation, huh…what in the fuck do you know about my present situation! You know, you three have a lot of nerve bringing me here and accusing me of child abuse!"

They all sat there and stared at me while I lost control. I didn't care though, I wanted to prove a point.

Miss Starks continued. "We interviewed Bella, and she said that this was the first time you hit her, so by law, we have to open a case on you, which will stay open for five years. This is so if it's a repeat offense, we'll consider it valid, which will result in removing Bella, and any other children you have, out of your home." She glanced at Mye, to give me a hint as to who was next.

They wanted to take my kids. After all I'd been through, they wanted to split my family up. I didn't speak. I wanted to let her words marinate in my heart before I reacted. Nothing could explain how mad I was. Before I got myself in anymore trouble, I demanded Bella come down from class, and issued her an early dismissal from school, so we could talk about this. I didn't give a damn what the school officials had to say.

"You all can go fuck yourselves! That's why these kids are killing everybody! If their parents had beaten their asses in the beginning, the world wouldn't be such a fucked up place. I live by the saying, You Spare The Rod, You Spoil The Child."

The Bible always came in handy when you needed it.

*       *       *

Bella hadn't said a word. I looked at her through the rearview mirror, and her face was tight as stone.

"That's how you do me?" I asked Bella, breaking the silence. "You tell them that I beat you? Do you know they'll put you in foster care?" My voice had gone from a whisper to a yell within a matter of seconds. Still, she hadn't said a word. "Bella, do you hear me talking to you?" I asked.

I'd hopped on the expressway at this point, not sure of where I was going, but managed to sneak another peek at her through the mirror. She just stared out of the window as if I was invisible. To her, I was always invisible. I was sick of being ignored by the world, and I refused to feel that way from a seven year old. Before I could think twice, I reached behind me and slapped her in the face. Between driving sixty miles per hour, and trying to get a good aim at her head, I swerved several times into other lanes. I got a few honks, but chose to ignore them until Bella got the point.

"Do you hear me talking to you?" I repeated. With my right hand balled up, I flung it behind me as hard as I could, catching her in the chest. I was aiming for her face, but anything would do. I brought my hand back for another blow, when the siren of a police car interrupted me.

I immediately pulled over, running over the loud, vibrating grate that alerts sleepy drivers, and stopped the car. The sound of the grate woke Mye up, and he started crying. As I reached for his pacifier, I looked at Bella through the rearview again, and said, "Don't open your damn mouth!"

"Hello ma'am," the young white officer said, as he crept alongside the car. "Do you know why I pulled you over today?"

I hated those questions. They were all so stupid. Who doesn't know why they were pulled over? I decided to play along with his game.

"No officer. What seems to be the problem?" I asked innocently.

"There was a report of a hit and run accident, and the witness gave your license plate number."

I looked at him and frowned. I just knew he'd pulled me over for swerving all over the road. "Hit and run...are you serious? You can look for yourself...there're no dents on my car anywhere. There has to be some kind of mistake."

"No, I don't think so," he responded sternly. "The plate that the witness gave us is an exact match."

"Like I said before, officer, you can check the car yourself. The proof is right in front of you."

He stopped talking to me and diverted his attention to Bella, who was crying her eyes out.

"Is she okay?" he asked.

"Um, yeah. She got a bad report in school today, so she's in trouble."

He looked back at Bella and smiled. "Hey, little lady, are you okay?"

I discreetly looked in my rearview mirror, and just when I thought she was going to say something, she caught my glance and nodded her head, yes.

"Okay," he replied, focusing back to me. "Ma'am, can I please see your license and registration?" With the music all the way down, all I heard were the sniffles from Bella, and Mye sucking his pacifier like something was gonna come out of it.

"Sure," I replied. The last thing I needed was a ticket, so I went through my purse, got my license, and as I opened up my glove compartment to retrieve the registration, a pistol fell out.

"Don't move!" the officer yelled, putting himself in a defensive stance. His loud demand instantly made Mye and Bella jump, and now they both were crying.

I froze where I was, slowly placing both my hands back on the steering wheel. "I don't know whose that is, sir."

"That's a concealed weapon, ma'am!" At this point, all his sympathy for me was going down the drain.

"I promise you, that's not my gun!" I yelled, wondering where it came from. "I was just in my glove compartment earlier, and that definitely wasn't in there."

"Ma'am, please step out of the vehicle!"

# 14 OSHYN

Luckily, after pleading with the officer to let me contact my family, I called Ms. Sara. She and Brian met me at station as soon as I got there, and while she took the kids home, Brian worked overtime to get me out. I wasn't sure if either of them believed that the gun wasn't mine, but they both still seemed to be on my side. I found myself downtown, and behind bars for three long hours.

"Oshyn Jones?" an officer asked, reading a clipboard full of paper. "Your bond has been posted and you're free to go."

I blew out a big breath of air, and was relieved that Brian had finally gotten a bondsman to bail me out. After escorting me to the processing area, and giving me all of my paperwork, including the information for my next court date, I was free to go. I knew I would be cleared as soon as they did a fingerprint test on the gun. I'd never touched that thing, and everyone would soon find that out. It still bothered me as to who'd put the gun in my car, and what was even more disturbing, was they'd gotten that close to me.

I walked out front to wait for my car, which had been

STILL A *Mistress: The Saga Continues* *By Tiphani*

impounded. The moment an officer pulled up with the car, I jumped in and dialed Ms. Sara's number.

"I'm out, Ms. Sara"

"Oshyn…what's going on with you…are you okay? Do you need help?"

"I really don't know what's going on," I confessed to her. I started to plead my innocence about the gun not belonging to me again, but decided not to. She probably wouldn't believe me anyway. "Do you mind watching the kids for me for a few more hours? I really need to be alone right now."

"No, of course not. As a matter of fact, you go ahead and let them stay the night. They'll be fine."

I wasn't sure if her proposal was to allow me more rest, or protect the kids from my uncertainty. Either way, I had the night off. Something that was well overdue.

After driving back home, I put my keys on the kitchen counter, and immediately picked up the letter from my mother.

The time had come.

Tomorrow was the day she was being released from prison, and I wasn't sure I was ready to see her. Part of me didn't even want to pick her up. I closed my eyes and imagined her standing there at the bus station, alone and thought that was exactly how she'd left me feeling when I found out she wasn't my mother …alone. I hated the selfishness and anger I felt toward her, but I couldn't just ignore my feelings.

I poured myself a glass of red wine and sat at the kitchen table. I drank the alcohol, despite the fact that I was pregnant, hoping to drown the baby in poison. Somehow that seemed easier to do than to get an abortion. Five glasses of Merlot later, I'd passed out, making the glass table my pillow.

*　　　*　　　*

Morning had come sooner than I expected, and my head felt like someone was beating it with a hammer. I instantly regretted that last glass of wine, and still didn't feel as well rested as I'd hoped. The letter from my mother was stuck under my arm, and I picked it up again to read it for the fifth time.

Against my better judgment, I talked myself into picking her up, because I needed answers that only she could give me. I needed to close at least one chapter in my life. I looked at the oversized circular clock in the kitchen, and saw that I only had an hour before she arrived at the station. I got up, jumped in the shower and rushed to get ready.

I hadn't been to see the person I called my mother in over eight years while she was locked up, and a lot had changed since then. There really wasn't an excuse for the length of time I went without seeing her, I just hated the fact that she was behind bars. In my mind, I'd rather not see her at all, than to see the only mother I knew locked up like some kind of animal. I know it was a selfish decision, but at the time, it was the only thing that got me through.

I got in my car and drove toward downtown. As I got closer, I found myself still wanting more answers about how she was getting out of a life sentence, but that was another conversation. I was just happy that she'd received another chance. At least one of us had some good news.

I decided to pick her up from the bus station without the kids, because I didn't want them to see something else they didn't understand. I didn't want them to see a reunion between me and a woman that I wasn't even sure I still knew. I wasn't sure how either of us was going to react, so this was my way of protecting them.

After arriving at the bus station, I got out of the car and walked inside, feeling very uneasy. My stomach began to do flips, and I felt like I had to throw up. At that moment, my body felt like it had a mind of its own. I tried taking deep breaths to calm my anxiousness, but the pungent stench of piss from the filthy station clogged up my nose.

*Damn, I'm glad I don't have to travel like this,* I thought to myself, while watching the dirty people unload off the bus. Even at this time of morning, the graffiti reddened station was filled with gang members who frequently threw up their gang signs. I calmed my urge to sit down, fearful that I would get shot, and chose to walk a little further until I found her. Even though I didn't have the slightest idea what she looked like.

"Oshyn?" I heard a small voice say from behind. I slowly turned around to see what face matched that voice. Her once joy filled eyes now looked extremely tired, as they rested on the bags that had developed under them. With nineteen years of prison under your belt, whose wouldn't?

Although she looked like the walls of hell had beaten her down, she was still beautiful. I stared at her while she stood in front of me, but never said a word. My eyes scanned hers thoroughly, trying to muster up some resemblance, but I got nothing. After I found out that Mahogany was really my mother, I began to realize that Roslyn and I really didn't share any similarities.

"How did you know it was me?" I finally asked.

She gave a quick smile. "A mother always knows her daughter," she responded, with her arms extended. I guess she wanted a hug.

"Please…don't start that!" I warned, backing myself away from her touch. "I'm not your daughter, I'm your niece, remember?"

All of a sudden, the tears began pouring out of my eyes, and I couldn't help it. There were so many mixed emotions going on inside me, that shooting up the place sounded like a great stress reliever at that moment. I wanted to hug her, yet I didn't want her hands near me. I was confused and it showed.

"Oshyn, you'll always be my daughter." She bent down, picking up a small duffel bag and embraced it, as if it were me.

"You ready?" I asked, brushing past her. She followed without uttering a word. I walked swiftly to the car, but when I turned around, I realized she wasn't behind me. A few seconds later, I watched as she limped through the crowd with a handicap I hadn't noticed earlier. I suddenly felt bad for not walking by her side.

"Do you need me to take you to the doctor?" I asked, once she and I got into the car.

"No, baby, I'm okay," she said with confidence. I guess after coming out of one institution, she didn't want to go to another one, even if it was a hospital. I couldn't blame her.

The ride home was an awkward silence. Maybe because it felt like I was riding with a stranger as opposed to a relative. When we made it to the house, this time I carried her bag for her. I also walked slowly, while she limped alongside of me.

"Are you hungry," I asked, as I motioned for her to take a seat at the kitchen table. I searched through the cabinets for food.

"Ahh…, a little hungry."

I always envisioned that if my mother ever got out of jail, we would talk non-stop about everything she'd missed. But I soon found that this encounter was far from my dream. We really had nothing to talk about, nor did I know where to start. I just studied her, sort of like how Celie studied Shug in the *Color Purple*. I ended up making her some box macaroni and cheese with beef sausage, which was the quickest thing I could find.

With every bite she took, I became infatuated, finally making up in my mind that I would never let her go. She was the last woman in my family standing, and I promised myself that I would never lose her again.

"I'm so glad to be here," she said, with a smile that screamed relief. That was one thing I noticed about her. After everything that she'd been through, she still had an aura of peace about her. It was like she was at one with herself and God, a place in my life I was hoping to get to one day.

"Me too," I answered, while giving her a bear hug. Her shallow breaths told me that I'd cut off a little of her circulation, but she didn't budge. She took it all in without complaining, happy to finally be back with her daughter. There were still a million questions that I wanted answered, but I didn't know when the time would be appropriate. She'd just gotten here, and I didn't want her to feel uncomfortable.

My hands fought the urge not to touch her, as I ran my fingers through her silver hair that nearly touched her waist. I was shocked that at only forty-seven she had a full head of platinum silver hair, but it was always said that premature grey was a sign of luck. And even though I didn't believe in luck, I couldn't argue with the fact that she was truly blessed.

"What's that?" I asked, pointing to a large scar that made its home on her neck. It was so big that I was surprised I hadn't noticed it before. *Maybe her long hair covered it.* Her wound had become a scar, whose appearance was almost monstrous.

"Oh, it's nothing," she responded, running her long fingers over the scar. "When I first got to prison, an inmate tried to punk me out of my snacks. Even though my chips and candy weren't worth fighting for, I beat her up in front of everyone. It was strictly a respect thing. If I'd let her get away with it, the rest of my life there would've been miserable. I would've been a target for countless and meaningless other problems. Her damages were so severe that she went to the infirmary, and that night, while I was asleep, her girls slashed my throat as an act of revenge. We both survived, but after that day, no one messed with me again."

"Wow!" I said. I was amazed that she'd even gone through that. I got lost in her gaze again as I stared at her. She reminded me so much of my grandmother that it was almost scary. "How did you get out of jail?" I asked, recalling the night in my mind when she killed my aunt…mother…whoever. Even though I was six when it happened, those images never left my mind, and I could remember them like it was the actual day.

"I'm not sure if your grandmother ever told you this, and knowing her, she probably didn't, but there's something about our family history that you have to know." *Oh no, not again*, I thought, as I readjusted myself in my chair. Whatever this blow was, I wanted to be sitting down when it came. "The women in our family have a history of mental illness," she informed, searching my face for a reaction.

"You think?" I answered back sarcastically. "That explains Chloe's psychotic ass and her fucked up mother…" I quickly stopped with all the profanity, realizing who was sitting before me. She was still my mother, and I had to respect her.

"Well, you and your grandmother may have been the only ones to escape the curse. The rest of us weren't so lucky."

"What does everyone have? What kind of mental problems?" I asked, not sure if I really wanted to know the answers.

"Your…Aunt Mahogany and Chloe were more of the psychopath and sociopath. I knew for a fact that Mahogany, and from what my mom told me, Chloe were both pathological liars. They never seemed to tell the truth on a consistent basis. They also weren't remorseful, or didn't feel any guilt from the wrongs they did. I saw it in my sister, and you could most likely relate to this in Chloe's situation."

My mind began to wonder while she continued to speak, thinking of all the clues and red flags that clearly indicated how sick Chloe really was. *I wonder why grandma didn't get her any help?* I couldn't help but think how things could've been a lot different for Chloe had she gotten some medication. I didn't understand how grandma could ignore the problem, if she knew about it.

"They always think that they have a 'right' to everything,

and they're often very promiscuous," she concluded. That was my confirmation. Who knew that being a hoe was considered crazy. In my opinion, that bitch needed to be in a straight jacket a long time ago.

"I still don't get it? You don't have any of those traits, and from what I remembered, you never did. So why do you think that you're sick?"

My mother was always the very well mannered woman in the bunch. The one that was soft spoken and polite. She was the hard worker, someone you'd want on your team. I just couldn't seem to piece together the link between her and crazy.

"I was diagnosed with being bipolar, even before the incident, by a family doctor." I wondered why I hadn't been diagnosed as bi whatever, because there was no doubt that I had too many highs and lows in my life.

"So, what do you being mentally ill have to do with them letting you out of jail? I mean, who in there isn't a little crazy?" I asked, while twirling my finger around in a circular motion.

"I'm not crazy," she replied, quickly correcting me. I felt a little resentment from her, and instantly saw the seriousness in her eyes of how sensitive this subject was for her. I had no right to make jokes.

"I'm sorry," I said, after realizing how inconsiderate I'd been. She nodded her head saying that it was okay. I hoped it was.

"There was an eighty-two year old black woman that I had befriended while in prison. She was serving a life sentence for murdering her husband and his mistress, and went to jail when she was only twenty-two. We shared the same pain, and out of that hurt, birthed a friendship that was stronger than blood. Although she didn't finish middle school, she was very well educated, especially in the area of law. She decided to review my case for me, and when she did, she found several inconsistencies, which led to me receiving a new sentencing hearing because of legal errors."

"Wow, your lawyer couldn't figure that out?" I asked, wondering why she had an inmate go farther in her case than the attorney who was paid to do it.

"That's what I said," she agreed, rolling her eyes. "In an unanimous decision, the court found that because of the inadequacy of my trial lawyer they would overturn the case."

"I still don't get it. What inadequacies?"

"My attorney, that the court assigned to me, was found incompetent for not investigating the possibility of an insanity defense for me. I'd been diagnosed bipolar way before going to jail, and it was left untreated. This wasn't an illness back then that was understood, and since everyone considered me crazy, I decided to not talk about it anymore. So when I found my sister having sex with my husband, I not only shot her, which should've been considered a crime of passion, but I wasn't in a state of mind that I could've made an accurate choice."

"Why did it take them so long to figure this out?" I asked angrily. "Your whole life! You've lost most of your life for something as simple as this."

"Yeah, but it happens more often than you think. My future was destroyed because of how little I knew, so I couldn't blame anyone other than myself. The Bible says that my people are destroyed because they lack knowledge, and I've learned how true that statement really is."

I smiled when she quoted the scripture from the Bible, because I was glad to know that at least she carried the tradition that grandma left behind.

"Well, at least you're out now, and that's all that matters," I said, trying to bring back some comfort to the situation.

"Yes honey, God is good and don't you ever forget that. Listen, I don't want you to think that I'm condoning what I did to your…to Mahogany." That was the second time that she corrected herself with her title. Maybe she felt uneasy. "I'm not using my illness as a scapegoat, because it is what it is. I'm simply free because my lawyer didn't do his job. Even though I'm sure that anyone in my situation would've done the same thing, it still doesn't justify the fact that I took some-one's life."

My thoughts drifted again while she spoke, and went to the night I found Chloe and Brooklyn having sex in Miami. *I defi-nitely would've been in my mother's shoes if that bitch, Chloe, hadn't lived,* I thought. God was good, even when I wasn't.

"Before your grandmother died, she told me that she'd revealed to you who your real mother was." That was the question that I wanted answered more than anything, and I was elated that I didn't have to figure out a way to ease it into the conversation.

"Yeah…she did. Why did you lie to me?" I asked, as those feelings of betrayal instantly came back up.

"Lie? Why did I lie to you? Little girl, you are my daugh-ter! From the moment you came out the womb, you were mine. No one lied to you, we just protected you from the truth. That's what mothers do. We protect our kids from the truth," she replied, tearing up. I was right behind her with the water works that were welling up in my eyes.

"Tell me what happened, please."

She looked down at her restless hands and then back up at me and said, "Mahogany was always a free spirit. She did whatever she wanted to do, and thought that the world owed her something. My mother lost control of her very early, like around fifteen years old. Mahogany started hanging around older men, who, even at her young age, toted her around as a trophy. She was beyond beautiful, with a body to match, so anything she wanted, she got it. Well, one day she got a little more than she expected, when a man that she'd stolen drugs and money from came knocking at her door. When she opened it, he demanded his money and product back, but it was long gone. She'd snorted all his coke up, and spent his money on clothes and jewelry. The next day, he forced his way into her house and raped her for two days straight, until he felt like the debt was paid off. When the police got to the house, they said that there was so much blood, it looked like someone had been murdered."

"Does anyone know who the man was?" I asked, secretly wanting to know who my father was.

"Yeah, streets talk. He was a hustler and a pimp. One of the toughest in Rochester at the time. Your grandmother tried getting out who the man was so she could have him arrested, but Mahogany would have rather died than to be considered a snitch. I don't know what persuaded her to mess with him, but she never learned her lesson. He ended up dying of AIDS sometime in the late eighties."

"So, when did she find out she was pregnant?"

"It was after the rape kit had been administered. She immediately went hysterical and demanded an abortion, but back then, no one was doing them. So with Chloe just born, and you on the way, she was going to be a single mother of two at the age of eighteen. I knew that if she gave birth to you, and you were left in her care, you would've been dead before your first breath, so I stepped up to the plate. I was only twenty-one, and couldn't have kids anyway, so I begged her to give you up, and promised that she would never have to lift a finger as far as you were concerned. With no other option left, she agreed, and as soon as you were born, you were my daughter."

"But...but, you said that I was born on the ocean, and that was how I got my name. You told me that you were on a cruise ship, and you pushed me out when you were seven months pregnant! Those were all lies?" I asked, feeling manipulated.

"I wanted to give you a story that you could tell your

friends. One of honor and fun. At the time, I'd always wanted to go on a cruise, but I couldn't afford it. When I looked into your eyes, I felt like I was on the ocean. That's really where your name came from. You were my Oshyn." I couldn't help but to understand why she'd chosen to lie to me. "Oshyn, are you okay?" she asked, as I cupped my hand over my mouth and started making gagging sounds.

I nodded my head yes, afraid that if I opened my mouth, my breakfast would come out everywhere. This pregnancy had begun to take its toll on me, and I was barely a few weeks. It was still something that I wasn't ready to share with her.

"I think I have a stomach virus," I lied. That's what mothers do, we lie to protect. Guess I learned it from the best.

# 15 CHLOE

I was satisfied with the fact that Oshyn had been locked down yesterday, even if it wasn't for long. The device that I'd placed on her car, told me that she'd only stayed there for a couple of hours. For some reason, I knew those sorry ass protect and serve people would let her go once she posted bond.

Where were the crooked cops when you needed them?

I instantly made a mental note to find someone on the force as soon as possible, so shit like this wouldn't happen again. After getting dressed for the day, I walked out of the guest bedroom and roamed around the halls of Mason's mansion, trying to find something valuable to take. Even though I'd been a guest for only a couple of days, I didn't plan on staying too much longer. Especially since Mason still hadn't made any advances toward me. Every night when I went to sleep, I expected to be harassed by his hard dick, either in my mouth or pussy, but he never tried. I knew my body could've been a playboy centerfold every month, so being that the old man didn't appreciate my physique, started to piss me off. Men would die to even get a whiff of my kitty kat, and here he was turning it down.

As I continued to look around, thoughts about my small problem with Mason raced through my mind. *Shit, I don't think he's gay because I haven't seen any fairies running around. Then again, this house is so damn big, it could be one around here.* I suddenly stopped dead in my tracks.

"I got it…maybe his dick can't get hard," I said to myself. "But if that's the case, Viagra or Cialis would do the trick." Whatever the problem was, his ass had to get in gear. I wasn't going to wait forever.

The house was very big, like a maze, and I quickly found myself lost with every corner I turned. The doors to every room looked like they belonged to castles, and everyone that I walked by was shut. My curious nature started getting the best of me, so before long, I quietly began opening every door I passed, trying not to alarm anyone. I didn't know who else was in the house at the moment, so I didn't want to raise suspicion.

By the time I got to the third room, I heard some faint huffing noises. Being the nosey person I am, I pressed my ear to the door to get a better idea of what the noise was, but the thick oak wood wouldn't allow a clearer sound. So, without hesitation, I slowly twisted the knob and opened the door slightly. From the angle where I stood, the only person I saw was an older woman in a fancy titanium wheelchair. Her skin was so sunken in, she resembled a skeleton.

*This has to be his wife,* I thought, as I immediately remembered him describing her condition. As I cracked the door open a little more, my eyes almost popped out of my head when I witnessed Mason, butt naked with his hard dick in his hand. *So much for being fucking impotent*, I thought, as my mouth hung open like Biz Markie. The more I looked, I realized that the old woman was naked too. He held a magazine in his left hand, while his right one stroked his dick as fast as he could. For an older guy, his dick still maintained a nice size.

"Shit, it looks like I picked the right room," I whispered.

I quickly went back into the hallway and slipped out of my clothes, trying to catch him before he finished. If this was how he got off, I wanted to show him what real fun was. After taking off my favorite pink thong, I opened the door, exposing my naked body, and proceeded to walk in the room. The half dead lady made me a little nervous, but hey, I was up for anything new.

"GET OUT!" Mason yelled, as soon as he realized that I was in the room. I ignored his command and ran over to him, falling on my knees to suck his dick. But as soon as my lips touched it, it went limp...immediately.

"What the fuck is wrong with you?" I asked, feeling offended.

"You have no right to be in here!"

He was hysterical at this point and refused to calm down. I looked over at his wife, and she never blinked once, making me second guess her existence.

"So, you would rather jerk off in front of a dead broad, than fuck me?" I asked, with my hands of my hips.

Now he looked offended. "GET OUT!" he yelled again, this time covering up his shriveled dick with the magazine.

"Fine!"

I walked out the room, picking up my clothes that were in the hall, and found my way back to the guest room. I quickly got dressed and decided to leave the house for a while, giving Mason some time to cool down or to jerk off, whichever came first.

*　　　*　　　*

Needing some new drama, I followed the directions on my transmitter that was connected to the tracking device under Oshyn's car. *Technology is a bitch!* I thought, remembering how small the dime-sized receptor really was. After driving for a few minutes, it lead me right to Oshyn's house. Just like the day before, I parked a couple of cars down and turned my ignition off. Oddly enough, I was willing to be patient in order for things to go smoothly.

However, I didn't have to wait long, because a short moment later, Bella came jogging out the house. *Man, Bella is getting so big.* I also noticed how much she resembled her mother, Apples. Her long legs were definitely going to make her some money when she got older. I couldn't help but think what my nephew would've been like if he were still alive. He was so handsome, even at six years old, and I had no doubt that, as he grew older, he would've looked just like his fine ass father, Trent. But just like his father, he'd gone to meet his maker, and I partially blamed myself.

My mind was redirected back to reality as I watched Oshyn walk out of the house, and Bella running up to her. It was good that Oshyn had decided to settle in the role as Bella's mother. God knows how she would've turned out if Apples's bitch ass was still around. Even though I didn't pull the trigger, that was one bullet who'd found the right person.

Following behind Oshyn was a woman who looked uncomfortably familiar. Holding on to Oshyn's baby, she was dressed appropriately in the eighty-two degree weather, wearing a cute laced tank top with a pair of jean capri's. Her skin was a bit worn and her posture sucked, telling me that she had a long, unforgiving life. I watched on as she intimately ran her fingers through Oshyn's hair. I sat in confusion for five more minutes, until they decided to make their way to the car. With my car a short distance away, I was close enough that I could hear the conversation slightly.

Oshyn grabbed her son from the woman's arms and slowly walked with her to the car. The stranger seemed to be held back by a slight limp. I sat low in my car with the window rolled down, as they got closer. I was beginning to think that this was a wasted trip until I heard Oshyn say, "I still can't believe you're home. I missed you so much, Ma."

I thought I was about to have a heart attack, as my heart rate took off like a speeding car. I sat up abruptly, trying calm myself down, as beads of sweat began to form on my forehead. "No, I must've heard wrong," I said quietly. I took my shades off to get a better look, and stared at the woman one more time. *It is her*, I thought, while I watched my Aunt Roslyn get into the car. *But how? She's supposed to be serving a life sentence for killing my mother.*

Although I was beyond furious, I put my emotions away to find some good in all of this.

Now both women would have to die.

# 16 OSHYN

The following Friday, my mother insisted on keeping Mye and Bella for the day, while I went to go see my lawyer. Even though she'd only been home for less than a week, she fell in love the moment she laid her eyes on them. And even though she'd never met Apples, she was overjoyed to take Bella in as her granddaughter. Like she said, "Any great friend of Micah's, is a great friend of mine!" I left them in her care in total peace, and had no doubt that she would handle everything.

Must've been those maternal instincts.

Everyone had adapted to my mother living with us very well, especially Bella. Her attitude changed considerably, and Mye rarely made a sound. I guess it was all the one on one time she'd been spending with them. I didn't care what anyone said, spending time with kids really made a difference in their persona. I was at a point in my life where I simply didn't have that time to give. She came just in time to lift my burdens.

I guess in talking to my mother, I realized just how smart

she was, even if she didn't have the piece of paper that society wanted you to have. If I hadn't learned anything else from our lengthy conversations, I learned to become knowledgeable on whatever life had stolen from you. For a moment, my hopes were up once again, and I prayed that I'd get my life back in no time.

"Baby, hand me those ham hocks over there," my mom said, while pointing her thin fingers toward the sink. "I'm gonna make some collard greens today."

I noticed that she enjoyed starting her meals in the morning. If nothing else, we had been eating like royalty since she'd been home. "Ma, how many times are you gonna cook collard greens? You've made them everyday this week!"

"As many times as I want to," she replied, with a hint of sass in her voice. "I'm finally free from all that jailhouse food," she continued, adding relief to her tone. "I..."

"Grandma, can I have this?" Bella asked, rudely cutting my mother off.

"Excuse me! Do you not see us talking?" I asked. I hated when kids interrupted adults while they were speaking. It was one of my biggest pet peeves. Bella continued holding the bag of chips up to my mother's face, totally disregarding what I'd said. "Um, little girl...did you hear me?"

"Oh, it's okay," my mother said quickly. I was upset that she'd come to her defense. Bella was lucky.

"Do it again!" I yelled, warning her. I was still in charge, and needed for her to know that. She walked away unaffected by my threat. "Ma, why did you do that? She needs to learn that certain things are just unacceptable."

"Listen, I missed your whole life. Simple things like this I yearned for. I craved for the idea of taking you to the park and pushing you on a swing. There were so many things I wanted to do with you that I couldn't, and I feel like I've been blessed with another chance. Now I got you, Bella and Mye. I know you think what she does is aggravating, but not to me. It may sound crazy, but I would've given anything while I was in jail, to hear you suck your teeth at me...anything."

I knew exactly how she felt. I too would give anything for everyone to come back and aggravate me for one more day...anything. I peeked at my watch, and saw that I had about twenty minutes until my meeting with the lawyer Shannon got me. I made sure that I looked my best for the occasion with my white Poplin short sleeve blouse and black wide leg trousers, both by Jean Paul Gaultier.

"Ma, let me take you out for a good time tomorrow. Maybe we can go to a nice fancy restaurant and eat."

"Out to eat? With all this food we just got. You're trippin," she said, while soaking the greens again for the third time.

"Just for tomorrow," I insisted. I went to the refrigerator and poured a cold glass of sweet tea. "You haven't been any-where since you got out. I just want to show you a good time. Hell, I could use a good time," I admitted to myself. "Just this one time...for me, please?"

"No. I'll pass on this one, sweetheart. You go out tomorrow with your friends and have a nice night out. I'll watch the kids while you're gone."

"Why don't you like going anywhere?" I asked my mother, while taking a sip of my tea.

"What are you talking about? I'm fine." I watched as she fumbled with the food. I knew that statement couldn't have been further from the truth. I could tell by her mannerisms that she was still institutionalized. Her dislike for society was apparent in the way her body tensed up when she went out-side. It was as if she wasn't physically comfortable if she was-n't at home. *Maybe life was just moving too fast for her*, I assumed, as I watched her struggle to adjust.

"Please, Ma, just for me," I begged, poking out my lower lip.

"Don't beg, it doesn't fit you well," she replied, as she

pinched my cheek. "Okay...okay, I'll go. But just this once."

I kissed her on the cheek for finally agreeing, and told her I'd be back from my meeting soon.

Before getting into my car, I looked around and took a deep breath of fresh air. The aqua blue clear sky and chirping birds made the eighty degree day perfect and worthy of a pair of my open toed Manolos. I learned early on in life that people treated you much better if you were dressed appropriately. It spoke volumes of your appearance, and it also let them know that you were on the same level as they were.

\* \* \*

I'd yet to meet the lawyer, but I sat in the Starbucks on Six Forks Road, wondering if everyone who came in was him. Moments later, my curiosity was finally answered, as a short and frail black man approached my table. *You've got to be kidding me,* I thought to myself, as I made a quick observation of his attire. He was 5'2, if that, and had on a disgusting brown suit that was visibly too large for his frame. *This has to be some kind of joke!* I looked around to see if I was being played, and found no obvious sign that this was a set up.

"Oshyn Jones?" he asked, with his hand extended.

"Yes, Oshyn *Rodriguez*," I answered, taking a mental note that I desperately needed to get to the courthouse. He grabbed my hand aggressively, and gave a shake that made me wince in pain. I guess that was his way of proving he was a man. It was apparent that he had the little man complex.

"My name is Sean Davis, and I'll be representing you in the civil asset forfeiture case. My good friend, Shannon Bourdeaux, has taken full responsibility for all of your legal costs."

I could barely concentrate on what he was saying, because it felt like I was talking to Gary Coleman. He looked like an adolescent playing around in his father's clothes, but at this point, I didn't have any other choices. It was either trust in the little man or lose everything that I'd worked so hard for. I redirected my attention to the only person that was able to help me.

"What about the concealed weapon charge? Are you handling that as well?"

He looked at me like I was some sort of thug. "Umm...I didn't know anything about a concealed weapon charge. I'll have to talk to Mr. Bourdeaux and get back to you concerning that. Your court date is not next week, is it?"

"Oh, no not at all."

He finally smiled. "Good, then I'll see what I can do."

At that point, I was a little ashamed of judging him in the beginning, because despite his size, he was probably one of the best lawyers in Raleigh.

"Thank you so much for taking on my case. It's been a month since the authorities seized my assets, so where are we right now in regards to retrieving my things?" I got straight to the point. I needed answers, and I needed them now.

"Well, Mrs. Jo...I mean *Ms.* Rodriguez, let me start off by educating you briefly on what the forces are that you're up against. Asset Forfeiture falls under two categories, civil and criminal. With Criminal Forfeitures, the government can only seize your things if you've been convicted of a crime. In this category, you're innocent until proven guilty. Civil Forfeiture, on the other hand, is much different. That's because your property, not you, is convicted of the crime. In this instance, your assets are considered guilty until proven innocent."

He paused, and waited for a comment, but I never said a word.

Mr. Bourdeaux had gone over a few things with me concerning this topic, and I just wanted to listen to everything he said before I spoke.

"From the information that I've conducted, I have good news and bad news."

"The bad news first, please," I insisted. At least with that out of the way, I'd be able to leave the table with something good. I was determined to.

"There's something in the system called 'equitable sharing', which allows most of the law enforcement agencies to receive a profit of up to eighty percent of the net proceeds. From my experience in fighting these kinds of cases, your money and your homes are long gone."

"That's unbelievable!" I said in disbelief. "How can they violate my life, steal what belongs to me and my family, and spend *my* money? I haven't even been convicted for God's sake! What's going on?" I asked, pounding my fist against the table. I kind of wished I hadn't done that with the same hand he gave me a death grip with, but just like him, I wanted to prove a point.

"Look, I know this is frustrating, but the more you keep your composure, the better you'll be able to handle the arrows that'll be thrown your way. And believe me, there will be tons of arrows," he warned. "The good thing is that we were granted a trial to get the process started in fighting this war. There was a non-refundable bond, and it was a generous amount of money, but Mr. Bourdeaux took care of it."

"So, we have a chance to win?" I asked, hoping that he had a simple yes or no answer. Of course, I wasn't so lucky.

"You're going up against the most corrupt gang in America...law enforcement. This is war, and if you're gonna win, you have to get off of the defensive side, and find your way to an offensive position." I found a sudden urge to want to play football after his scenario. "To beat them, you have to find a way to make them fear and respect you. It may sound impossible, but it's been done. You have to be willing to attack them personally. Hit them where they hit you...their pockets."

The little man was on his game after all. I would've liked more concise answers, but I was content with what he'd discussed with me. We talked for a little longer, and he gave me a few instructions to follow regarding my case, before we said our goodbyes. After grabbing an iced tea, I headed toward my car, and quickly realized that I couldn't remember where I'd parked.

Downtown Raleigh was getting bigger than ever, and the construction made it almost impossible to remember where my car was. Just when I thought I had an idea of where to look next, I ran into someone I didn't necessarily want to see.

"Hey Oshyn, wait up!" he said, as he ran across the street. "Oshyn, wait!" I kept walking until he caught up to me, demanding my attention. "Oshyn!" Cody caught up to me, panting loudly. *Must be a cigarette smoker,* I thought, as I watched him attempt to catch his breath. I noticed that he wore a pair of Paper Denim and Cloth jeans, topped off with an Armani t-shirt. I don't know why I even noticed, but I did. I wasn't interested in him, but I liked his style.

"Remember, I met you at Home Depot a few weeks ago?"

I remembered him all right, and he was even more attractive than the first time I saw him. "Is everything okay with you?" he asked, almost in a whisper. "When you ran out of Home Depot that day, I knew something was wrong. And then when I got home later on that night, it was plastered all over the news."

I couldn't help but notice how much he resembled Robin Thicke. His ice blue eyes stared into mine with such concern, but I was no fool. Brooklyn had also stared at me with the same emotion, and I wasn't going to fall for it again, especially with a white guy.

"Um, I'm fine, thanks. Look, I'm sorry for being such a bitch but…" I looked up at the sky in mid-sentence, and decided to keep my problems to myself. "I have to run, so if you don't mind…"

"Wait," he said, grabbing my arm as I started to walk away. I was beginning to notice that this was a habit for him. I stared at his hand and then back at him, and like the first time, he got the hint. "All I wanted to know was if there was anything I could do to help? Anything at all?"

"No!" I said again at his repeated attempt to assist the 'poor little black girl'. At this point, I was very aggravated. "I mean, my God, what is it that you want from me anyway? I have no business! I have no money! I'm basically homeless, and on top of all of that, I'm a rape baby! My first-born and best friend is dead, and now I'm trying to get a divorce, so no, I don't want you or your help. Just…just leave me alone," I demanded, as I ran away in tears.

I knew all of that was uncalled for, and I was convinced I'd just had a nervous breakdown. He didn't deserve that, but my anger was waiting to be poured out. Unfortunately, he happened to be there to receive the overflow. After finally getting in my car, I dug into my purse, looking for something to wipe my eyes with. When I pulled out a piece of tissue, a business card with Brooklyn's name on it fell out.

I held it in my hands, rubbing my fingers across his name, and dabbed the tissue on my cheek, trying to catch the countless tears. *How did I get this,* I wondered. I figured he must've slid it in my purse the day at the grocery store. I couldn't remember us being that close, but he always found a way to make things happen. I had the urge to throw the card out the window, but there was something in me, something bigger that decided to keep it.

I missed him.

I took a whiff of the black paper, and briefly caught his scent as I started the car. I didn't stop crying until I reached the house.

"What's wrong, Oshyn?" my mother asked, as she immediately came to my aid. The house was in perfect order, and I could smell the ribs she had barbequing on the grill. Bella was at the table doing her homework, and Mye was in his grandmother's arms being spoiled. He deserved it though, he'd been through a lot as well. It was so nice to have her back home.

"Look, Ma, I need to talk to you, but not in front of them."

"Of course." She went upstairs and put Mye in his crib, and told Bella she'd be right back. We went to the kitchen table and sat down.

"What's going on, baby?" she asked, pulling my hair away from my damp face.

"I'm pregnant again, Ma…I'm pregnant!" I couldn't believe that I was telling her this, but I had to. Despite the anger I harbored in my heart when she first got here, we'd become closer. I needed her help and I figured that in order to get it, I would have to be honest. "What am I going to do?" I asked, in between gasps of air.

"Everything is going to be okay, baby. I'm here now. I'll take care of everything. Who's the father? When am I gonna meet him?"

I bit my lower lip and peeled a piece of dry skin that sat there. I didn't want to tell her, but I had to. "His name is Shannon. Shannon Bourdeaux."

"Shannon…Shannon…why does that name sound so familiar?" she asked herself out loud.

"When grandma died, he came to the funeral. Then the FEDS came and seized everything, and it was him that gave us this house to stay in." She looked around the room as if she'd seen a ghost. "What's wrong?"

"If my memory serves me correct, he was my father's closest friend. Mom told me stories about the both of them when I was a child, some good, some bad. They were both involved with the Mob though," she warned. "When Daddy died, Mom said that Shannon never left her side. Does he know anything about the pregnancy?"

"No. I didn't know how to tell him."

My tears began to dry up after I knew I had her support. That's all I needed, was for her to have my back.

"You have to tell him right away. You can't hide anything from a man like that. Tell him now!"

I took heed to her warning, and called Shannon right away, insisting that we meet as soon as possible. He made arrangements and told me that a ride was on the way to pick me up. I was nervous as hell, but ready to tell the man I barely knew that I was bearing his child.

# 17CHLOE

"Where is that bitch going?" I said, ducking down in my car as Oshyn rode by. *I hope she didn't see me.* The white man who chauffeured her in the black Maserati looked vaguely familiar, but I couldn't really focus in on him in the dark. I'd been staked out in front of her house since she came back from downtown, and waited patiently for the perfect time to make my grand entrance.

I watched the rest of the family interacting through the bare windows, that revealed their every move. *Wow, I thought only white people refused to put up curtains.* I looked on as the woman who took my mother's life, braided Bella's hair, sent her upstairs, and then rocked Oshyn's baby to sleep, a baby that should've been mine. After taking him upstairs, she finally retired to the living room and turned on the TV. I knew at that moment, it was time for action.

I didn't know how much longer Oshyn was going to be out, so I had to make this quick as possible. I didn't want for her to walk in, even though it wouldn't matter. I wanted her ass dead anyway. I got out of the car, and ran over to her precious convertible that sat in the driveway. I wore black from head to toe so that my presence wouldn't be easily detected. After looking around for the perfect rock, I scratched the word BITCH on the driver's side door, then stood back like an artist to admire my work. Even though I could barely see it, I knew I had a masterpiece.

At that moment, I was motherfucking Picaso.

*On to the next event,* I thought, as I looked toward the house. However, it was right at that moment when I realized I didn't know how I was gonna get inside. I couldn't believe that I hadn't thought the plan all the way through. There was no way I could break a window without causing obvious, unwanted attention. This wasn't the hood, and any noise other than the birds chirping, would've been attended to immediately from some nosey white woman.

*Think, think, think,* I told myself. It finally came to me. *The front door,* I suddenly remembered. *Rich people rarely lock their front door. Especially the way Oshyn ran out of here.* She never turned around to make sure it was locked. I made my way from the driveway, and walked casually toward the front door. If there were any witnesses, I didn't need them reporting a suspicious person creeping around the house, so I maintained my effort to look normal.

I placed my hand over the cold gold doorknob and slowly twisted it open. "Jack pot," I mouthed, as the door slowly opened. I silently hoped it wouldn't squeak. After stepping inside, I closed the door just as carefully, making sure there were no signs of an intrusion. I tiptoed along the hardwood floors, not really knowing where to go. The air was stuffy and hot, making it hard to breathe. *That bitch still doesn't believe in AC,* I thought to myself, remembering all the days Oshyn complained of being cold. She always blamed it on her low iron count.

I poked my head out and peeked around the corner, before walking into the next room. When I finally saw Aunt Roslyn slouched down in a plush reclining chair reading her Bible, I smiled. Even my nipples got hard from the slight rush. The TV lit the room up, making it just right for my element of surprise. I would've preferred it darker, but I had to work with what I had. I patted my side, making sure that my weapon hadn't fallen out of my pocket as I ran out the car. I knew it was a stupid thing to check for at this point, but it was always better late than never.

I walked in the living room, hiding nothing from my victim as I stood before her.

"Oshyn?" she said, squinting as she looked up. She quickly sat up in her chair when she realized that I wasn't her beloved daughter.

"Hey Auntie, it's me, Chloe. Do you remember me? Do you remember killing my mother?" I asked sarcastically. She didn't say a word, and clutched her Bible close to her heart, hoping that it would protect her from my demons. "Answer me, old woman!"

"Chloe? Baby, what are you doing here?"

"No, the question is, what are you doing here? You're supposed to be in prison for the rest of your life, but somehow…you're not!" Her eyes protruded in concern as she watched me take the hunting knife out of my pocket. I ran my black leather gloves over my hair that kept getting into my face. It was too short to put into a ponytail, so I had to deal with it.

"Letters. I wrote you countless letters, trying to explain what happened, but you never responded. Not once did you write me back or come to visit, and although I understood, I just wanted a chance to tell you my side of the story."

She was right. She had tried over and over again to reach out to me, but I refused to forgive her for what she'd done. Against my better judgment, I listened to her as she spoke. Even though I came here to do one thing and one thing only, there was something in me that still wanted to hear whatever she had to say.

"Yes, I did it. I took your mother…my only sister's life, but it wasn't me. I'm not sure if your grandmother ever told you this, but we all suffer from mental illness, everyone except for your grandmother and Oshyn. Chloe, I heard that same voice in my head that you're hearing right now, and it told me to kill her. Please, please, I beg of you, please don't make the same mistake I made. Don't do this, baby. Don't do this," she pleaded with me. She laid her blue Bible on the arm of the recliner, and slid to the edge of the chair. She took her hand slowly and extended it toward me. "Come here," she whispered. "Everything is going to be okay."

I looked at her, and started to wonder how a family that could hate each other so much, look so much alike. She sat there in a manner that my grandmother once did. Her hair, so silver, rested in one long wavy braid over her shoulder, just like my grandmother's. And then there was her face that was a scary reflection of my own mother. How could I want to kill a woman who was the symbol for our generation? She was right. I did hear those voices, and for a moment, I wanted to shut them up and run into her arms.

I took a step forward, ready to surrender when that voice came back into my head. *What the fuck are you doing, you stupid bitch? How can you betray me like this? Out of everyone that has turned their back on me, I never in a million years would've thought that you'd do the same. A truce? You're getting ready to make a truce with the woman who took my life? I was the only person on this earth who has ever loved you, and this is how you repay me?*

"No," I whispered to my mother. "No, I didn't betray you…come back!" I demanded of her. But there was silence. I'd hurt my mother's feelings, and there was only one thing I could do to make her forgive me.

"Where are the kids?" I asked, holding a death grip on the

knife.

"You leave those children out of this!" she demanded, and immediately rose to her feet. "If you have a beef with me, handle it with me, but leave those babies alone!"

"I want you, the babies, and your daughter all dead!" I screamed.

With no time to prepare for the attack, Roslyn lunged toward me in an attempt to save her family's life, but was stopped in her tracks by the knife that quickly made its home in her chest. She gasped for air as the blood began trickling down her shirt. Money is a motivator for most crimes, especially in my case, but today, my motivation was different. It was bigger than money. It was revenge, and I wouldn't stop until my mother's death had been avenged.

"Die, bitch!" As I twisted the knife around, ripping her chest apart, she never let go of the partial hug she gave me. I wanted her death to be slow and painful, just how my life had been, and it was. I stabbed her repeatedly as she fell to the floor. Then without hesitation, I stood over her body, lifted up her chin and slit her throat from ear to ear. She gasped for air, while I struggled to lift her butchered body back on the recliner. I pressed the button, which allowed the chair to lie back, and covered her body with a blanket I found nearby.

With the lights and TV off, she looked like she was sound asleep. Making my way upstairs, I rapidly searched for the kids. As luck would have it, the first room I found belonged to Oshyn's baby. I walked over to the crib where the baby laid, and gently touched his face just like I would've done to my child, if Oshyn hadn't killed it. She took my future with my seed and even with Brooklyn. He loved me, I knew it. He wanted me to be the mother to his child, not Oshyn.

The baby looked just like his father, and I was beginning to miss, once again, something I never had. Dreaming about what could have been, I suddenly had a change of plans. I took out

Oshyn's folded up birth certificate that I'd put in my back pocket before I left Mason's house. I looked it over one more time before placing it in the baby's crib, next to his stuffed dinosaur. I wanted her to know that I was responsible for this. I wanted her to know that I hated the fact we were more than cousins.

I grabbed a blanket and wrapped the baby up before lifting him out of the crib. It felt good to be holding a part of Brooklyn in my arms. I made my way back into the hallway, and searched two more rooms before finally finding my next target. I looked at Bella as she slept soundly in her twin bed, oblivious to the fact that the new family member in her life was now gone. "I hope you enjoyed your grandmother's short stay," I whispered.

Forgetting that I had to make this quick, I walked over to Bella's bed and picked her up. Throwing her small body over my only available shoulder, I made sure to get a good grip as she hugged my neck. Bella was so knocked out that she never even realized that she was being carried out of her room.

Carrying them both downstairs felt like carrying two small sacks of potatoes, but it was easier than I thought. With Bella dead to the world, I didn't have to struggle at all for her cooperation. On the way out the door, I walked passed the dead body, just as a devilish grin spread across my face. My aunt looked just like a sleeping beauty.

"Sleep tight…don't let the bedbugs bite," I childishly said, as I made my way to the door. After leaving out the front door with my extra baggage, I quickly walked to my less than attractive car, and laid Bella in the passenger seat, while laying the baby in my lap. For the life of me, I couldn't understand why I hadn't bought a new car with the money Agent Tate and I had stolen from Oshyn. I guess in a sick way I wanted her to know that I was responsible for all of her pain before I could enjoy it.

As I drove away, I tried to imagine what Oshyn's reaction

would be when she arrived. I would've loved to kill her too, but the fact that she was going to be tortured by what she saw when she came home, was well worth the wait.

"Are you glad you have a new mommy," I said, patting my sleeping nephew on his back.

# 18 OSHYN

I rested my head against the window of the Maserati, while the driver sped away into the night. I was exhausted from being out all day, and wished I could've picked another day to tell this man about my pregnancy, but it was imperative that it was done tonight. I needed a clear conscious, and knew I would feel better once he was informed. We'd only had sex that one time, but I still felt like I was his slave. There had been plenty of times that I wanted to run, find somewhere else to call home, but quickly realized that I had nowhere to go.

I'd become dependant on him to care for us. It was the kind of dependency that I hadn't felt since I was with Micah's dad, Trent. Dependency that I said I would never feel again. I went back on my word. I was beginning to no longer trust myself.

As Shannon's driver parked in an alley of a small restaurant, my stomach started to do several twists and turns. The closer I got to actually seeing Shannon, my fear returned as I began recalling how violent he'd been. This was so unlike me to be so afraid. Life had worn me down, and I was just a puppet. After parking the car and opening the door, his driver led me into the building and right to Shannon's table. *I thought he had money*, was all I could assume, wondering why he would've brought me to such a place.

The restaurant, called Q's, wasn't a place that I'd assume he'd frequent. It was small, nothing too fancy, but exceptionally clean. Maybe this dump was a reflection of how he thought of me.

Small. Nothing too fancy. Exceptionally clean.

I looked at his diamond wedding ring as I sat down, and wondered where his wife was. And then I questioned myself as to if he even had one. *If I had a husband, he would never*...I stopped dead in my thoughts, realizing that I *had* a husband and he *did* do this to me. I had changed my mind. Just that quick, I'd changed my mind, and no longer wanted any part of this circus that I'd created for myself.

"Have you found Chloe yet?" he asked, interrupting my thoughts.

He was stern and straight to the point, just like the first time. I looked for ways to find an answer to that question. My leg started to tremble underneath the table. I was afraid of what his reaction would be when he found out that I hadn't even begun my search. Hell, I didn't even know where to start. I could tell by the Jeroboam Fuente lighter he used to light the Cuban cigar with, he had eloquent taste. That lighter set him back at least thirty-two hundred dollars. I got nauseous as he pulled on the illegal cigar, blowing the communist smoke in the air. *I'm pregnant*, I wanted to scream, but I took my time with sharing the news.

"I'm not going to ask you again, Oshyn! Damn, didn't you learn anything from our first encounter?"

I cleared my throat. "No." I tried giving an excuse, but nothing seemed to come out. I was speechless.

"No? It's been weeks since you've been in my house, and you still don't have anything on her?" His thick eyebrows frowned, showing me his displeasure. "You have five days to find her, or something about her. If not, you're getting the fuck out my house. Live in the streets and die for all I care, but you will leave my house!"

"Wait," I interjected, suddenly finding the urge to talk. "You can't put us out. I'm…I'm pregnant!" I blurted out, before giving any real thought to what I was saying. I didn't want to be his whore or even his mistress. His eyes looked at me as if he was shocked. Like he was unaware that his little men could still march up a hill. I hated to be the one to tell him that they could.

"And what does that have to do with me?" he asked.

"It's your baby, Shannon. This is your baby!"

His piercing laugh made my flesh crawl. "Don't try that ghetto shit with me, bitch. If you're after money, don't even waste your time, because a thousand dollars a week is all you're getting until you find Chloe," he replied. "Besides, don't include me with the group of men you've probably been fucking."

Tears instantly welled up in my eyes. I couldn't believe he was actually treating me like some type of whore. "I haven't been with a man in a year, before you decided to rape me."

Obviously I must've struck a nerve, because he changed his tune slightly. "Well if it is mine, you'll abort that baby first thing in the morning. I'll arrange for your pick up at…"

"Abort! Listen, I didn't want this as much as you, but Shannon, I can't kill this baby! Please, let's discuss this."

"Didn't you fucking hear what I said? That was all the discussion I'm going to have," he said, looking around. "What makes you think I want that thing? Either you get the abortion tomorrow or I'll abort both of you! As a matter of fact, now your five days has been decreased to one. I want you out of my fucking house!"

I couldn't believe my ears. I was so close to feeling a sense of security, and now it was being taken away from me right under my nose. In a matter of seconds, I'd gone from a five-day deadline to being homeless as soon as tomorrow,

"Are you serious?" I asked, careful not to piss him off any more than I already had.

He got up from the table, and before walking away said, "Oh, and find your own fucking way home!"

"What? It took us more than thirty minutes to get here? How am I going to get home?" I cried, as he continued to walk out of the door. He never looked back.

Distraught, I took my phone out my purse, and dialed 411. I got in contact with the cab company and gave them the location to where I was. Forty long minutes later, I hopped in the back seat, still puzzled as to what had happened, and told the driver where to go. I grabbed my stomach, wishing I hadn't decided to tell him so soon. It was too late at this point though. The damage was done.

When we pulled up to my house, I gave the cab driver his fare and a decent tip before getting out. I stood in the dark, facing the house, not quite ready to go inside. I couldn't tell my mother what had just happened. She didn't deserve anymore bad news. The air outside was still, and no matter how hard I tried, my feet wouldn't go toward the place I called home. I had an icky feeling inside that something wasn't right, but convinced myself that it was my pregnancy. Besides, my entire life wasn't right.

I went to sit in my car just to clear my head, and reached in my purse. Despite the feelings that told me no, I grabbed Brooklyn's business card. I couldn't fight it anymore. I needed to talk to him. I took my phone out and slowly dialed his number.

"Hello?" his deep voice said over the phone.

I swallowed my fear and said, "Brooklyn, it's me. I need you…it's important!"

# 19CHLOE

After all that I'd done, I still wasn't satisfied. I needed to physically see the pain in Oshyn's eyes when she found out what had happened. I needed to go back to her house. Back to the murder scene. With both Bella and Mye still asleep, I drove down to the country to drop them off at Mason's house. I hadn't been back since his morning's 'jack off session', and I didn't know where he stood as far as me living in the house, much less bringing two children into the mix.

After pulling into the driveway, I picked up Mye and Bella, who were still sound asleep, and let myself in the house with the spare key Mason had given me. I still couldn't believe he trusted me that much to give me access to his house, but I didn't complain. Maybe he wanted some company. Lonely people would do crazy things for companions, and obviously companionship was all he needed, because pussy sure wasn't.

I walked straight toward the guest room and turned the light on, trying my best to be quiet. I gently placed the kids on the bed, and was surprised that they never made a sound. *Damn, these kids can sleep through anything.*

"Chloe." The sudden voice startled me. I jumped back to see Mason standing at my door with a navy blue silk robe on. By the looks of his attire, you would never assume that he was such a weirdo. I walked closer to him, trying not to disturb the children.

*Maybe he finally came to his senses.* "Yes?" I said, in a seductive tone.

"I wanted to apologize…you know…about earlier," he struggled, peering over my shoulders the whole time. He wanted to know who else was in the room. This was, after all, his house.

"Um, I understand," I assured him, while rubbing his arm. "I had no business roaming around like that, invading your privacy. I'm the one who should be apologizing."

He kept staring at the bed, never giving me any inclination that he'd heard a word I said. His attention was focused on something else, and it wasn't me.

*So much for wanting some ass. Something is definitely wrong with this dude.* "Listen, I can't explain them right now," I told him, pointing at the kids. "But I need another huge favor from you. Can you watch them for a couple of hours while I go and get the baby's medicine? They'll sleep the whole time. I'll be back shortly."

Finally he smiled. "No problem. I've always wanted grand-kids," he said. "You go on, they'll be safe."

I quickly got myself together before he changed his mind, and was back out of the house in no time. I took out the trans-mitter that tracked the device on Oshyn's car, and saw that she was no longer at home. *Maybe she's already seen the body and noticed that the kids are missing,* was the only thing I could think of, as I noticed she was about twenty miles away from her house. But I could care less where she was, I went straight to her location to finish my plan.

I made it to Oshyn's destination on Oakwood Avenue, in less than twenty minutes and turned off my lights, parking next to a mini mart on the corner. It was unusually quiet, being as though Saint Augustine's College sat a few yards away. But most of the kids were out for the summer. There were a few feigns here and there, but other than that, it was pretty deserted, which was strange for this area. I, at least, expected to see a shoot out while I was there.

"What's her uppity ass doing in this area?" I asked myself, as I continued to look at my surroundings. Suddenly, I noticed Oshyn standing in front of the campus with an unidentified man. "Oh, so she's out here creeping, while her mother is at home dead," I said to myself. I needed to see what was going on and who the person was, so I got out the car to find some answers. I figured that I'd be less noticeable on foot anyway.

I hid behind the corner store, and watched them from a few feet away as they seemed engaged in a heavy conversation. However, I was hit with a blow to the head when the unidentified man, finally stood under a street light, which gave me a better view.

There they were, Oshyn and Brooklyn, standing side-by-side and staring at each other like two lovesick puppies. I quickly felt like I was about to lose control. My blood began to boil, and my skin tensed up as I watched Brooklyn caress Oshyn's arm. This was the first time I'd seen my former lover in a year, and in no way did I expect our reunion to be like this.

He would be mine, no matter what it took, and that was a vow I planned to see to the end. I picked up my phone and made a call. I had a problem that needed to be solved.

"Hello."

"Nino," I whispered, "I need a favor."

Nino was a body builder nigga I used to fuck with back in the day. His body was banging, thanks to all the steroids he took, and he stayed high on coke. His lifestyle was fucked up, but he was the perfect man for the job. For the right amount, no form of torture was off limits.

"Who is this?" he asked, sounding high as usual.

"It's me, Chloe."

He paused for a second. "Chloe? Chloe with the good ass pussy? Is that you?"

"Yeah, it's me. Listen, I need a favor."

"Hold up, I haven't heard from you in over a year, and you calling for a favor?"

I let out a huge sigh. "Look, I don't have time for small talk right now. Can you do it or not?"

"What do I get?"

"What do you want?" I asked, hating the fact that we were on the phone for this long.

"Pussy. I want some of that good ass pussy...I can taste that shit right now."

"Look, nigga, now really isn't the time," I said, still talking low. I didn't mind being fucked by his rough ass since Mason wouldn't give me any, but I had a mission to complete. "Maybe I'll let you play in my ass after everything is taken care of, okay?" He loved to toss my salad.

That was all I had to say, before he got off the phone and was on his way. Luckily, Nino didn't live far away, so a few moments later, he called to let me know he was in the area. I instructed him to wait a block away until I gave him the okay, and described what I wanted to be done. He was certain that my request would happen flawlessly.

This needed to be perfect, there was no time for mistakes.

I watched in disgust for forty more minutes, as Brooklyn continued to caress Oshyn's skin, and whisper sweet nothings in her ear. I could tell by the way Oshyn smiled that she hadn't been inside her house yet. She was happy to be where she was, and wasn't showing any signs of a woman who'd just lost her family for the second time.

Finally, after giving each other a small peck on the cheek, Oshyn got in her car, and they both said their goodbyes. Little did Brooklyn's ass know…it was show time.

When Oshyn was clear off the scene, I rushed to call Nino, before Brooklyn got away. He was walking toward his car, and just like clockwork, Nino's van came screeching through, hitting Brooklyn at full speed. I ran out to the street and stood over my former man as he laid on his back in agony. It wasn't until he opened up his eyes, did he realize who I was.

His eyes became the size of golf balls, which told me I was the last person he expected to see. "You were supposed to wait for me!" I screamed. "After all this time, I really thought you loved me. For a whole year, you've strung me along and now this. I find you with this bitch? Nino, get him!"

Without a second thought, Nino picked him up like a rag doll, as Brooklyn tried unsuccessfully to fight back. With the force he was hit with, I was sure he didn't have the strength to fight back. Blood had begun trickling down his face, and he moaned loudly, showing signs that he was in severe pain.

I accompanied Nino into the back of his van, while he put Brooklyn on the floor.

"You should've picked me. Oshyn can't love you like I can."

I rubbed his face as he continued to squirm in pain. A squirm that I'd felt in my heart since the day he left. He was hurt and probably needed help, but he would get none today. Revenge was all the medicine he needed. It would at least make me feel better.

With Brooklyn moaning in pure pain, Nino took his time and snorted up two lines of cocaine, which sent him into a daze.

A spaced out look.

A look that didn't look good.

Almost instantly, he became the Incredible Hulk. He began licking his lips profusely, and his breathing turned into loud pants. He went over to Brooklyn and yanked his pants down.

"No...No!" Brookyn yelled, as Nino forcefully pulled his underwear down, then exposed his own rock hard dick.

At that moment, I also wanted to tell Nino no, because I surely missed both of their manhoods. The sight of the two muscles instantly made my panties wet, and my clit went out of control. However, my desire to be fucked didn't last long when Brooklyn screamed to the top of his lungs as Nino forced him over on his stomach.

Brooklyn struggled to defend himself, but with the three hundred pound monster on his back, there wasn't much that he could do.

"AAAAHHHHHHHH!" was all I heard, as Nino shoved his dick in Brooklyn's ass. The pressure was so much that every vein in Brooklyn's face and neck came bulging out. I squirmed at the sight of shit that oozed out his ass. It was obvious he had lost control of his bowels.

Nino pounded his body against Brooklyn, and seemed to enjoy his screams for help. His body was so big that Brooklyn didn't stand a chance against him. Sweat rolled down Nino's face with each thrust he made, and all Brooklyn could do was lay there, as his manhood was taken away.

Satisfied with what was going down, I'd seen enough. I let myself out the van, leaving behind Brooklyn's screams for help and Nino's grunts of pleasure.

# 20CHLOE

I drove back to Mason's house with a smile on my face the entire time. Finally, I'd gotten some closure to the pain that everyone had caused me. I would've paid anything for Oshyn to watch her beloved Brooklyn being fucked in his ass. However, what was waiting for her at home was well worth her missing the action. Fully convinced that Nino would kill Brooklyn after he was done using his booty as his playground, I knew that he was finally out of my life forever. If he didn't want to play by my rules, he wouldn't play at all.

Pulling up into the driveway, I got out of the car and walked into the house. I didn't know what my next move was. What I was going to do with two new kids, two new kids that I hated. Bella reminded me of her mother, who I'd always despised, and Mye was a combination of two people who betrayed me. As I walked to my room, I decided that I'd hit the road, despite the fact of how tired I was.

Once in the room, I flipped on the lights, and saw that the kids were still asleep. I looked at the antique clock on the wall, and noticed that it was going on three o'clock in the morning.

Time always seemed to fly by when you were having fun. I was preparing to take the twelve-hour ride to Rochester, New York, and I couldn't take Bella with me. She was too old, and I was more than sure she would talk. She would ruin my plans.

I sat on one of the chairs, which were placed at the foot of the bed, just to get my thoughts together. I needed to find a way to get Mason to keep Bella for me for two days tops.

"You're back." Mason said, startling me.

*Since when did his ass start sneaking around? Maybe he's trying to get me back.* "Why are you up so late?" I asked, as he stood at the door.

"Just wanted to check on the kids…make sure everything was okay. Didn't want them to wake up in such a strange place with no one to explain where you were."

"Ahhh," I said, with fake sincerity. "That's so nice of you."

"Okay. Well, you all have a good night and…"

"Wait…Mason. I have another favor to ask of you." I knew Mason was tired of my favors, but he was the only one in my corner right now.

He came a little closer to me, wondering what I wanted this time. I had yet to explain who the kids actually were, and I knew that soon he'd want an explanation. "These are my sister's children. Her boyfriend beat her up very badly, and she's at the hospital in critical condition. I have to take the little boy to his grandmother's house in New York until his mother is able to care for him again. Her father will be picking her up when I get back," I said, pointing to Bella.

"Oh…I'm sorry to hear that."

"Me too. He almost killed her. I was wondering if you could watch my niece for me, no longer than two days, and I'll be out of your hair forever."

He rubbed his chin with his hand, as to contemplate my request, and said nothing for a while. "I just don't want her to be afraid when she wakes up. Does she know about anything that's happened?" he finally asked.

"Oh, no. She doesn't know anything. It's been a pretty stressful situation for everyone. I'll understand if you can't help. You've done so much for me already and…"

"No, I can do it. I'll just hire some clowns and stuff like that to keep her happy. She'll have a great time."

Even though we weren't having a sexual relationship, he was like putty in my hands. "Oh, thank you so much," I mustered up, along with some tears. "You have no idea what this means to me and my family."

"Anytime, Chloe. Just be careful out there." He left the room, giving me some time to get myself together.

I went into my purse and took out a bottle of pills. Pills that had gotten me through my roughest times in Asheville. Pills that made my depression and panic attacks manageable. I opened the child proof bottle, and placed five cream colored pills in my hand. The funny shaped tablets had the word 'ZOLOFT' written on one side, and the 100MG dosage on the other. I knew five pills were probably over doing it, but that was the whole purpose. Looking in my purse again, I grabbed my favorite pocket knife, and crushed the pill into tiny pieces before I was finally satisfied with the results.

I grabbed a bottle of orange juice off the nightstand, that I hadn't finished from earlier that morning, and dropped the powder inside. It dissolved almost immediately. "She should have a terrible case of diarrhea," I said laughing.

I got up from the chair and walked over to Bella. After struggling with her a while, I finally got her to sit upright. She rubbed her eyes and struggled to comprehend what was going on. I held the tainted juice up to her lips, forcing her to drink it all. She took several large gulps, and before long, the glass was empty.

That was it.

That was all I needed for the medicine to kick in. In a short time, she would be in another world, and that's exactly where I wanted her. Bella opened her eyes to see what was going on, and then stared at me to see if it was all a dream. When she realized that she was awake, she jumped up, almost crushing the baby.

"Chloe?" she asked unsure. "Where's Aunt Oshyn?"

I smiled. "There is no more Aunt Oshyn!"

Bella bent over and bit my arm as hard as she could, catching me off guard. She was fending for her herself, and her new brother. I couldn't blame her, I would've done the same.

"Ouch!" I screamed, before knocking her down to the floor. "You little bitch!"

"You killed my mother! I know you did…"

Even though I knew Quon had pulled the trigger, I decided to take the credit. "I sure did…I hated that bitch!" *And if you don't stop, I'm gonna kill your little ass too.*

She stood up and stared at me. If looks could kill, I'd be dead. I tried not to make too much commotion, because I didn't want Mason to show up again. So we just stood there eyeing each other like wild animals, ready to attack.

However, it wasn't long before she was out cold.

# 21 OSHYN

As long and painfully hectic as my day was, meeting up with Brooklyn made me forget my woes. I remembered running up to him and digging my face into his shoulders, trying to hide from the pain. I never wanted him to let go as he tightly wrapped his arms around me. After explaining my living situation with him, leaving out the fact that I was pregnant, Brooklyn assured me that he would take care of everything. That was all I needed to hear. Now, I didn't have to worry about being homeless.

We put a plan together to get me out of the house, and I was sure that everything would work out. I felt safe again. I finally felt like someone was in my corner, other than my mother and my children. And then he kissed me. He put those wet lips that once belonged to me, on top of mine. To my surprise, I felt a tingle in a place, I was sure wasn't working anymore. Before Shannon, there had been no other man inside of me since Brooklyn, and I was beginning to want him back.

When I arrived back at home, I got out of my car and

dragged myself up to the front door. Even though I still didn't want to tell my mother how the discussion went between me and Shannon, I was excited to reveal that I had a solution. For once, I finally had a solution. Before walking into the house, I paused, closed my eyes and said a silent prayer to God, thanking Him for all He'd done for me. *I guess He is on my side when I thought He wasn't,* I concluded, almost wondering why I doubted Him. I'd been through a lot, but He always kept me. Even in the midst of my own mess, He kept me.

I opened the door and walked inside, noticing that for the millionth time I'd left it unlocked.

"One day somebody is gonna come in here and steal everything I got," I said, as I turned around and made sure the door was locked. I wasn't as quiet as one should be when they walked into a house at twelve o'clock in the morning, but I knew my mother was awake. She was a night owl, and had promised to wait up for me, so we could talk.

I thought about turning on the dining room light, but noticed that all the other lights were off. I threw my keys and my purse on the glass table in the foyer, and took my shoes off in the dark. Normally my mom had the TV on, even if she dozed off, but tonight everything was off. I was kind of upset that she didn't wait up like she'd promised, but I was sure the kids had worn her out. What I had to tell her was nothing that couldn't wait until the morning.

I softly walked past the living room, and saw what appeared to be my mother laying back in the recliner. As my eyes struggled to adjust to the dark room, it looked like she was sound asleep with blankets covering her body. *How in the world is she sleeping with all those covers on her as hot as it is in here?* I thought to myself. For me, that would've felt like pure torture, but apparently she liked it. I thought about giving her a kiss goodnight, but didn't want to risk waking her up, so I mouthed goodnight and made my way upstairs.

*Go and check on the kids,* I heard a strong voice say to me, as I eased my way past their room. It was loud, very dominant, and sent chills up my spine. I wanted to go in each of the kids' rooms to see if everything was okay, and give out goodnight kisses, but decided against it. In a way, it felt like I was checking behind my mother, like she was incapable of handling things. I knew they had been in the best care, so at the time my overprotection seemed silly. Besides, I didn't have the patience to deal with Mye right now if he happened to wake up. I just wanted to climb in my bed and go to sleep. *There's always the morning*, I said as I went into my room, and laid on my comfortable king-sized bed.

*     *     *

Morning came much sooner than I'd expected. I had planned on sleeping in, but the rays that beamed through my window refused to let that happen. It was so nice having a live in caregiver. It felt good not having to worry about getting everything situated before the kids got up. I sat up in the bed and took a deep breath. As I inhaled, I quickly realized that something was missing.

On school days, my mother normally prepared breakfast for Bella before I dropped her off. However, on this particular morning, that aroma didn't fill the house. *Maybe she decided to take the morning off and give her cereal,* I assumed. I got out of the bed, put on my thick terrycloth robe, and went to check on things.

When I walked by Bella's room, I noticed that she wasn't in the bed. "Oh, my God! It's nine-thirty!" I said to myself, as I stared at her Dora the Explorer clock. School started at eight thirty, so she was extremely late.

I was surprised that my mother hadn't woken me up to take Bella to school, but from the quietness in the house, I thought that she might've overslept as well. I went over to Mye's room and looked in his crib, noticing that he wasn't there either. *Where is everybody?* I picked up a piece of paper that replaced my son, wondering why it was even there as I unfolded it.

My heartbeat raced so fast that it felt like it was going to pop out of my chest. With my own eyes, I examined the birth certificate that belonged to me. This was the very document that I couldn't find in my grandmother's house after she'd died. Seeing all the pain it had caused me, I thought she'd thrown it away. *How did this get it here,* I wondered.

I quickly ran downstairs, and was shocked to hear how quiet it was. The loss of sound in a house, that's normally so noisy, was spooky. It felt like I was being watched. I walked a little faster to the kitchen, and immediately became worried when my family was nowhere to be found.

"Ma?" I said, trying to get an idea as to where she was. With no reply, I went to check the living room, which was where she'd fallen asleep. "Ma!" I whined, wondering why she hadn't answered me. As I walked a little closer, I felt in the pit of my stomach that something wasn't right. It was the same feeling that I got when…when…

I lifted the blankets off my mother and screamed. A scream that should've broken all the glass in the house. I turned around and threw up everything that was inside of me, as I witnessed my mother's dead body lying face up in a waterfall of blood. Her head nearly decapitated. *The kids*, I thought, after realizing what was happening.

"Beellllaaaaaaa!" I screamed, as I ran frantically all over the house, trying to find them. "Where are you?" I hollered, in a panic state. I'd begun to hyperventilate, and the walls were closing in on me. I ran to the foyer and dug in my purse until I gripped my cell phone. My hands shook uncontrollably as I dialed 911.

"This is 911 dispatch, please state your emergency," an unenthused operator said over the phone.

"She's dead! My mother is dead, and my kids are missing…please help me!"

"Ma'am, what happened?" the operator asked, finally coming to life. I continued to search frantically all over the house for my children for the second time. I knew in my heart both of them weren't here, but I had to check.

"I don't know what happened! My mother…she' gone…there's blood…my kids."

"What do you mean, ma'am?" she asked, just as confused as I was.

"What do you think I mean, lady! Someone killed my mother and my children are gone! Where are the fucking police?"

"Calm down, ma'am, and stay on the phone, they're on the way."

I knew that she was just trying to help, but I wasn't in a calming down mood. My mother's head was barely attached to her body, showing all the muscles that had been severed. Knowing that the kids were missing gave me hope that they were still alive. *Who could've done something like this,* I asked myself, wondering if Shannon hated me that much.

A million questions ran through my mind, as I tried to piece the puzzle together. *How long have my kids been gone? What type of evil person would do such a thing? Are they even still alive?* No matter how many people I wanted to blame for this, the only person, who was sick enough to do something like this was Chloe. I knew at this point, without a doubt, that Chloe was behind this. My intuition told me so.

The longer I stayed in the house, the longer it felt like the walls were closing in on me. It started feeling like a ton of bricks had fallen on my chest. I fell to the floor, gasping for air.

"Outside," I whispered through my hyperventilating, to someone who wasn't there. I managed to open up the door, and tried helplessly to pull myself outside. I crawled with all the energy I had left to the front step. It felt like I needed an asthma pump, and I didn't even suffer from the chronic illness.

The noise that the sirens made consumed the air with its urgency. It seemed like hundreds had come to my aid, but it was only one. Neighbors came out of their million dollar homes to see what the ruckus was. As I laid on the ground, trying to catch my breath, flashbacks of the night Trent put me out the house while I was eight months pregnant raced through my mind. *At least it's not snow on the ground this time.* I was physically drained by the time the paramedics and police cars pulled up.

"Ma'am, are you alright? Are you hurt anywhere?" a very tall EMT asked.

"My son, my children…they're gone…please help them," I pleaded with him. He checked my pulse, and commented about how faint it was. I was taken to the back of the ambulance, while a team of officers ran in the house to help whoever they could. Little did they know she couldn't be helped. I just hoped that her death wasn't as painful as it looked.

The EMT placed an oxygen mask over my mouth, and instructed me not to speak until I'd calmed down. I sat up on the stretcher, while they placed the yellow crime scene tape all around the house. It looked like something right out of a movie. I watched as the neighbors huddled in small groups, and pointed to the house like they were sightseeing. I'm sure they never thought in a million years that a murder and kidnapping would've happened right under their nose. Hell, it happened right under mine.

"Oshyn Jones?" a female officer asked. She looked at me for a few seconds. "Have we met before?" she asked.

I shook my head yes, with the oxygen mask still attached to my face. I held it there tightly, feeling like if I were to let it go, my whole face would fall to the ground. Everything about me felt so unstable. She did look oddly familiar, but I didn't have time to figure out whether she was a friend or a foe. I had to find my kids. "Are you the one that found the body?" she asked, with her notepad out.

"Yes, that's my mother," I cried through the oxygen mask. "My son and daughter are missing. Whoever did this took my kids too!" The tears fell down my face at the thought of losing anybody else. I could only imagine what made Chloe this unstable.

"The investigators have confirmed that your mother has been deceased for several hours. At least some time last night. However, you called about the homicide and kidnapping not even a half an hour ago."

I took the mask off of my mouth and twisted up my face in confusion. "Last night? I just found her like that this morning!"

"Things aren't adding up, Mrs. Jones," she replied, as if I was a suspect and not the victim. "Did you stay here last night?"

I shook my head up and down. "Yes."

"Well, if you stayed here for the night, why did you wait so long before you called for help?" Her tone had become more accusatory and less helpful, as she searched for an answer that I didn't have.

I remembered coming home, thinking that my mother was asleep. I remember ignoring my gut feeling that was telling me to check on the kids. Everything was adding up now, but it was too late. I watched helplessly as officers ran in and out of the house, trying to piece together this mess they were now trying to blame on me.

"Oshyn!" the officer said sharply, snapping me out of my daze. "What happened last night?"

"I don't know. I…I wasn't home. I mean…I left, but it was just for an hour or so…I think. I can't remember!"

"Oh yeah! So now you weren't home. How convenient.

You want me to believe that your mother was just fine before you left the house. Then you waltz out to handle some *business* in the wee hours of the morning, and that's when someone comes in, kills your mom and takes your children. You come back several hours later, or so you think, and go to sleep with a decapitated woman on your couch and two missing children. How does that story sound to you?"

I had to admit, the story did sound like I was trying to cover something up, but that was honestly what happened. With a story like that, I knew I was fighting a losing battle.

"I don't know what you're trying to get at officer, but I'm the victim here. My children are missing. You have to find them, please."

She looked at me with no sympathy in her eyes and said, "What's the baby's name?"

"Mye Storie."

"Aren't all of our children our stories? I didn't ask you that, I asked you what your child's name is."

"His first name is Mye, and his second name is Storie. My son's name is Mye Storie Rodriguez. Please find him!" I pleaded with her again, ignoring her sarcasm. If this were under any other circumstances, I would've fucked her up. But since I needed her help, I put up with her bullshit.

I crossed my arms across my chest, as the officer watched me suspiciously out the corner of her eye. I wasn't sure how much time I had, but I knew that she was wasting most of it. I wasn't sure if it was my intuition or not, but something wasn't right.

"Mrs. Jones, do you mind if I take you down to the station for some more questioning? It's standard procedure."

"Standard procedure my ass. Why are you talking to me in such an accusatory tone? I just found my dead mother's body and my kids are gone!" My chest heaved up and down, as I tried to gain control of my breathing once again. "Please, just find whoever did this!"

"Your son…Micah I think his name was? You got a pretty penny for his death, didn't you? I was at that scene too."

That was it, that's where I remembered her face. I still couldn't piece together where she was going with this, in her sarcastic tone. "It's no secret that you're in financial ruins right now. With your business gone, your bank accounts frozen, you could definitely use the extra cash. The insurance money from the deaths you planned will come just in time, like it did with your other son, Micah!"

A surge of cold air filled my lungs. I wasn't sure if I was hearing right, but if I was, she was accusing me of killing Micah, and now my mother. She was accusing me of kidnapping my babies and setting this whole thing up. For a slight moment, I thought about telling her who I felt was up to the whole thing, but I decided against it. I figured that it wouldn't do me any good at this point. I was like every other black face in the justice system…guilty until proven guilty.

I continued to inhale what air I could, as I watched them carry my mother out of the house on a stretcher wrapped in a black body bag.

"You're a smart girl. I'm sure you didn't let too much time past by without taking life insurance out on her. I wonder how much you're going to get for your mother?"

That was the last straw. I lunged for the officer with all my might. I punched her in the face, catching her off guard, and went in for the kill. I'd been beaten down mentally enough, and couldn't take anymore. It wasn't long before her fellow officers came to her rescue and pried me off of her. I was unruly and resisted everyone who touched me.

"Get your fucking hands off of me!" I screamed, as they tried restraining me. I was thrown to the ground face first, and held there until another one of the officers got their cuffs out. "What are you doing? Get your fucking hands off of me! I'm not the criminal!" I screamed again, this time crying.

"You have the right to remain silent, everything you say can and will be used against you in a court of law. You have the right to an attorney. If you can't afford one, one will be appointed to you…"

The whole world stopped existing once I was read my Miranda rights for the second time in less than a month. I continued to fight, refusing to let them take me easily.

"Please…someone, find my kids. Time is running out!"

No one would even acknowledge me. I'd attacked one of their own. I was no longer a victim, but a suspect of a brutal crime. News cameras had now entered into the equation, and snapped pictures as they carried me away kicking and screaming. "WHERE ARE YOU TAKING ME!" I continued to yell.

# 22CHLOE

It felt good to be back home. Rochester, New York was where I was born and raised, and I hadn't been back since I left with Mr. Bourdeaux's money. Those were the days. I decided to come back at the perfect time of year. The snow was gone and the flowers were blooming. I thought about all the good times I had while I was here. It made me want to move back permanently. Even though most of my friends were dead or in jail, I knew that it wasn't an option. I'd done too much shit to come back now. This visit was strictly business.

"Sweetheart, do you want anymore pop?" Ms. Louise asked, while I sat in a daze on her battered porch.

"No, ma'am," I answered, thankful that I still had her around. I called her right after leaving Mason's house, and told her that I was coming home. She asked me where I was staying and after telling her a hotel, she insisted that I stay with her. That was my real intention anyway.

She was an old woman in her seventies, and had lived on Alphonse Street her whole life. She was the neighborhood mother, grandmother, rehabilitation center, and food shelter.

Though she smoked, drank and cursed like a sailor, her heart was full of love.

"Your baby sleeps like a grown man," she said, probably wondering why he'd been asleep for so long now. Little did she know I spiked his drink with a small dose of Tylenol PM. His ass had been crying since we left Mason's house, all the way here. Nothing I did soothed him. Maybe I wasn't fit to be a mother, but Ms. Evans didn't have to know that.

I'd told her he was my baby, because in theory, he was. Oshyn owed me after killing my baby, so I was gonna find a way to make this work, even if it killed me. Ms. Evans sat in a chair that I was certain was as old as she was, and lit her cigarette. She crossed her skinny frail legs, and pushed her oversized seventies style glasses further up her nose.

"Chloe, What's going on?" she asked, as if she knew I'd just killed my aunt and kidnapped my sister's son. She was the only woman in my life, other than my mother, who cared about me.

With my back facing her, I looked at the littered, gang-riddled neighborhood that I once ran to for comfort. My eyes got a little misty as I watched the cars drive up and down the streets with their systems blasting, and crackheads walking around aimlessly, trying to find their next hit.

I was sick of this life. I wanted her help. I wanted to cry out to her and confess about all the wrong that I'd done. I wanted to lie in her arms, like Oshyn did in grandma's, while she stroked my hair, and told me that everything was going to be okay. That it wasn't too late to turn my life around, to go to school and get a degree. To find a husband, my own, who would love, honor, and cherish me. I wanted her to tell me that God actually did love me, but I couldn't.

Still sitting on the porch step, I said, "Nothing. Nothing's going on. I just broke up with my son's father, and needed to get away, that's all. Just needed to get away." I was sick of lying. Sick of hurting. Her silence let me know that she didn't believe me, but it was okay. I knew her well enough to know that she wouldn't harp on the situation.

"Child, I still can't believe you cut off all that long purty hair of yours. You baldheaded like some dyke. You smoking dope?" she asked, still puffing on her Virginia Slims. I laughed at her comments, wondering when the shit talking was going to start. She couldn't help it. She'd been doing it all her life. "How's your cousin Oshyn doing? I haven't heard from her in years."

The sound of Oshyn's name made me sick. "Ah…I don't know. I think she's living in Raleigh, but I moved to Houston after I left Rochester. I haven't spoken her," I replied, lying through my teeth. I just couldn't bring myself to tell her the truth.

I jumped off the porch as I heard a series of sirens getting closer and closer to where we were. "Child, you act like you ain't never lived in the hood before. What you got bad nerves for? Who you did wrong?"

I watched as the cops raced down the street and past the house. "Nobody…I haven't done anyone wrong," I lied again, as I sat back down on the broken wood. I swear old people always had an answer for everything. "Why don't you move from this area, Ms. Evans? I could put you up somewhere nice."

"Nice? Hell, this is nice! I was born and raised in this house, and I'm going to die in this house. I raised all my kids and grandkids in here, and this is where I belong!" She was adamant on staying here. This is where her love was.

I looked around again, and saw that she still had the best-manicured yard on the whole block. Even though dope boys took over the area, they made sure that nothing happened to her. Hell, she had raised half of them.

**WAAAHHHHHH! WAAAHHHHHH!**

I put my head in my hands, dreading the fact that the baby

was awake. I thought I had at least an hour more to relax, but…oh well. I got up, walked past Ms. Evans to get into the house, and headed toward one of the bedrooms. Once I picked him up, I immediately noticed that he was beet red and had a temperature. His wailing in my ears made my head pound, so I fixed him a bottle and went back outside with him to get some cool air.

"Child, give me that baby," Ms. Evans ordered, with her hands extended out. As soon as her used wrinkled fingertips touched his skin, he stopped crying.

"How did you…?"

"Oh, it comes with practice. I've been along this road a time or two," she replied, trying to make me feel better. "This baby has a bad fever, Chloe. With all that sleeping he's been doing, and feeling how hot he is, you need to take him to the doctor. He's too young…"

"No! I mean, no, I can handle it," I said, lowering my tone. I'd forgotten for a second who I was talking to. "It'll go away soon, I'm sure. Don't you have any home remedies that you used back in the day to get rid of stuff like this? It's just that…I don't like doctors, and I never have since I had him. I had a rough delivery." She looked me dead in my eyes, almost as if she wasn't buying any of the things I told her.

"Who in the hell do you think I am…the witch doctor? Home remedy my ass. I said this damn baby needs some medicine. So, don't back talk me, little girl!"

She rocked him in her arms as only a grandmother would, and he seemed content. A content he hadn't displayed since I took him from his crib. I was convinced at this point that I wasn't mother material. I'd initially made plans to ditch Bella off somewhere, and keep the baby to myself. I wanted to raise him as if he really was my son, but with his constant wailing, my fairy tale ending wasn't an option.

Just that quickly, I decided to get rid of the baby and sell him to someone. I knew several wealthy couples that couldn't have a baby on their own, so it seemed like the perfect plan.

"Ms. Evans, I was wondering if you could keep the baby for me? It wouldn't be but for a couple of days. I'll pay you for it."

"But you just got here. Child, you know I don't keep no kids! Y'all young kids having these babies, you take them with…"

"Please?" I asked her again, with a hint of desperation in my voice. "Just for a little bit, until I can get myself together again. I think I'm suffering from postpartum depression." She looked at me again with her questionable eyes that magnified through her thick glasses. I thought for a second that I'd taken it too far with the depression thing, but oh well, the damage had been done.

"Fine! I don't know what you're up to, but you better bring your ass back here in a week, cause I ain't raising no more fucking babies!"

I got up, went back inside the house and grabbed my bag that I'd never unpacked. I knew I had to hurry up and get out of before she changed her mind. I dropped her a few hundred bucks on the table, and walked down the steps without saying goodbye.

"Aren't you gonna say goodbye to your son, girl?" she asked, still rocking him back and forth. "You better not be on that crack shit!"

"Nah, he'll be alright," I mumbled, as I kept walking.

"Trifling…" was the last words I heard Ms. Evans say to me. I didn't care though. I knew that he was in great hands, and by this time next week, he would have a whole new family, and my pockets would be thicker.

# 23 CHLOE

It was the wee hours of the morning by the time I pulled into Mason's driveway. The air was still and warm, maybe seventy degrees, which was a step up from the chilly air in Rochester. It had been a full forty-eight hours since I'd had some rest, so I was beyond tired. Almost to the point of being delusional. With the drive I'd just made, I barely had time to sleep. I'd tried to sneak in a few naps at a couple rest stops along the way, but I never got comfortable. My mind wouldn't give me any peace. All I could think about was how they'd caught the D.C. Sniper, and I didn't want to go out like that.

I got out of the car and made my way toward the front door. My plans were to get Bella, and dump her ass off somewhere. She was in the way, and I didn't have a need for her. I used my key to let myself inside, and went directly to the guest bedroom. Surprisingly, I couldn't find a sign of Bella anywhere.

"That little bitch!" I said, knowing she'd run away or told Mason everything that happened.

*I knew I shouldn't have left her with Mason's old ass.* I ran through the halls, hoping that she hadn't gotten too far, and stopped in front of Mason's infamous 'jack off room'. When I opened the door, ready to ask him where Bella was, my mouth almost hit the floor.

Bella's mouth had been duct taped, along with her feet and hands. Her clothes had also been completely removed from her small body, which trembled in fear. It was the same fear that reminded me about the night her mother died. She struggled to breathe, crying heavily as Mason stood over her butt naked. His dick was extremely hard. *This seven-year old girl is what arouses him? Not me*! Mason's face read deranged, and luckily I'd gotten here in the nick of time. I saw it in his eyes. It wouldn't have been long before he raped her.

"Mason!" I said firmly, scaring the shit out of him. He apparently didn't know that I was looking at his sick intentions from the door.

"GET OUT!" he screamed. It was just like the last time I'd caught him jerking off in front of his half dead wife. I peeked over at Bella, and noticed that her tears had stopped. We locked eyes, and I no longer saw her fear. Hate and anger replaced what she felt inside.

"Let her go," I demanded, as I walked closer to him.

"GET OUT! LEAVE US ALONE!"

Mason stepped toward me like he was ready to kick my ass for interrupting, but that wasn't gonna happen. Using my hood survival skills, I quickly searched the room for a weapon, and noticed a long metal log pole against the fireplace. Without a second thought, I rapidly made my move, and ran over to the weapon, to grab it for safety.

Mason stepped even closer to me, not threatened at all by my new line of defense. I raised the pole high into the air and swung it down, cracking him on the head. He hit the ground with a hard thud, and I watched as the blood slowly oozed out of his head. I looked down at his pitiful body and noticed that his dick was still hard. Viagra was the only pill I knew would keep a dick that stiff, even when you weren't in the mood. From the looks of it, that hard on was going to last him another hour or so.

"I'm gonna force you to like a grown woman's pussy," I said to him, as I took off my jeans and panties. I bent down and jammed my knee into his chest, cutting his breathing short. He flapped around, like a fish out of water, while he struggled for air. I removed my knee and straddled over his dick that was still hard.

"No, please don't," he pleaded, crying like a bitch, while I forced his weapon inside of me. It was big, dangerous, and satisfying. He tried his best to get me off of him, but he was too weak. Besides, as horny as I was, he didn't stand a chance. I pounded my pussy up and down on his dick in between my pants of pleasure and his cries of being violated. I was finally in control.

Sick of hearing him whimper, I reached my hand over to his neck, and wrapped my fingers around his throat. As he gagged, I bounced on his cock even harder, and held on for dear life. I felt like a cowboy on a raging bull.

His dick had been drowned in my pussy. This was what I needed. This was all along, what I wanted. I lifted myself off of his dick, and rushed to sit on top of his face. His muffled cries, tickled my pussy as I moved it around in circles on his mouth. Surprisingly, it felt good.

"Open your mouth!" I demanded.

He refused to follow my instruction, so I brought my pussy up to his nose, and rubbed my clit up against it. He fought that too, trying to move his head back and forth and from side to side. Being both pleased and frustrated at the same time, I stood up and grabbed the pole again. I repeatedly beat his body with the hard metal. Hopefully I'd managed to crush his dick, a dick that wanted to molest an underaged girl. A dick that wasn't satisfied with me. I knew I had some nerve being the moral police, but the shit that he was into was unforgiving. She was a child. He was a pedophile.

He was moaning in pain when I threw the bloody pole over his body. That's the way I wanted him, in pain. I wanted his ass to remember what he'd tried to do every time he pulled his dick out. I put my clothes back on and stepped over him, walking up to Bella. As I went down to pick her up, she wiggled around violently, refusing to submit.

"What in the hell is that smell?" I asked, as I inhaled another whiff. When I looked at Bella, the strong smell of urine reeked from her naked body. "That sick bastard!"

I fought Bella's muffled screams and uncontrollable body movements as I carried her outside. With no time to lose, I didn't bother to remove the tape before throwing a sheet around Bella and picking her up. We needed to get out of there fast. When he reached the car, I threw her in the passenger's seat, then jumped in.

"If you promise not to scream, I'll take the tape off your mouth."

She shook her head up and down, as if to say she agreed to my terms. I snatched the grey tape off her mouth, and she flinched in pain. She bent down, almost immediately, and threw up all over the car. *Damn, as if the car wasn't already fucked up.* When I thought that she was done, I went to help her out, but she bent down and bit my arm again.

"You dumb bitch," was all that came out, right before I punched her in the face. With the way my fist landed on her eye, I knew that it would be black in no time.

"I hate you!" she screamed, defiantly.

She was tough, refused to give in. But I liked it. It reminded me of myself.

"Fuck you, little girl," I replied.

She needed to learn a lesson for putting her mouth on me again. I now had two bite marks that sat right next to each other. I quickly got out the car and walked around to the passenger's side. After pulling her out of the car, I moved toward the trunk and opened it.

"Here, you can ride in here."

"Noooo!" she begged, right before I placed the tape back over her mouth. I was sure that the time in the trunk would show her some respect.

# 24 OSHYN

"Yo, when can I get my damn phone call?" one of the gorilla dyke looking girls kept asking. I still couldn't believe that this was my life. I sat in the holding cell for almost four hours, and I still didn't know what was going on. At this point, all I could do was just sit and pray that they were looking for Mye and Bella.

I put my head in my hands and started to rub my eyes, which still stung like hell from the pepper spray the police had sprayed in my face. My back also hurt a bit from them shoving me on the ground, but there was no need in complaining. It wasn't gonna help the situation. They still refused to tell me what was going on.

"What's your name?" the dyke asked, turning her tone from aggressive to a bit sexy. Without looking up, I knew she'd turned her attention to me. I ignored her advances, and decided not to speak. I wasn't in the mood to make new friends.

"I asked you what your name was?" she said again, this time a little louder, with a hint of impatience in her voice. By the way she carried herself, it seemed like she always got her way. I looked at her six foot, two hundred pound frame, and still decided not to speak. If I was going to be in here, I wasn't gonna get punked by anyone. I was going to get respect or die trying. She stepped a little closer, invading my breathing space, and asked for the third time, "Your name?"

I got off the bench and stood in her face, challenging her to whatever she wanted to do. If she knew that she was fucking with a ticking time bomb, I doubt very seriously that she would be in my face. She tried her best to intimidate me, but I stood my ground. By the way she handled herself, I knew that no one had tested her before. She was one of those chicks that relied on their size to scare people off. However, she picked the wrong bitch today.

"Oshyn Rodriguez-Jones, let's go!" the short stubby officer said, from the other side of the holding cell. I took my precious time, as I looked the gigantic gorilla girl up and down before I left. I was positive that this situation we had going on was going to end with someone being rushed to the infirmary...and it wouldn't be me.

I made my way outside the cell, wondering where I was being led. Even though I didn't stay long the last time I was in jail, I was sure that they didn't let people out that easy, especially when assaulting an officer was involved. After four hours in the joint, I hadn't even gotten my one phone call yet. *Maybe they're taking me to the interrogation room,* I thought as my allegations were confirmed. I sat in the hellhole for another fifteen minutes before two officers came in.

I looked up and rolled my eyes, as I watched the officer I'd assaulted take a seat. A red-headed female detective, who looked no older than eighteen, followed her. The assaulted officer's right eye was beginning to show its damage already. I was shocked that she even showed her face, but then again, not really. Revenge was a motherfucka.

"So we meet again, huh, Ms. Jones?" she taunted. I

flinched as she called me by Brooklyn's name again against my permission, but it didn't matter. I began to wonder where he was, hoping that he'd seen everything on TV, and was on his way to rescue me.

"I don't believe that we were formally introduced. My name is Detective Shay Johnson, and this is my partner, Detective Lea Baker."

Her tone was calm and confusing. After our showdown earlier today, I expected there to be more anger. But there wasn't. She was cool, mannerable, even a bit nice. I definitely had to be on my A game, because something was up. After she finished talking, I never acknowledged her or her friend, who sat off to the side. I had nothing to say.

"Oshyn Mone Rodriguez, now Jones. Born July 4th, 1981, and raised in Rochester, New York. Had your first son, Micah, several months early when your baby father kicked you out of the house in the middle of a snow storm."

She slid the newspaper clipping my way that captured the whole story of what had happened to me that day. I was shocked and felt violated that she felt the need to pull up my dirt.

"You moved to Raleigh after that, and started up your own real estate firm. You did very well for yourself too, I might add. Your gross income in your first year of business was well over four hundred thousand. Seems like you and your family had become quite accustomed to living a nice lifestyle."

"Is that a crime?" I asked.

"Would you look at that? The dead does speak," Shay said to her white counterpart.

I wasn't in the mood for anymore of her shit, but she continued on as if I hadn't said a word. "Then you met the love of your life, Brooklyn Jones and just like a fairy tale, you have the engagement party of the year. Our undercovers were all over the place taking pictures. That's right, they were your photographers for the night. Let me tell you, you take some amazing photos," she added, passing them along for her partner to see.

The white girl reached for the pictures anxiously, as if we were long lost girlfriends reminiscing about the past. Her partner thumbed through them, and smiled as she handed them back.

"Would you like to take a look?" she asked, handing the pictures to me.

I only stared, never blinked, nor extended a hand. The white girl then sat them down on top of the newspaper clippings, while muttering, "Suit yourself."

Shay organized more of her things, as she proceeded on with my biography. "Not too much longer after that, your son, best friend, and her child's father, are found dead in *your* home. You were not only pregnant, but also wounded, along with your best friend's daughter, Bella. The murder weapon is found next to you, along with your prints on it, but somehow you got away. You claimed that there was someone else to blame for all of this, and yet all the evidence pointed to you. Nonetheless, you walked away from the murder scene over three hundred thousand dollars richer from the life insurance policy that you'd taken out on your loved ones."

Both officers watched me like a hawk to see what my reaction would be, but I remained very calm. I'd watched too many *NYPD Blue* shows to get upset over nothing. I knew what they were up to.

"Now," she continued, "you have a new baby, and your lucrative business gets seized by the FEDS for money laundering and tax evasion, and your bank accounts are frozen. With no husband to look after you, you have to find a way to survive by any means possible, right?" She paused, waiting for a response. I again said nothing. "So you killed your mother, who you didn't really know that well anyway, and you killed your kids, staging a kidnapping for them, just to complicate things a bit."

"No...no, my children are still out there. Please find them," I pleaded, breaking down.

She'd hit a soft spot.

My kids were the only thing the officer said to me thus far that made a difference. I needed for her to know I had nothing to do with my mother's death, and that Mye and Bella were still out there. The first few hours in a kidnapping were critical.

My time was almost up.

"Sure they are," Shay replied, looking at me like I was full of shit. "Look, Oshyn, you can talk to us. I mean, with everything that you've been through, I'm sure I would've done the same thing if I were in your shoes. For heavens sake, a human being can only handle but so much, you know what I mean?"

Her sympathetic tone was fake. Just like her bad weave.

"Look, I didn't do this!" I pleaded once again, hoping that someone would look in my eyes and see my innocence.

"Sure you didn't," she said again, ignoring my plea for help.

She slapped some pictures on the desk that showed my mother's dead body. Her blood saturated clothes revealed her gaping wounds, and I immediately turned my head. My stomach couldn't handle seeing her like that again.

"She was stabbed in her head, neck, throat, back, chest, stomach, and arms. She had twenty-four stab wounds in all, and her head had been partially decapitated. Your mother died a painful death, drowning in her own blood." Shay waited for an answer. "Do you want to tell us what really happened?"

"I told you before," I answered, "I didn't do this. I left my house around midnight, and came back an hour or two later...I can't remember. When I got there, I saw that everyone was asleep, so I went to bed myself."

"Oh, so now you saw everyone sleeping?" Shay asked me,

as if she was on to something.

"Well, it appeared that she was sleeping. The house was dark. When I saw my mother's silhouette on the chair, I didn't want to wake her, so I went upstairs to my room. I didn't go into the kid's room either. I just went straight to sleep."

Shay let out a small chuckle. "Sure you did. Tell us about this alibi you say you have. Where were you last night between the hours of twelve and two, and we need a contact for whoever this *alleged* person is."

I thought long and hard about how I was going to answer the question. I was still pregnant by this old married, very wealthy white guy, and I wasn't sure if I wanted to reveal that. I also knew that any involvement with Brooklyn wouldn't look good either.

"Did you hear me? We need to hear your alibi," Shay ordered.

Regardless of what I told them, I knew they would find a way to make my situation look even worse than what it already was.

"I was with a friend of mine, Brian. He worked for me at the office. He'll confirm that I was with him last night," I lied. Had to. I just hoped that Brian would be on point. If not, I was in deep shit.

"Oshyn, stop the bullshit! We have fingerprints at the scene of the crime that links you to the murder. Not only that, we also have a bloodstained footprint at the scene of the crime that belongs to you. There is also an eyewitness that said she'd testify that she saw you running out to your car with the baby and the little girl over your shoulders! The game is over...you're fucked!"

*Is she kidding me?* "Fingerprints? I fucking live in the house, what are you talking about? I'm the one that found my mother dead, of course my finger and footprints are going to be there, you fucking genius. And an eyewitness? Did that nosey ass bitch tell you what model and color the car was that

I supposedly drove away in? Because if so, you're that much closer to finding the person that actually committed the crime. You're wasting your time here, genius."

I knew that name-calling was a low blow, but I wanted to show her how retarded she sounded by saying some dumb shit like that. There was an abrupt knock at the door, and whomever it was, let themselves in.

"Your little meeting here is over. Did you ask my client if she wanted a lawyer while she was being interrogated?" he said, as he took a seat next to me.

I almost fell over on the floor when I saw who he was. With his black tailored suit and his briefcase by his side, Cody looked like a man you didn't want to cross. I was totally shocked that he was even here. The last time I saw him was when I blurted out my whole life story and ran away from him downtown. The world was turning out to be a very crazy place.

I parted my dry and cracked lips to say something, but he looked at me with those Carolina blue eyes and instructed me not to speak. "Any other questions you have for my client will be asked through me," he announced.

It was funny that as soon as he got there, they had nothing else to say. He'd completely shut the party down. Half an hour later, I was a free woman again.

"Thank you so much," I said, to the familiar stranger. I immediately felt upset with myself for being as nasty as I was every time I saw him. *You never know when you're gonna need someone.* He was the last person I expected to come through for me. "How in the world did you know what was going on?" I was still clueless as to what Cody was doing here, but grateful that he'd posted the two hundred thousand dollar bond to get me out. Even though I still couldn't figure out why he would do something like that. I hoped that this wasn't some sort of set up because I'd been through enough.

"No problem. I guess you've figured out by now that I'm a lawyer." He smiled. "I was actually at home relaxing when I saw the story on the news. When they said you were in jail for assaulting an officer, I knew you needed my help."

"Thank you so much," I mouthed again. I felt myself starting to cry. I was so overwhelmed with everything, I couldn't contain myself.

"You don't have to keep thanking me. Honestly, it was my pleasure. This kind of feels like the date I wanted to take you out on," he replied, trying to lighten up the mood.

"Can I use your phone for a minute?" I asked. I didn't mean to cut him off, but my phone was dead, and I knew Brooklyn was probably wondering what had happened.

Cody handed me his blackberry.

I dialed my husband's number.

*Please hold while the Nextel subscriber you are trying to reach is located.* I held on, desperately hoping that the call would go through. I wasn't so lucky.

"Hello, Brooklyn…this is me, Oshyn. Please call me as soon as you get this."

I walked away from Cody, and dialed Brooklyn's number a few more times, only to get the same response: *Please hold while the Nextel subscriber you are trying to reach is located.* "Brooklyn, it's an emergency! She took my kids! I gotta get in touch with you!"

I went back over to Cody and placed the phone back in his hand.

"Is everything okay?" he asked.

"No…it's not."

We walked down the street from the jailhouse, to his car that was parked in one of the garages.

"Oshyn, you were charged with assault on an officer, disobeying a police officer, simple assault, and resisting arrest. You're looking at nine months in Wake County Jail if convicted."

There it was again. Another blow to the head, and it seemed like the power punches wouldn't stop coming.

"Cody, I have to worry about all of that later. I didn't kill my mother or kidnap my kids, but I know who did. I need your help getting my family back before it's too late."

"If you say you didn't kill her, I believe you. I'll find your kids and clear this whole thing up, if it's the last thing I do." He looked down at the ground, then back at me. "I hate to be the one to say this, but there's a very good chance that your kids may not be alive."

I shook my head. "No, they are! I can't explain it, but I know in my heart that both of them are okay. I just need to find them before it's too late!"

"Look, Oshyn, it's all over the news that you're the prime suspect of the murder/kidnapping, and the motive is money. You aren't allowed to leave town."

"Not allowed? What the fuck are you talking about, not allowed?"

He threw up his hands. "Don't shoot the messenger," he responded, showing his dislike for the tone I'd taken with him. "You've been told by the police not to skip town for any reason."

I looked at him, feeling paralyzed from the neck down. I couldn't move, couldn't breath. I wondered, why now? What was the reason for Chloe coming back after all this time?

"I'm so tired," I said, holding my head. I noticed how hot I was. It felt like I was coming down with a fever. I couldn't afford to be sick right now, so I decided to rest and let my body relax for a couple of hours.

"I got a hotel room for you for as long as you need it," Cody said, as comforting as he could.

I forced a smile. "You've done so much for me, but I don't have any money to compensate you for any of this." I wanted to know what his true motives for being this nice were. I was beginning to learn that nothing in life was done for free. I wasn't giving up any more pussy just because someone was being nice.

"Believe me, it's all over the news about how much money you don't have. Just consider it an early birthday gift. Seriously, I take at least two pro bono cases a year, and this is my first. Really, it's my pleasure."

After talking for a few more minutes, he finally took me to a nearby Target for a few necessities, a cheap tank top and some shorts. Then, he checked me into the Hilton, and made sure I was in a safe place.

"I'll call you tomorrow," he said, giving me a small black traveling bag before he left the lobby area, and made his way back to his car. I didn't even have a chance to ask him what the bag was for before he jumped in his car and drove away.

When I got to the room, I immediately walked over to the bed and buried my face in one of the pillows. I was out cold within a matter of seconds.

*"Oshyn! Oshyn!"* I heard a voice whisper in my ear. *"You've got to get those babies back before it's too late! Oshyn..."*

I jumped out the bed saturated in sweat. My clothes were so wet it looked like I'd jumped in a pool. I could identify that voice from anywhere. It was my grandmother warning me to get the kids back. As always, she knew something I didn't. This time I took heed in the urgency of the whisper, got up, and rushed into the shower, trying to put together a plan. This was war, and I knew just who to call!

# 25 OSHYN

With the hotel phone in hand, I picked it up and checked the voicemail to my cell phone. I needed to see if I had any messages from anyone, specifically Brooklyn. He was the only one that had been where no man had been before. He had reached a piece of my heart that was unattainable to the rest of the world. He was the only person that could help me end this mess.

Nothing.

There were no messages from him. Not even one.

I had a sinking feeling that, regardless of what he told me the night we met, the relationship we once shared was gone. I needed to realize, no matter how hard I tried, it would never be the same. A feeling instantly crept into my body that I would have to find my children alone. I left a few more messages on his voicemail, but felt no optimism about getting a call back.

I was on my own.

I dialed another number for help.

"Hello?" a groggy voice answered on the other end. "Who

is this?"

"It's me, Oshyn."

"Oshyn?" Brian cleared his throat. It was going on six o'clock in the morning. "Oshyn, what's going on? I've been trying to reach you for days."

"Yeah, sorry for calling you this time of morning, but…"

"No, no…you're fine. Where are you now?" Brian asked, interrupting me.

"I'm at the Hilton on Wake Forest Road. It's a long story on how I got here," I responded. At that moment I burst into tears.

"Are you alright?"

"No, I'm not," I replied, in between sniffs.

I was having a nervous breakdown and at this point, chills had accompanied my fever. I was falling apart and trying to hold it together the best way I could.

"Look, whatever it is, don't say it over the phone. I'm on my way," he ordered, before hanging up.

After trying to get myself together, I paced the room, wondering what I was going to do, when I spotted the small bag Cody had given me when I first checked in. I figured it may have been something he thought I needed, so I grabbed the black nylon bag, and opened it up to see the contents. Inside, sat a small bundle of money, which looked to be about two thousand dollars, my car keys, and an uneven folded note that read:

*Here is some pocket money, just in case you need to move around. If you need anything else, call me. We'll get to the bottom of this.*
*Cody*

An angel in disguise is what Cody was. When all of this was over and done with, I was going find a way to pay him back. I sat around the hotel room for an hour, trying to get my thoughts in order. I'd grown impatient waiting for Brian to arrive, so I gathered my things and left the hotel, only to be greeted by my Benz that had been parked out front. Cody was a lifesaver…literally. I was relieved that I still even had my car. I was sure the police would've seized it by now, along with everything else, but it was still here. And to think, I wanted to get rid of it. I was learning fast, the hard way, to be thankful for everything that I had.

However, as I walked closer to the car, it was at that same moment when I realized the word BITCH had been scratched on the door. It stopped me dead in my tracks. Another clear indication that Chloe was up to her old tricks again.

*Who else would be this fucking stupid?* "I cannot wait until this maniac is out of my damn life!" I screamed.

It was a good thing that I was the only one in front of the hotel at the time, because with all the bad publicity I'd been getting, I'm sure they would've called the police. I began to walk closer to the car, even though I didn't know where I was going. But pacing the floor of the hotel room had started to make me a little crazy. I did everything I could to keep my mind from wondering where my kids were. I was in the process of unlocking my car, when Brian pulled up.

"Were you leaving me?" he asked, jumping out of his car. It almost seemed like he had an attitude.

"Mye and Bella are gone! Chloe took my kids…I have to find them!" I yelled.

Brian listened intensely as I told him the entire story, refusing to miss any details in the process. I didn't want anyone else thinking that I was involved in any way.

"So that's it," I concluded. "Brian, please help me find the kids!"

If anyone could find Chloe, I knew he would. He was well connected.

"Don't worry about a thing, I'll find that bitch if it's the last thing I do!" he promised. I felt relieved and a bit confident that he would help get the job done. I just hoped that it would be in time. "Let's talk in a few hours. I'm gonna make a few calls. I know somebody who can find anyone. I'll have a lead on Chloe's ass in no time."

"And what am I suppose to do until then?" I asked.

"The same thing you were going to do before I pulled up…nothing!"

His sarcasm made me laugh, but not for long.

There was really nothing that could keep my mind off of reality. Every time I closed my eyes, I saw my mother's dead body. She had just come back into my life and now she was gone…forever.

Caskets.

I'd seen enough of them to last a life time.

More than twenty-four hours had gone by, and the critical time for recovering kids was almost near.

If statistics were right, the chances of finding them now, were slim to none. The police were expecting them to be dead, while I on the other hand, expected life.

I didn't believe in statistics.

I refused to give up.

*      *      *

Three more agonizing hours went by before Brian finally called me back. I'm sure the hotel was gonna have to replace the carpet once I left.

"Oshyn, I got a lead!" Brian screamed, over the phone.

"Oh my God! Are you serious?" I asked, a bit uncertain that he was able to pull something off so soon. I didn't want to get my hopes up for no reason and then find out that the information he had was useless. "What's up?" I asked anxiously.

"There's an annual event in Cary tonight called The Millionaire Mogul's Conference. It's only for the elite, and in order to be invited, you have to have at least a million dollars in liquid assets to come. The hosts of the event pride themselves on keeping their guest list exclusive, but I found out from my source that Chloe was going to be there."

I immediately needed a paper bag to contain my hyperventilating. I was under so much stress at this point that my hair had begun to fall out, which was all I needed.

This was a favor from God that I was sure my grandmother had set up. I would give anything for all of this to be over with, but I knew that I would have to go through Chloe to end it. I wasn't in the mood to go to some fancy gala, but I had to. My children were in danger, and I was their only hope.

"I can't believe this. I can't believe you found her so soon," I replied. "She's probably been under my nose the entire time."

"Knowing her conniving ass, she was. Listen, my source was able to muscle us two fake journalist badges, so we can get in. I'm on my way over to give you the badge, along with something else."

"Thanks," was all I could manage to say before we hung up, although my heart wanted to say more. Brian had really come through for me, like all the countless times before. He was a lifesaver, and I appreciated him more than words could express.

Thirty minutes later, there was a knock on my hotel room door. After looking through the peephole, I removed the huge lock and let Brian in.

"Here," he said, holding up a white couture Chanel gown.

"What's this?" I asked, looking completely surprised.

"It's my wife's wedding gown. I knew you needed something to wear tonight, and since both of you are about the same size…"

I shook my head back and forth. "Are you crazy? I can't wear your wife's wedding gown!"

"Yeah, I am a little crazy right now, so try not to get any-thing on it. That way I can sneak it back in the closet before she finds out it's gone," he replied, with a slight laugh.

This man was crazy. I couldn't believe what lengths he was willing to go in order to help me out. After going back and forth about the dress a few more minutes, I finally gave in and tried it on.

It fit perfectly.

The innocence of the gown allowed me to be discreet, yet beautiful at the same time.

"I'll go with you," Brian insisted.

"No, this is something I have to do alone. You've done more than enough," I replied. "But, I do need to borrow your car. I can't pull up to that type of event with the word BITCH on the side of the door."

He understood about me not wanting him to go, and hand-ed over his keys. With only a few hours before the event start-ed, I told Brian goodbye and started preparing myself for a night full of chaos.

\*　　　\*　　　\*

At nine o'clock sharp, I pulled up to the venue, and was in awe at how much money was there. New and old money con-gregated around for a night of promised fun. No wonder Chloe was coming. *A bitch like her wouldn't miss an opportunity like this, even if her life depended on it*. The valet opened my door and escorted me out onto a red carpet, where I was bombarded with flashing light bulbs and cameras from the local news channels and journalists. I instantly became sad as the picture takers reminded me of my engagement party. An engagement party where Apples was by my side, while all of my loved ones waited inside to celebrate with me.

Brooklyn made that night unforgettable.

I hid my face while the rest of the guest basked in the

glory of fame. Besides, I was still the prime suspect in a murder and kidnapping case. Pictures were the last thing I needed. I needed to stay under the radar for a while. After flashing my fake journalist badge, I finally made my way into the gigantic ballroom, and made sure my eyes were focused and sharp as an eagle.

I wasn't here for fun.

I was determined to find Chloe.

While everyone else mingled their way through the crowd, I examined the room as hard as I could. I was as cordial as I could be considering the circumstances. I still wasn't sure what I was going to do once I found her, but it didn't even matter, as long as I knew where she was.

I continued walking around the ballroom, feeling completely out of place, when I ran into someone.

"Oh my goodness, I'm so sorry!"

I turned around to apologize for my clumsiness once again, when I saw that it was my grim reaper, Shannon Bourdeaux, standing in front of me.

*Damn, can life get any worse?*

# 26CHLOE

It didn't take me long for one of my sources to find Oshyn's baby some wealthy parents to live with. He was actually in high demand, and I had the honor of going with the highest bidder. It was surprising to see how many couples had difficulty having kids. Seemed like all those bitches in the hood were poppin' their babies out left and right, while responsible parents couldn't get pregnant to save their lives. Looked like I'd found a new niche, and it was in demand.

It had been about thirteen hours, and Bella still lay motionless in the trunk of my car. I hadn't even checked on her yet. Guess I hoped that she would just die in there. Unlike Oshyn's baby boy, I hadn't found anyone for her. She was too old and would talk. The little bitch just wasn't an asset.

The couple who were willing to take the baby, were middle aged, in their forties, and had tried desperately for years to have a child. I didn't want to know their business, but the wife insisted. She said that she'd tried everything to get pregnant, but nothing ever worked. She was sure that this was a blessing from God.

It didn't take much for me to sell the couple on the baby once I let them know that he had the biggest grey eyes they'd ever seen. It also helped that they thought I was the mother. Actually, the more I thought about it, I was pissed that I hadn't thought about doing this before. With all the dudes I'd fucked, I could've made millions if I'd just allowed myself to get pregnant.

The wife asked why I wanted to give the baby, up and I explained to her that I just couldn't take care of him anymore. She guaranteed that he would be in great hands, and thanked me profusely for granting her wish. I then drafted up a fake birth certificate with two alias names on it, which would allow them to file for adoption. However, I told them they didn't have to wait for the adoption to be finalized before they could take his little ass. All I needed was the money.

I thought I had everything figured out, including where the pick up was suppose to take place, but the proud new parents insisted on meeting with me face to face first. I assured them that it wasn't necessary, but they wanted to ease my mind about letting them have *my son*.

They invited me as a guest at The Millionaire Mogul's Conference in Cary, so they could formally introduce them-selves, and more importantly, give me the twenty thousand dollar down payment for their new bundle of joy. If it had been anywhere else, I would've protested, but a chance to be in a room full of millionaires was too good to pass up. I could always use a place to network, and this was the prime opportu-nity to reel in some new clients.

When I left the hotel room where I was staying, I stopped at the mall and picked up a black Tommy Hilfiger piece. It was something I wouldn't normally rock on a regular night for an event as big as this, but it would have to work for now. Looking glamorous would make me too suspicious. I was here on business.

An hour later, I pulled up to the massive event, and was

amazed at the number of people who were in attendance. *Wow, I can smell the money from out here,* I thought. As a smile began to creep across my face, it quickly disappeared as I thought about the small problem I had.

Before pulling up in front of the building, I pulled my car over, grabbed a Burger King bag that I had earlier and got out. I looked around to see if anyone was looking before I opened the trunk to see if my problem was still alive. I silently hoped she wasn't.

"Bella," I said softly.

There was no response.

*Shit, maybe she is dead.* "Bella," I said again. This time I gave her a little push. Bella slowly moved her head toward me and opened her eyes. She appeared incredibly weak. Even though it didn't look like she could cause any trouble, I had to make myself clear. "Don't even think about making any noise when I leave this car, you little bitch. Don't fucking move," I ordered, before tossing the half eaten hamburger inside.

After slamming the trunk, I hopped back in the car and headed straight toward the valet. As I stepped on the red carpet, I couldn't believe how many news cameras were there. *Wow, are they expecting some type of celebrity? Shit, I knew I shouldn't have worn this dress,* I thought, as I pulled on the plain unattractive material.

Once inside, there was a woman standing off to the side, holding up a sign with the fake name I'd given. The proud parents told me that their assistant would be there to escort me in. I guess they wanted to make sure I was taken care of as soon as I walked in, and I couldn't complain. *I should be treated like royalty anyway.*

"India Shaw?" a tall beautiful woman asked me as I approached her.

"Yes, that's me," I replied, with a huge smile. I hadn't had sex since I'd raped Mason, so her gorgeous appearance immediately made my pussy wake up. *I would love to be in between your legs right now.*

"It's nice to meet you. Follow me."

*Oh, I'll be more than happy to follow that ass*, I thought, when she turned around to walk away. As I tagged along behind the woman, who reminded me of Tyra Banks, I watched as people walked by draped in their finest attire. I guess they were trying to prove who had the most money. Even though I was ready to get the whole ordeal over with, I wanted to see who had the most money as well.

As we walked a little further, I realized that the crowds of people were becoming thinner. This was an area where no one was. "Where are we going?" I asked, suspiciously.

She gently grabbed my hand and led me into the women's bathroom. When I walked in, she made sure no one else was in the stalls, and then locked the door. Right before I could ask her anymore questions, she moved closer to me, outlining the edges of my lips with her tongue. *What the fuck is this shit?* I wondered, even though I didn't want her to stop.

I was nervous that this would potentially ruin the transaction, but it didn't matter. If pussy was want she wanted, then I was gonna provide. I sat on the counter of the black marble sink and lifted my dress above my waist. I watched as the beautiful woman kneeled down and inched her face between my thick thighs. She slowly began to kiss my skin, making my kitty drip with anticipation. *Good thing I didn't wear panties*, I thought, as she began making her way to my pussy. I realized how much of a hassle it would've been to get them off.

She sucked on my clit, like a jolly ranger, and moved her fingers inside of my treasure until it drowned in the juices that were flowing out.

"Ah, right there, baby," I moaned, when she found my spot. I reached for my zipper and finally got my dress undone. I needed her hands, her mouth, her tongue on my breasts. They were swollen and needed some attention.

She stayed downtown for several minutes, enjoying the taste of what I had to offer as someone started to bang on the door. But it didn't matter. They could've stayed there all night, because I wasn't gonna let her stop until I had an orgasm. As she stuck her tongue in and out of my pussy, I could feel my legs starting to tremble.

I knew what that meant.

I could tell by the smile on her face.

When she stood up, she licked the cum that surrounded her mouth, and brought it to my nipple. She bit it, softly. I cringed at first, but loved every second of it. After sucking on my sensitive nipple, she took my entire breast and swallowed it in the mouth.

While I moaned, she crept her fingers back in my pussy, and massaged my insides, while I convulsed. I was in heaven and couldn't figure out how I'd gotten here. I let out another moan of ecstasy and seconds later, our intimate moment was over as soon as it started.

"It was nice meeting you, gorgeous," she said, sticking her hand out for a hand shake. *These damn rich people are crazy*, I thought, as I extended my hand toward her in return. I put my clothes back on, and we both freshened up before leaving the bathroom. Luckily, who ever was banging on the door, had decided to leave.

I was on cloud nine, as my new sex partner led me back to the party. I pranced around as seductively as I could, trying to subliminally command all eyes on me, when I saw the living dead staring me right in the face. My face went cold as ice.

*How in the hell is he still alive?* I asked myself, staring at the gruesome birthmark that was shaped like Italy on his face. The Mayor was hunched over in a wheelchair, with a young blonde nurse by his side. *Looks like he still hasn't learned his lesson by messing around with white women.* I was sure that the multiple stab wounds I'd placed in him were more than enough to end his life, but that apparently wasn't the case.

I quickly turned around and proceeded to walk the other way, when I saw Oshyn and Mr. Bourdeaux standing right next to each other. It was also just my luck that they noticed me at the same time. I hadn't seen or heard from him since I stole his money, and I had a feeling that our paths would cross again, but not here. Oshyn began walking toward me, her pace quickly turning into a slight run. The fire in her eyes indicated that she knew I was the one to blame for her mother's murder and the kidnapping of her children.

Just when I thought I had run out of all options, the unthinkable happened. "Chloe Rodriguez, you're under arrest for the illegal adoption of your son," my beautiful escort said, accompanied by the middle aged black couple that I was supposed to meet. I couldn't believe that the bitch who'd just finished eating my pussy, was the same one who was arresting me. I looked at her, as a devious smile appeared on her face. She never said anything, only licked her lips and rubbed her stomach as if she was full. I bet she was.

"Shit!" was all I could get out, as the entire room looked in my direction. When Oshyn saw the woman place handcuffs around my wrists, she stopped and backed away slightly. We locked eyes for a second.

Confusion was in mine.

Death in hers.

For once, the tables had turned.

# 27 OSHYN

It had been a year since I laid my eyes on her, and I was much angrier than I thought I'd be. Just for a moment, my mind wandered to the day I found Chloe in the bed with my man, who was now missing in action. Sweat ran down my face, while I watched her slip through my fingers once again. I was crushed at the mere thought of how close I was to finding out where my kids were. The fever that I'd recently acquired seemed to have taken a turn for the worse.

I didn't know what my next move was going to be, as I watched the three undercover officers arrest my sister and drag her off to jail. *I wonder if she's getting locked up because they finally know the truth.* However, as crazy as it seemed, this wasn't the right time.

I needed her out.

I needed my questions to be answered. Once Chloe was locked up, she would probably never tell me where my kids were.

Our eyes never left each other's gaze until she was out of the building. I came back to reality as soon as I felt Shannon pulling me by my arm. I knew what he wanted, but I still didn't have an answer.

"Did you take care of your problem?" he asked, cornering me up against the wall. Everyone's attention was so focused on Chloe, that no one ever noticed my silent plea for help.

"Move out of my way!" I gritted through my teeth. I was sick of his shit, and no longer willing to be threatened.

His thick eyebrows frowned. "What the fuck did you just say to me?"

"Move out of my way!"

I cringed when he grabbed my neck. His hold was so strong, it felt like he was trying to choke the life out of it. After struggling for a few short moments, I finally pulled myself out of his grasp, and ran away as fast as I could. As soon as I got outside, everything started to spin. I felt dizzy, and the light abdominal pain that slowly began to take place, didn't help either.

"Ma'am, are you okay?" the valet asked. "Do you need to go to the hospital?"

I was sick.

I knew I needed medical attention, but that was precious time I couldn't spare. My unborn baby probably needed help, but my son and Bella were somewhere out in the world...lost. Wondering why they weren't with Chloe almost drove me insane. I ran off without answering the valet's question, then jumped in Brian's car and started driving back to my hotel room. After placing my cell phone on the car charger, I picked it up and tried calling Brooklyn one more time.

"Hello?" a soft voice answered. The sound of the woman's voice instantly sent chills through my body. *So, is this why he couldn't call me back in my time of need*, I wondered.

"Who is this?" I asked.

"This is nurse Perkins at Wake Medical Hospital. I'm answering the phone for Brooklyn Jones. Are you related to him by any chance?"

"Nurse? Where's Brooklyn? Is he okay?"

"I'm only allowed to give information to immediate family," she informed me.

"Well...I'm his...his...wife," I finally got out. "I'm Mrs. Jones. What's wrong with my husband?"

"Well, Mrs. Jones, you may want to come down here right away. Your husband was found on the street. He's been beaten up pretty badly."

"Oh my goodness...I'm on my way!" I yelled, before hanging up.

I silently cursed myself for thinking that Brooklyn was up to his old tricks again. Here he was lying up in the hospital, while my mind placed him elsewhere. It was at that point when I began to think about how much I still cared about him. How much I loved him. How much I needed him.

\*     \*     \*

"Hey, you can't park there!"

I ignored the whiny voice of the overweight security guard who wobbled over to me. I'd parked in a handicapped spot, and he immediately noticed that I didn't have the famous tag dangling from my rearview mirror. I got out of the car and closed my door, trying to ignore his determination to get my attention.

"I said that you can't park there!"

"Will you leave me alone! It's an emergency!" I screamed.

"Lady, everybody in the hospital has an emergency. Go park your car in the garage like the rest of the world!"

I heard it in his tone.

He spoke to me like I was a child.

I peeked over his shoulder, and saw how far the parking garage actually was, and let out a huge sigh. It was a journey I didn't feel like taking. It was a walk that I refused to do. I didn't have time to explain myself. Brooklyn needed my help. Everyone needed my help. I brushed his protruding stomach slightly as I walked past him.

"Lady, did you hear me?" he asked.

"Look," I said, just before entering the revolving doors, "your fat ass better leave me the fuck alone!"

I didn't mind getting a ticket at that point. I just wanted to be left alone. When I entered in the building, I walked up to the information desk, asked for Brooklyn's room number, and was directed to his floor.

A short elevator ride later, I walked up to the nurse's station and demanded to see my husband. I knew it wasn't their fault, but I was tired of waiting.

"I'm here to see Brooklyn Jones!"

"I'm sorry, only immediate family members are allowed to see him at this time."

"I'm his…I'm his wife, Oshyn Jones. Where's my husband?"

"Oh, okay, Mrs. Jones. Please wait one moment while I call his doctor out here to speak with you," a nurse replied.

I paced back and forth in the hallway, waiting for answers. I watched as all the doctors walked around in their scrubs waiting for their day to be over, while people lay dying, waiting for cures to their illnesses. Hospitals always freaked me out. This was the same place my mother refused to go to be treated for her limp, and I wasn't any better. I refused to get treated for my fever that had gotten considerably worse.

"Mrs. Jones?" a woman asked, after tapping me on my shoulder. I turned around, and saw a short black woman with a Nia Long haircut. "I'm Doctor Christie Linton. I've been treating Mr. Jones since he got here."

"What happened to him? Is he alright?"

"Mrs. Jones, your husband was badly beaten up, and has suffered a concussion. At this time, I believe he's suffering from temporary amnesia and…"

"Amnesia? What are you talking about? When did this happen?" I asked.

I was overwhelmed with the urge to get information. It had only been a few days since I'd seen Brooklyn, and I couldn't believe what I was hearing. I was beginning to think that I had a curse. That everyone that came into my life would eventually be hurt.

"He was found lying in the middle of the street on Oakwood Avenue two days ago. The owner of the store, I believe the woman's name was Teesha, brought him in. He doesn't remember what happened to him that night, but his memory is coming back slowly. The only reason we knew his identity was because of his driver's license."

I couldn't believe what she was saying. *This must've happened the night we were together.* "Who did this to him?"

"We don't know…he doesn't know. This type of memory loss is normally associated with a trauma of some sort. It can last any where from one day to two weeks. Some patients recover and remember the memories that were lost during the trauma. However, some patients never recover the memories of the attack, or the event that happened immediately before."

"Can I see him?"

She shook her head. "Of course, follow me."

I trailed behind her as we walked silently down the hallway. The hospital scent of latex and sanitation made me a little queasy. "Here we are. Let me know if you need anything." She pushed her thick black Chanel frames up on her nose before walking away.

Brooklyn's lips had been busted wide open. Blood saturated bandages covered the top half of his face, and desperately needed to be changed. An IV was placed in his arm and his left eye was badly swollen.

"Brooklyn," I whispered in his ear. He appeared to be sleeping, and I didn't want to startle him by being loud.

"Brooklyn, it's me, Oshyn. Wake up."

I cringed as he struggled to peel his eyes open. It looked like it hurt to move the slightest muscle, but I was glad to see him still alive. He looked over at me and appeared to smile.

Grandma would've said that it was just gas.

Maybe it was.

"Hey Oshyn," he managed to say. His voice was barely a whisper.

I grabbed his hand. *At least he remembers my name.* "Hey baby, how do you feel?"

"Where's Micah?" he asked, ignoring my question.

"Micah?"

"Yeah, I want to see our son."

I wanted to cry, but decided against it. I had to be strong. "Baby, Micah is dead."

He really did have amnesia.

"Dead? What do you mean he's dead? Oshyn…what are you talking about?"

"Babe, Micah died last year, remember? We have a baby boy named Mye." I dug in my purse to show him a picture. "What happened to you?" I asked, while he examined the photo of *our* baby. "Please tell me, who did this to you?"

"I don't know. I don't remember anything."

"Do you remember meeting me that night?" I asked.

He shook his head no.

"Do you remember our baby?"

"I think so," he responded.

I held my head down for a second, before looking at my husband in his beautiful grey eyes. "Well, he's gone," I blurted. I didn't want to stress him out, but the reality was clear. My children were still gone.

Brooklyn looked confused. "Gone? Where did he go?"

"They were kidnapped. He and Bella were kidnapped," I replied, speaking softly. Every time I said those words, it tore me apart.

"Bella. That name sounds so familiar."

While he was trying to make sense out of all of this, my phone began ringing. I was surprised I even got service in the hospital. "Hello?"

"Mrs. Jones, this is Detective Lee Baker. We've found your daughter, Bella, and she's alive."

*Oh my God!* I couldn't believe what I was hearing. "Where did you find her? What about my son? Where is he?"

"We arrested Chloe Rodriguez in connection with all this. After searching the car she was driving, we found your daughter in her trunk. She was severely dehydrated, but the doctors got her fluid levels back up. She's in the emergency room at Wake Med."

"Oh my God, I'm here! I'm in Wake Med now...where's my son?"

The Detective seemed hesitant, but finally responded. "He wasn't in the car, so we're still unsure. However, we're working hard to find him."

I couldn't believe that my son was still missing. After dealing with the death of Micah, there was no way I could face burying another child. He would have to be found. I thanked the detective for the information, and then quickly hung up. "I'll be right back," I said to Brooklyn.

"Wait, where are you going?" he struggled to ask.

"The police found Bella, but Mye is still missing. I'm going down to the emergency room to get her, and then find our son!"

Hope had resonated back in my heart, and I knew that if Bella was still alive, it was a good chance that Mye was too.

"I'll go with you." Brooklyn said, before I made my way to the door.

"You can't...you're hurt. Stay here and rest."

"I'm a little banged up, but I can still walk. I'm going with you!" He slid out the bed, without waiting for my approval, and fell to the floor. I watched him struggle to get up and put on another hospital robe, so his ass wouldn't be exposed. He tore the tubes out his arms and then placed them around me for support.

"Are you sure you wanna do this?" I asked. I knew the nurses would be running in at any moment.

"Yeah, I'm sure…let's go."

We slowly walked down the hall, as Brooklyn winced in pain from each step he took. I knew he was in no shape to be walking, but the more I thought about it, I didn't want to do this without him. I was tired of facing everything alone. After walking past the empty nurse's station, I prayed all the way down the hall that no one would make us turn around. Luckily, we continued to walk as if we were invisible.

When we got down to the emergency room, I watched as people looked at Brooklyn like he was crazy. I guess they thought he was trying to leave without being discharged, and I couldn't blame them. He did look out of place with two hospital robes on and a pair of dusty looking socks. An emergency room attendant directed us to Bella, who was in the care of a nurse.

"Oh sweetie," I blurted out, when I saw the black eye she wore. She was also attached to IV's, and looked extremely weak. "Is she going to be okay?"

"Yes, she'll be fine. Are you alright sir," the nurse asked Brooklyn, as he winced in pain. "Are you sure you've been discharged?"

"He'll be fine," I answered for him. He needed all the energy he could get. I walked closer to Bella and held her hand. It was lifeless. "How long will it be before she can leave?"

"Are you related to this child?" the nurse asked.

"Yes, she's my daughter."

"We want to admit your daughter and monitor her for at least a few more days. We ran a urine sample, and found traces of Roothie, better known as the date rape drug, and Zoloft. I'm not sure how all of this happened, Ms…"

I looked at Brooklyn. "Mrs. Jones," I said.

"Mrs. Jones, I'm not sure how this happened to her, but your daughter has obviously been through a lot. I'm surprised that she's doing as well as she is."

"Date rape drug? Zoloft?" That seemed to be the only words I heard. There was no telling what Chloe had done to my child. All I could do was thank God that she was alive, but cringed at the thought of what could've happened to Mye. "Do you mind if I have some time alone with her?"

The nurse looked a little hesitant at first, and I couldn't blame her. I'm sure she thought I was an unfit mother, and that I'd let this happen. "No…sure. But just remember, she's a little weak." The nurse walked away and left the three of us alone. But from that comment, I knew she thought I was some sort of child abuser.

"What are you doing?" Brooklyn asked.

"I got to get her out of here." I took the two needles out of Bella's arm, and with all the strength I had, picked her up off the bed. All she had on was her hospital gown, but I didn't care. All I cared about was getting my child out of there.

It took a while, but we finally made it out of the hospital.

# 28 CHLOE

I'd been in the county jail for twenty-four hours, and I still wasn't any closer to getting out. I looked down at my index finger that was covered in black ink, and thought about my life. A life that was about to take a drastic turn.

A life that no one even cared about.

Even though my bail had only been set at thirty thousand dollars, I still wasn't able to pay it. My money wasn't in my possession, and there wasn't anyone who I could call for help. Right now I couldn't even call a client.

"Rodriguez!" an officer yelled. "You have a visitor."

As the officer opened the holding cell, I couldn't help but think who the visitor was. I just hoped it wasn't Oshyn. I wasn't in the mood to talk about something I had no plans on discussing. When the officer led me into a small interrogation room, I immediately became confused. *Why would my visitor be in here*, I thought, as the officer told me to sit down, then closed the door.

I sat in the uncomfortable steel chair, staring in the two-way mirror and smiled. They probably thought they were intimidating me, but I was gonna show them otherwise. However, when the door finally opened, and he walked in, I knew I was fucked.

"Chloe Rodriguez...so we meet again?"

Agent Tate came in the small, cold room, and paced around slowly. He smiled at me. I knew that whatever chance I had of walking out of here had instantly been lost. I was guilty, and I knew he would make sure everyone else found out.

"I see that you've gotten yourself in a sticky situation," he said.

"Fuck you!" I replied, sticking up my middle finger.

"Oh, don't worry about anything, you will be fucked, and raw if I may say so myself. I'm gonna make sure that they bury your ass." His smile was brighter than the sun. "I'm sure you know by now that the Mayor from Asheville is still alive, so you're fucked big time."

I wanted to wipe the smile off his face with my gun. "Let's not forget... I still have something on your bitch ass," I warned.

He walked over to me and whispered in my ear, "Oh, if you're talking about the tape. Well, me and a couple of other agents ran up in your hotel room, and found the tape in your duffel back, so don't worry about that." He walked away then turned back around. "Oh, by the way, I'm gonna make sure the federal charges against your sister, Oshyn, are dropped.

I was furious. After all the hard work I'd put into taking Oshyn down, seeing the plan fail right before my eyes made my blood boil.

"Chloe?" a man said, opening the door slightly. He peeked his head through, and briefly showed his face to me and Tate. I didn't answer. Figured I'd let the bright orange jumpsuit I had on speak for itself. "Chloe, my name is Cody Reed, and I'm going to be representing you."

Agent Tate looked at me, then back at my new lawyer. I could tell me having a lawyer wasn't part of his plans, but hell, it wasn't part of mine either. I was just glad to catch him off guard.

"Can you excuse us, please?" I said to Tate. "I need to speak with my lawyer." I spoke to him like I was in charge again, even though I was far from it.

"Yes, please, I need to speak to my client alone," Cody added.

It felt good watching Agent Tate leave, even though I'm sure he was gonna be on the other side of the glass.

Cody made himself as comfortable as he could on the hard chair and steel table, where he placed his briefcase. I gave the lawyer an uncomfortable stare as he positioned himself in the chair a few times. He looked like someone I'd seen before, but I quickly brushed it off. He could've been anyone, hell, probably an old client for all I knew. But as much as I tried brushing him off, I still couldn't stop thinking about it. I never forgot a face.

"We're going to get you out of here today, Chloe," he informed.

"Wait. How am I going to post bond without any money?" I was very skeptical, and for good reason. At this point, everyone was a suspect.

"I'm going to post the bond for you. If they need any additional information, you'll have to come back and submit that, of course."

*Since when do court appointed lawyers post bail?* I wasn't concerned with anything he'd just said to me. Whatever he wanted to do was fine. All I wanted to do was get out. And once I was free, no one was going to see me again.

*         *         *

An hour later, I flinched a little as I sat on Cody's tan leather car seats. It was so hot, it felt like my skin had melted. He turned on the AC as soon as he hopped in the car and started driving.

"I hate the summer months," he said, patting his forehead with an expensive looking handkerchief. "I'm more of a fall type of guy."

"Where are you going?" I asked, while trying to ignore his weather report. Normally, the only strangers who convinced me into their cars were my clients, but this time I had nowhere else to turn. I needed Cody's help to get my car, so I could get out of town. I needed him to help me get out of this mess.

He looked at his Louis Vuitton watch and said, "There was somewhere I was supposed to be earlier, but because of your case, I'm running incredibly late. If you don't mind riding with me briefly, I'd appreciate that. Then I'll drop you off whereever you want to go."

I wasn't too interested in being his sidekick, but it seemed like I had no choice. From the tone in his voice, it wasn't really a question. He got off of the busy intersection and turned on a scenic route that looked like it led to nowhere. We were the only car on this road for miles, and I knew something was wrong.

"Where are we going again?" I asked, wanting to know where all the other cars had gone.

"I have to meet one of my clients in his warehouse. This is where all of our meetings take place," Cody responded, with a sinister grin. Don't worry, it's right up the street."

A chill instantaneously ran through my body, as I realized I had nothing to use for protection. Even the Tommy Hilfiger evening gown that I'd put back on from the conference, hindered my ability to move like I was supposed to.

Right up the street, turned into a forty minute drive on a

deserted road. When he finally arrived, the abandoned building resembled something that should've been in a Friday the 13th movie. I hoped like hell that Jason's crazy ass wasn't in there.

Cody insisted that I come in, despite my choice to stay in the car. "You can't stay out here by yourself. Come on, it'll only take a second," he replied. "Trust me."

He couldn't have picked a worse choice of words, because it was at that moment, I knew something was about to happen. But what could I do. Without some type of weapon, I was helpless.

As we walked closer to the door, I realized that there were no other cars present. "Hey, when is your client going to show up?" I turned around and asked, greeted by the barrel of a gun.

"Very soon, Chloe," Cody responded, as he motioned for me to enter into the building. I remained calm, trying to search my mental database of who he could be. I'd done so many people wrong, he could've been anybody.

When we walked inside, I looked to my right and saw a chair, accompanied by ropes, a can of gasoline, and a few other materials, which led me to believe that this was premeditated.

"Who are you?" I asked, hoping that he'd reveal himself. I didn't know much, but I knew that whoever went through this much trouble to kill me, definitely wanted me to know who he was. I was convinced that no one would go through all this trouble without wanting to be recognized.

He ignored my question and forced me into the chair. It took him several minutes, but he tied my hands and my feet together like a pro. I struggled to get them loose, but the more I moved them around, the tighter it got.

"Please…just tell me who you are. What do you want from me?" I pleaded with him. "What do you want from me daddy," I said, changing my helpless cries into a seductive tone. "Is this your fantasy?"

If nothing else would free me, I was sure that my pussy would. He watched me through his aqua blue eyes, as my tongue danced around my lips. I opened and closed my legs the best I could with my ankles tied together, and desperately hoped that this was working.

He walked over, and without saying a word, flipped open a pocketknife. The blade looked to be no smaller than four inches, but the closer he got, the larger it seemed. I winced a little as he glided the blade along the right side of my face. I was trying to show no fear, but it wasn't working.

"Who are you?" I asked again. I was prepared not to get an answer. "Ahhhhhhh!" I screamed. He took the knife and carved it into my cheek. He then placed his left hand on the top of my head, to balance himself, and continued to cut into my face with no remorse. I pleaded for him to stop as the blood poured down my face. "Ahhh…noooooooooo!" I screamed. When he finally stopped, he looked at his work and smiled, like a proud sculptor.

"Who…are…you?" I managed to get out one more time.

"Remember Mr. Bourdeaux?" he asked, holding my chin up with his hand. "He's my father!"

# 29 OSHYN

"I have to go," I told Brooklyn, after I hung up the phone with Cody. Brooklyn, Bella and I were all at the hotel, when I'd gotten the word that Chloe was at some warehouse. Just when I thought all my luck had run out, something always strengthened my faith. I was so happy that I could literally smell my son's sweet breath on my face. My heart told me that he was still alive, it just wouldn't reveal to me where he was.

"Let me go with you," Brooklyn said, as he struggled to get up. He still wasn't himself. I remember lying next to him the night before, wishing he would kiss me. Wishing he would turn over and tell me how much I meant to him. Wishing he would make love to me. Maybe he didn't remember. I'd taken my own initiative to remind him of how he felt about me, but before I got a chance to kiss him, he flinched.

He panicked.

I left him alone and cried myself to sleep, wondering what had happened to him. To Bella. To my son.

"I don't know. You and Bella aren't strong enough to go with me now…you'll only slow me down."

"We're not going to separate!" he instructed, in his New York accent. He stood up and struggled to put on his pants along with the tacky Carolina Panthers t-shirt and tennis shoes we managed to get from the same Target Cody had taken me to.

I had no time to argue with him now. I guess since he'd decided to discharge himself from the hospital by walking out with me and Bella, he felt the need to be with me at all times. With his determination, it seemed like a losing battle anyway. I picked Bella up, who was sleeping, and we all went down to the car.

I followed the directions that I got off of my navigation system, frustrated regarding how many times I'd gotten lost. A forty minute trip had turned out to be an hour. *This expensive piece of shit,* I thought to myself, as I wondered why my Benz kept spitting out the wrong information, quickly forgetting how blessed I was to even still have the car.

When I finally pulled up to the building, I looked around and hoped that I was at the right location. There were no other cars there, and I couldn't call Cody for help, because the signal in my phone had died. I had no other choice but to go inside for a closer look.

"You two stay in here," I told Brooklyn and Bella. He agreed, not having too much energy to get up anyway.

I walked in and was greeted by the stale smell of gasoline. The building felt like a sauna, and with the gasoline stench, it forced my dizziness to return. I held on to the wall as I forced myself to continue on. *I didn't come all of this way to turn back now.* I took a few more steps, before I heard a groaning sound that was coming from around the corner. I hesitated for a moment before I looked. It sounded like a wounded animal, but I was still skeptical, and wanted to know for myself.

I slowly inched my head around the corner, and that's when I saw Chloe tied down in a chair. The red container of gasoline that made me nauseous upon entering had been spilled over her and on the floor. Her face had been gashed open, and blood was everywhere. I didn't know who would do this to her, and more importantly, didn't have time to find out. She didn't look too good, and I needed as much information out of her as possible before she was unable to speak at all.

"Chloe!" I said, trying to get her to focus. "Chloe!" I couldn't believe that she'd cut off all her hair, as I grabbed a chunk of it to hold her head up. "Chloe!" I repeated one more time.

"Oshyn? Is that you?" she asked, half smiling.

"Where is he, Chloe? Where is my son?" I begged. I could tell by the look on her face that she definitely wasn't gonna give the information up quickly. I wanted so badly to be able to call the police, but I couldn't. If I wanted this done right, I knew I had to do it on my own.

"Chloe! Where is my son? Please just tell me!" I said again. I felt myself losing control, hoping not to kill her before I could get an answer.

"I'm…sorry…Oshyn," she answered, barely. I was dumbfounded. The last words that I expected to come out of her mouth was that she was sorry.

"Just tell me where my son is, Chloe, please!"

"I'm sorry O…"

"WHERE'S MY SON!" I yelled, shaking her vigorously. I was at the point where I could care less about her apologies. It was too late for her remorse and for her repentance. I wasn't God. She'd caused too much pain to be granted forgiveness. I simply wanted her dead.

She laughed very hard, coughing in between her comedy show. "I said that I was sorry, bitch!"

It was almost as if she were a completely different person. In just a matter of seconds, she'd become arrogant, almost invisible like the Chloe I knew. Not the apologetic fake that tried to trick me seconds before. "And what is this talk about having a son? I don't recall any of this," she said, continuing on with her monologue.

"Why? Why are you doing this to me?" I asked, not being able to hold the tears in any longer. I was trying my best to stay strong, but it was inevitable. I just wanted to know the obvious...why.

"You stupid, bitch! You stole everything away from me. My mother. My baby. My man. They didn't love you! None of them did, and you stole them from me. You don't deserve to be called my sister!"

I looked in her eyes, and for a brief moment, saw me inside of her. She was indeed my sister, and at this point, I couldn't say that I was any better than her. I'd stooped down to her level, and was just as guilty as she was. As soon as I fixed my mouth to respond to her ridiculous accusations, our family moment was interrupted.

"Shannon?" I asked. I was puzzled as to why the father of my unborn child was here.

Chloe looked up and her eyes widened. "Mr. Bourdeaux," she gasped in pure fear.

"Hello ladies. Oshyn, I see you found the building without any trouble?" I wasn't sure if he expected an answer, or if he was just thinking out loud.

"What are you doing here?" I asked, attempting to rid my face of the tears I cried minutes before.

"My son was kind enough to arrange this meeting with you all," he responded, as he focused his attention on the door.

"Your son?" was all I could muster up, as I watched Cody walk in. They embraced each other tightly, and then stood next to each other as they faced us. They were almost identical. Betrayal was all I felt as I watched this horror story unfold right before my eyes.

I immediately thought how careless I'd been when I realized that I didn't have a weapon. As sick as I was, I was left to fight for myself unarmed. I still didn't know what these two had up their sleeves, but whatever it was, I knew from the looks of Chloe, there was going to be more blood. I immediately regretted telling Brooklyn not to come in.

"Have a seat," Cody said, pulling a gun out of thin air. For a slight moment I thought about fighting him. I knew that once I sat down, it was over for me, but I was too weak to even run. I thought it was best to do as I was told. Cody tied me up quickly, then stepped back to admire his work.

"Why?" I asked him. That seemed to be the question of my life. Why?

"Well, Oshyn," Mr. Bourdeax said. "Last year this bitch stole a million dollars from me. She blackmailed me and took my money. I knew that I'd find her through you eventually and that's what I did."

"But what do I have to do with anything? I didn't take your money," I said confused. "Don't you care that I'm pregnant with your child?"

Chloe looked at me like I had a disease.

"Bingo!" he replied, as if I'd answered the million dollar question. "I can't risk having a baby, especially with someone like you. And I can't risk being blackmailed again. So I'm going to have to kill both of you, and close this chapter of my life!"

# 30OSHYN

Shannon and his psychotic sidekick, Cody, were both dressed in fine Italian suits, but behaved like two street dudes. For a second, I assumed that they wouldn't hurt us because of their attire, but then the thought of the mafia crossed my mind. They were trained to kill, no matter what they had on.

"But I met you at Home Depot," I said to Cody, out of the blue. "How did you know who I was?"

"Nothing was coincidental, my dear," he answered, rubbing his finger on my face. "I bugged your car and followed you there. Followed you to your job, and watched the FEDs seize all your shit, courtesy of your sister, Chloe. I followed you to your hotel, and waited downstairs until you finished fucking my father. Everything was planned."

I'd never felt more violated than I did at that very moment. My whole life had been under surveillance, and it all happened right under my nose.

"But, you were at my grandmother's funeral," I said to Shannon. I hoped that a little guilt would bring some humanity to their hearts, but I was wrong.

"A funeral?" Shannon asked, laughing. "I'm the one that had your grandfather's head cut off and sent to your grandmother."

My eyes almost came out of the sockets. "But why?" I asked, shocked that he was the one responsible for my grandfather's murder. I never knew him, but grandmother always spoke very highly of him, and demanded that we did the same. To me, that was true love.

"We were business partners and best friends, but the two simply didn't mix," he said, shrugging his shoulders non-chalantly. "He stole some diamonds from me. Twenty thousand dollars worth, which was a fortune back in those days. I forgave him, but told him in order to spare his life, he would have to let me fuck his wife. I knew that my request was a death sentence, because Joe Rodriguez was a prideful man. He said no, and with that, his head went in a box and was delivered by yours truly."

"She knew," I whispered to myself.

"Your grandmother?" he asked. "Yes, she knew. I told her that I would take care of her and her kids, but she refused to take my money. I even recall one afternoon leaving a briefcase filled with thousands of dollars on her front step, only to return to a neighborhood raining with shredded money. I respected her heart. A man was lucky to have a woman like that by his side."

I could've really gone without the tribute to my late grandmother, but I went along with his reminiscing for as long as he'd talk. Chloe was no good to me dead, and my son was hopeless with me six feet under. Shannon calmly walked over to Chloe's chair, and leveled the knife he'd pulled out his pocket up to her face.

All tied up, she looked at him with no fear, and spit directly in his face. He smiled at her, and in a matter of seconds, sliced her left ear off. Her howling was unbearable. I wanted to cover my ears, but with both my hands tied together, it was impossible.

He held her diamond studded ear in his soft hands and said, "Next is your eye, and after that, your tongue."

"No! Please..." I said, feeling hopeless. For the first time in a while, I felt like finding my son wasn't going to happen.

"Oh, don't worry. We're not going to torture you. One self-inflicted gunshot to the head should do the trick. A murder suicide is what they'll call this," Cody said. I hung my head down low and slammed my eyes shut. In the midst of Chloe's painful screaming, I tried to find silence.

I needed to hear from my grandmother. I needed a clue of what to do next. I needed her wisdom on how to handle this situation. I needed her God. I struggled a bit to reopen my bloodshot eyes, and noticed a shadow in the corner. Not sure if it was help or another accomplice, I prayed for the first.

I could tell by everyone else's activities that they were unaware of the intruder that was lurking in the dark, just a few feet away from us all. Shannon, after speaking with Cody, returned to Chloe's side. For the first time ever, I saw the fear in her eyes. Her whole body flinched when he raised his hand to scratch his face. He laughed at the power he had over her and then continued with the torture.

"Stick out your tongue," he commanded, with the knife by his side. She refused to obey his insane request. "Stick out your tongue!" he demanded again, this time dragging the tip of the knife on the outline of her lips. The blood started to trickle down once again, but she still refused to submit.

"Chloe, please tell me where my son is!" I begged again. I knew that with her tongue missing, I was never gonna find out where he was. "Chloe, please!"

She stopped her whimpering for the first time since her ear had been removed, turning her head slightly to look at me. She smiled that evil smile, and focused her attention back to Shannon. With pure rebellion, she stuck her tongue out with pride, and almost urged him to slice it off. I moved around in my chair as much as I could, trying to inch my way toward him. I wasn't quite sure what I was going to do once I got there, but it didn't even matter, seeing as though I was getting absolutely nowhere.

I held my head down again and slammed my eyes shut. I felt defeated and at this point, couldn't wait for my turn.

**POP! POP!**

Two gunshots were all I heard. My eyes were still closed, because I was afraid to see what the afterlife looked like. I wiggled around a little, only to realize that I was still thinking. Death felt oddly like reality.

"Oshyn, are you okay?" I heard Brooklyn say.

I quickly opened up my eyes and saw Shannon and his faithful son, Cody, laying a few feet in front of me, dead. I peeked over at Chloe, and saw that she was still alive.

"Are you sure they're dead?" I asked, thinking back to those movies when the villain always has nine lives.

"Yeah, I'm positive," he confirmed. He took a knife and ripped the rugged ropes off of my hands. I quickly brought them in front of me, and rubbed them as gently as I could, noticing the slight bruising I got from them being tied too tight. I looked at Brooklyn, and wondered where he got the gun. It didn't matter though, because it had saved my life.

"Come outside for a second and get some air," Brooklyn insisted, as he limped toward the door.

*Some air*, I thought to myself. *Who could think of getting some air at a time like this? Does he not realize what's going on?* There were still some unanswered questions that I needed to know.

"Chloe!" I screamed. "Where's my baby?" She wouldn't move. Didn't budge. I started to have second thoughts on whether she was alive or not. Brooklyn fell against the wall, and I helped him up until he got his balance. He seemed weaker than he was earlier.

I muscled my way out of Brooklyn's arms, and struggled to get to Chloe, before he stumbled to the ground again. I took my hand and slapped her as hard as I could, forcing her blood to splatter everywhere. She opened her eyes, staring at me. Yet, saying nothing.

"Come on," Brooklyn said, holding onto the wall for support.

Needing to get away from Chloe before I used the same gun to end her life, I helped him up and we made our way outside. I looked at the purple and pink sky as the sun went down. *One more night without my son.*

"Brooklyn, where's Bella?" I asked, while peeking through the back window. I was trying to make sure that she was okay, but instead, all I saw was an empty seat.

# 31 CHLOE

Bloody and all alone, I laughed at the fact that I'd survived, and that Cody and Shannon lay in front of me dead. My vision was blurred and I couldn't see straight. I thought I was delusional when I struggled to focus in on a little girl standing in front of me with a gun by her side.

"You killed my mommy," she said bitterly, fumbling around nervously with the gun she picked up off the floor. I finally realized that it was Bella.

"Put that gun down," I warned her. "You might shoot your eye out." I laughed at my reinterpretation of my favorite movie, *The Christmas Story.* Judging from the seriousness on her face, she didn't think it was all that funny.

She started to cry, and for a second, I felt her pain. I was the same age when my mother had been taken from me, and I remembered what that day was like. "I'm sorry," I said, hoping that my apology would mend any wounds that she would carry with her through life. "Please, don't do this," I reasoned with her. She was young, hell, a baby still, and had so much life to live. "Please don't go through life like me, Bella. You still have opportunities for a second chance."

"No more second chances," the freckled face little girl said as she raised the gun. "Where's Mye?" she asked, before pulling the trigger.

# 32 OSHYN

"What was that?" I asked Brooklyn, startled from the noise that sounded a lot like gunshots. I gathered up all my energy, and ran as fast as I could back toward the building. It was a choice that never proved smart for a white woman in a horror flick, but this was real life. Against his better judgment, Brooklyn limped after me, barely making it.

I fell to my knees once I saw what had made all of the ruckus. Bella stood in front of me with a gun by her side. Chloe was dead. I crawled over to Chloe on all fours, while Brooklyn grabbed the gun out of Bella's hand.

"WHERE'S MY SON, YOU BITCH? WHERE'S MY SON?" I received what one would when talking to a dead person…no response. I fell to the floor, in a mixture of her blood and gasoline, and rocked myself back and forth. Brooklyn came over and attempted to pick me up, but I flung my arms back in defense.

The moment was here.

I'd lost my mind.

"Baby, we have to get out of here," Brooklyn warned. Even

though we were in the middle of nowhere, we were still unsure as to who else knew about this night. I could assume that no one did, but that would've been a mistake. This night turned out to be full of surprises.

I finally allowed Brooklyn to talk me into going back to my car and I sat there, with Bella in the backseat, while he left and went back in the building. I heard a loud explosion inside, and sat up wondering where he was. I watched a little at ease as he struggled to run out toward the car before he got hurt. We all witnessed the building go up in flames as we sped away into the night.

"Bella, what in the hell were you thinking?" I yelled at her. "What happened?"

She sat in the backseat sobbing uncontrollably, as she tried getting her words together. I could only imagine the trauma she would endure growing up after taking another person's life.

"I...I didn't want to lose you again," she managed to say, in between cries. She took in a couple more breaths before continuing. "Right before I shot her, I asked her about Mye and she held her head down, then whispered someone named, Louise."

\*       \*       \*

Eighteen hours later, we were in Rochester, New York on the east side of town. Alphonse Street is where my intuition told me my baby was. Brooklyn pulled up to the old house, and I quickly let myself out of the car. The porch was full of visitors, like it was when we were growing up. I held onto the hood of the car for balance, as I walked around it and made my way to the front door.

"Is Ms. Louise here?" I asked, taking a whiff of the fried chicken they were cooking.

"Sweetheart, my mother is dead," a girl with long braids

responded.

"No!" I cried out.

"I know, I know. She meant a lot to all of us," her daughter said, trying to make me feel better.

"No, she has my baby, Mye. Please, do you know where he is?" I asked her desperately. She stared me in my eyes, and called for a woman named Mimi to come out of the house. The woman opened up the screen door, and in her arms, she carried a child that was wrapped up in a blanket.

"You this child's mama?" she asked. Her deep southern accent sounded like she was a former slave.

"Yes!" I replied, as I grabbed him out of her hands. Both women stood next to each other as I unwrapped him gently. His grey eyes met mine and he smiled, showing off his dimples. I kissed him until my lips hurt.

"Before my mother died, she instructed us not to give this baby back to some woman named Chloe. She knew that he didn't belong to her, and she was sure that you would come back to find him. Before mama died, she made us promise to beat that bitch's ass for even stealing somebody's baby."

I laughed at the thought of Ms. Louise saying that. It sounded just like something she'd suggest. Brooklyn and Bella came to my aid and helped me back into the car. Before we pulled off, Brooklyn moved the blanket off of his son's face to look at him.

"Oshyn, this is my son." He smiled. "I remember." Tears streamed down his face as he stared into eyes that looked just like his. They were identical. He looked at me and said, "Forever."

"Forever," I responded.

# EPILOGUE

Two weeks after finding Mye Storie, I miscarried the baby that lived inside of me for only a short time. I guess that explained the fever I couldn't get rid of. In the end, I think God knew what was best.

After receiving help from someone named Agent Tate, all the federal charges against me were dropped. He even managed to pull some strings to get the gun charges dropped as well. In the end, everything was linked backed to Chloe, especially when they found the knife she used to murder my mother in her car.

Once the pain healed a little more, Brooklyn and I renewed our vows a few months later, and have been inseparable ever since. We moved to the sunny island of St. Tropez, where we were sure no one would ever recognize us.

Bella adjusted to the island lifestyle, quickly, and her attitude has done a complete three sixty. She's also very protective over the whole family, which I'm not too sure is a good thing.

I was sad at the thought of never being able to visit Micah's, Grandma's and Apple's gravesight again, but it was a choice I had to make. They all lived in my heart anyway.

Even though I wished for Chloe's body to rot in hell, there was something inside of me that wanted God to have mercy on her soul. I didn't know why, but I didn't want her to suffer as much as I initially thought. I know, I know, it didn't make too much sense to me either, but I was trying to learn how to forgive.

**Doing**

**HIS TIME**

Who said dating a baller was easy?

**NICHELLE WALKER**

Every little girl dreams of meeting Prince Charming and living happily ever-after. But in the hood the Prince Charmings are ballers and we dream of living happily ever Rich! Now imagine being swept off your feet and upgraded from a nobody into a ghetto superstar. Imagine a life with nothing but the best things that money can buy. When Emerald met Dollar he quickly upgraded her into a overnight celebrity. Spoiling her with the hottest whips, the finest clothes, the fliest jewels and an unlimited cash allowance. Emerald represented a baller s chick to the fullest; she lived, breathed and swore by the hustlers anthem Ballin! The night Dollar asked Emerald to marry him; she knew all her blood, sweat and spit had paid off. She d be forever fly; Emerald knew the life of a baller s wife could only get more luxurious. But when a drop goes bad and Emerald's back is pushed against the wall. How much will she be willing to sacrifice to stay at the top?

**Author website: www.nwhoodtales.com**

## Who Needs A Job When You're A Paper Doll

As a young girl Karen Whitaker dreamed of becoming rich and famous, promising to buy her mother that huge house on the hill with a Rolls Royce parked in the driveway. Her desire for material things turns into a grown woman's obsession with money, power and sex. Now of age, Karen possesses the brains of a scholar, beauty of a diamond, and a body that a Coca-Cola bottle would envy. She knows how to get what she wants even if it means taking advantage of those who trust her most. Greed and passion for tantalizing sex throttles her into compromising situations that may destroy her career and crumble her picture perfect relationship with a multi-millionaire. Take a journey into her intriguing story as demons from her past strike to unravel her fairytale life thread by thread. In the end, will she escape her dark clouds or be exposed as one money-hungry, conniving vixen?

Visit Nicolette Online @ www.myspace.com/paperdollthebook

**Available At Borders, Waldenbooks and Independent Bookstores Nationwide**

Drama is no stranger to Tiara James. With a mom on the verge of becoming an alcoholic and an alcoholic crack-addicted father who use to beat her mom in front of her, who could blame Tiara for finding a family on the streets. She lost people who she loved and trusted the most to death, jail or betrayal. From welfare, section 8, jail, drugs, abusive relationships and lies, Tiara's future seems uncertain. Brace yourself as Tiara James takes you on a rollercoaster ride in her footsteps, in her hood, telling her story.

**Visit http://lashondadevaughn.page.tl/Home.htm**

# Life Changing Books Titles

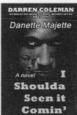

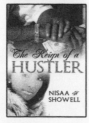

# ORDER FORM

**MAIL TO:**
PO Box 423
Brandywine, MD 20613
301-362-6508

**FAX TO:**
301-579-9913

| Date | | Ship to: |
| --- | --- | --- |
| Phone | | Address: |
| E-mail | | City & State:            Zip: |
| | | Attention: |

Make all checks and Money Orders payable to: **Life Changing Books**

| Qty. | ISBN | Title | Release Date | Price |
| --- | --- | --- | --- | --- |
| | 0-9741394-0-8 | A Life to Remember by Azarel | 08/2003 | $ 15.00 |
| | 0-9741394-1-6 | Double Life by Tyrone Wallace | 11/2004 | $ 15.00 |
| | 0-9741394-5-9 | Nothin' Personal by Tyrone Wallace | 07/2006 | $ 15.00 |
| | 0-9741394-2-4 | Bruised by Azarel | 07/2005 | $ 15.00 |
| | 0-9741394-7-5 | Bruised 2: The Ultimate Revenge by Azarel | 10/2006 | $ 15.00 |
| | 0-9741394-3-2 | Secrets of a Housewife by J. Tremble | 02/2006 | $ 15.00 |
| | 0-9724003-5-4 | I Shoulda Seen it Comin' by Danette Majette | 01/2006 | $ 15.00 |
| | 0-9741394-4-0 | The Take Over by Tonya Ridley | 04/2006 | $ 15.00 |
| | 0-9741394-6-7 | The Millionaire Mistress by Tiphani | 11/2006 | $ 15.00 |
| | 1-934230-99-5 | More Secrets More Lies J. Tremble | 02/2007 | $ 15.00 |
| | 1-934230-98-7 | Young Assassin by Mike G | 03/2007 | $ 15.00 |
| | 1-934230-95-2 | A Private Affair by Mike Warren | 05/2007 | $ 15.00 |
| | 1-934230-94-4 | All That Glitters by Ericka M. Williams | 07/2007 | $ 15.00 |
| | 0-9774575-2-4 | The Streets Love No One by R.L. | 05/2007 | $ 15.00 |
| | 0-9774575-0-8 | A Lovely Murder Down South by Paul Johnson | 06/2006 | $ 15.00 |
| | 0-9791068-2-8 | Changing My Shoes by T.T. Bridgeman | 05/2007 | $ 15.00 |
| | 1-934230-93-6 | Deep by Danette Majette | 07/2007 | $ 15.00 |
| | 1-934230-96-0 | Flexin' & Sexin by K'wan, Anna J. & Others | 06/2007 | $ 15.00 |
| | 1-934230-92-8 | Talk of the Town by Tonya Ridley | 07/2007 | $15.00 |
| | 1-934230-89-8 | Still a Mistress: The Saga Continues by Tiphani | 11/2007 | $15.00 |
| | 1-934230-91-X | Daddy's House by Azarel | 11/2007 | $15.00 |
| | 1-934230-87-1- | The Reign of a Hustler by Nissa A. Showell | 11/2007 | $15.00 |
| | 0 0711304-0-1 | Teenage Bluez | 01/2006 | $10.99 |
| | 0-9741394-8-3 | Teenage Bluez II | 12/2006 | $10.99 |
| | | | Total for Books: | $ |

Shipping Charges (add $4.00 for 1-4 books*)  $

Total Enclosed (add lines)  $

*For credit card orders and orders for over 25 books
please contact us @ orders@lifechangingbooks.net
(cheaper rates for COD orders)*

*Shipping and Handling on 5-20 books
is $5.95. For 11 or more books, contact
us for shipping rates. 240.691.4343*